The beast was coming.

He could see it now emerging from the shadows: a dark, fluid shape, an immense black rocket-shaped shark swimming through the air with its mouth open and dozens of gleaming interlocked teeth on display. When it reached him, those teeth would part as the jaws opened and then it would bite him in half. There was no escape.

The growling got louder.

It was no shark. It was the '59 Caddy El Dorado eating up the night. Still, it was a shark. It had the sleek fins of a guided missile, gleaming bone-white trim, and a glistening black hide. Its bullet taillights were the color of blood, its headlights lit like glowing baleful eyes, its chrome grill morphing into the fang-filled mouth of some primeval nightmare from the dawn of the world.

As it came closer, Flynn realized the growling was the sound of its engine—the triple-carb V8 that could bite down with 345 horsepower when the mood struck and launch it forward at 130 miles an hour.

It would have him.

It would feed on him.

Its jaws would crunch his bones to splinters.

Crying out silently, he kept trying to move, dragging his feet as the growling of the Caddy got closer and closer and he could feel the heat of its engine and the sweet, clean smell of the oil pumping through it.

Its front bumper nudged him and he went loose and greasy with abject terror. He looked back one last time as its mouth opened to swallow him whole and he saw two grotesque forms sitting in the front seat. He didn't know what they were, but they certainly weren't Toddy or Bones.

In fact, they weren't even human.

SYMBIOSIS

BY TIM CURRAN

1

"We're gonna take a ride now, Flynn. Just you and me in this here street-hungry shark, which calls itself the El Dorado," Toddy said, his mouth grinning like a jagged knife cut in his pallid face. "Yes, sir, just a nice little drive in the country to distant places and while we drive, you're going to do some thinking. You're going to decide who lives and who dies. Just like the Grim Reaper, you're going to make a choice because life is all about choices, now ain't it?"

2

1980

Flynn was a new kid and he wanted more than anything to fit in seamlessly. To become part of the greater whole and sometimes that was just the hardest thing to do. New kid. New school. And in eleventh grade yet. This was not the time to be starting fresh. Pecking orders were well-established, cliques organized, and circles rigidly closed to outsiders. Dropping into the socially ordered world of Compton High, he made nary a ripple. A week into it, he was politely ignored. A month into it, he was a target. Maybe they smelled new meat. Maybe they were standing back and trying to figure where he might fit into things. Whether he was cool enough to hang with the popular ones or athletic enough for the jocks, tough enough for the dirtbags or smart enough for the brains. Then, second week of October, Flynn made the decision for them. He got his tray in the lunchroom—spaghetti—and solemnly made for his usual unoccupied corner beneath the big posters announcing the upcoming Halloween dance. Of course, he never saw the outstretched leg and never did find out whom it belonged to. It was just there and he hooked his own foot around it and took the plunge, face-first. The lunchroom exploded with laughter and Flynn tossed his tray aside, covered in tomato sauce and pasta from crotch to chest, stomping away.

Decision was made: Flynn was a dipshit.

Flynn Connors had been a fairly popular kid back in Chicago. He lettered in track and field, dated pretty cheerleaders, and had more friends than he knew what to do with… now that same Flynn Connors, who'd walked high and proud back at his old school, had landed here at Compton High and promptly fell flat on his face.

He could do no right. He said the wrong things at the wrong time, fell over his own feet in gym, was clumsy and foolish and idiotic. Whatever magic had impelled him back in Chicago, leaked out of him at Compton (probably with a high, squeaking flatulence), leaving him deflated. The jury was most certainly in: he was a dick (and a limp one at that). Take equal parts stupidity, incompetence, and self-doubt, shake it up and down and all around like an iced martini and what you poured out—spilling most of it, of course— was the new, inept, and socially unacceptable Flynn Connors, the proverbial left hand and rusty third wheel, wingnut extraordinaire, the piss in the pudding every time.

But how could it be?

How could it have happened? He'd been on top last year, or nearly. And now he had sunk to the lower rungs of the food chain, a mud-sucking bottom feeder. The magic had died and, Jesus, this was no good at all. This was wearing the scarlet letter and the perpetual KICK ME sign.

He was a legend in the world of dipshits now. They'd never let him forget or live it down. In one fell swoop he'd destroyed his future.

After his performance in the lunchroom, it got worse. The doors were thrown wide open and the target on Flynn's ass was so big everyone saw it. Every jerk in school tried to repeat that hilarious maneuver and some days it seemed like he was dancing through a gauntlet of outstretched feet. But that was only the half of it. There was Icy Hot in his jock in gym class. The dish soap strategically placed around the rim of his pop bottle so that when he gagged and coughed, he blew bubbles. There were groups of popular girls that broke into gales of laughter every time he passed. The signs taped to his back that read KISS ME I'M A FAG and I WEAR PINK PANTIES. The love letter from him to Candy Horace, a massive and violent girl with unpleasant Neanderthal features that proceeded to shove him on his ass every time she saw him. And, the icing on the cake: the none-too-subtle messages scrawled on his locker in permanent marker, FLYNN SUCKS DICK and TWINKLE, TWINKLE, LITTLE FLYNN, BEND HIM OVER SLIDE IT IN, for all to see.

It was a living hell.

The sort of things that might push some students to drugs, the razor, or random bursts of violence—but it only pushed Flynn deeper inside himself so that it felt like day by day he was wearing an extra three inches of padding just to absorb the blows and humiliation. Slowly, he became desensitized, withdrawn, antisocial. Maybe he looked like a sixteen-year-old boy from a distance, but if you got in close, you saw the truth: he was a bag of hay, a scarecrow pretending to be a sixteen-year-old boy. He was a non-entity—dead and empty. The only thing with depth were his eyes and they were like old wounds, pockets of scar tissue.

He needed help.

And then, one day, he found it. Or it found him.

3

Here's how it happened:

Two weeks before Halloween, he opened his locker to find that he'd had visitors. His notebook was shredded to confetti. His jacket had been slit right up the back. And then, as an added incentive, somebody had opened his folder, taken his bio report on flatworms, and inserted a particularly slimy and vile dog turd between the pages and closed it again. Squeezing it shut so that the offending loaf was smeared into a smelly blob that had oozed out like melted chocolate. Even the plastic cover was soiled. There was no way to save any of the report. He stood there, swimming in the pervasive, unrelenting stench. A note was taped to the back of his locker. It read: A GIFT FROM YOUR FRIENDS.

He was mortified, his face hot and his throat constricted, his belly lurching in waves like he might vomit at any moment; but he did not vomit. He put on no show of any kind. For surely, in those crowded hallways, eyes were upon him, endlessly amused, waiting to see what Dorko's reaction would be. Trembling, his guts twisting, he slammed the door closed.

And that was how he met Chad.

Chad was a heavy, round kid with freckles and sandy blond hair combed into a wild birds' nest. "You getting tired of this shit?" he said. "You had enough yet?"

Flynn swallowed and swallowed again. "What's it to you?"

"I'm your friend," Chad said. "I'm probably the only one you got."

But Flynn wasn't so sure of that. He knew who Chad was. They were in the same English class. He didn't associate much with the others. In fact, they gave him a wide berth. But that didn't mean he wasn't in on it with them. Didn't mean that at all. Because standing there, staring at him, Flynn had a real ugly feeling inside. Like maybe Chad was real bad news. A rope waiting to become a noose.

"You get tired of it," Chad said. "I'll help you. You let me know."

Then he just walked away.

Two uppity jocks, Norm Kinder and Bobby Swinn, were coming up the corridor in their football letter jackets. These two tormented Flynn maybe a little worse than the others. But despite their rank, position, and social standing, they got out of Chad's way. No "Hey, fatso" or "Step aside, lardass." Nope. Nothing like that. They gave him a wide berth as if something about him turned them white inside. And maybe it did at that.

In third period government class, Flynn was ostracized to the point that he was shuffled into the far left corner with the losers, nerds, and those kids who weren't real big on hygiene. Daryl Smite, a thin kid who was rarely seen without pimples on his nose and an Asimov or Star Trek paperback lovingly cradled atop his armload of textbooks and binders, was one of the few that openly engaged in chat with him.

Daryl was a math whiz who was taking college classes as a junior—physics and trig—and already had his sights set on a career in astrophysics and quantum mechanics. While the other "losers on the left" (as they were known) picked their noses, trembled, played with their Texas Instruments calculators, or just plain tried to be unseen. Daryl liked to chat endlessly about the Voyager space probe and the perihelion of Comet West.

Flynn asked him about Chad.

"Chad?"

"You know, Chad Reese. Kind of chubby."

Daryl brayed with laughter, getting ugly looks from the popular kids. Unperturbed, he said, "Kind of? That's like saying a fish kind of swims." He giggled at his own joke. "What about him?"

"Seems like he'd be a target for Norm and Bobby and the rest of those dickheads, but they leave him alone."

Daryl looked suddenly more than a little nervous. "Yes. Well. Um. The thing is, Chad is not someone to mess with."

"And why is that?" Flynn asked.

Chad was big, but he was soft and dopey and perfectly harmless. He practically had a FUCK WITH ME: I WILL NOT FIGHT BACK sign on his forehead.

"Well, you know…um, the thing is," Daryl said, repeatedly swallowing as if something was stuck in his throat.

"He's got a badass brother? He carries a gun? His old man's a Hell's Angel…what?"

Daryl sighed, looking around as if he feared he might be overheard. He reminded Flynn of a dissident living behind the Iron Curtain that was afraid to speak his mind.

"Let's just say that you don't want to piss him off," Daryl whispered. "Things have a way of happening to his enemies. Enough said."

Much as he tried, Flynn could not get him to say anything more than that. For the rest of the hour, he politely ignored him. Apparently at Compton there were things you talked about and those you didn't. The way Daryl acted, you would have thought old chubby Chad was in the Mafia or something.

4

Later, Flynn slipped out of fifth hour bio only to find Norm and Bobby loitering in the hallway, both looking big and mean in their football jackets. They instinctively zeroed in on him, of course.

"Well, well, well, if it isn't my favorite little cocksucker," Norm said.

Bobby grinned, amazed as always at how Norm came up with things like that. He liked it so much he had to repeat it: "My favorite little cocksucker. I like that."

Norm beamed with pride. "How's it going, faggot? I hear you started shaving your pussy."

Flynn bristled. He could have turned the other cheek as usual, but it had been going on so long by that point that he'd run out of cheeks. All the humiliation and bullshit boiled black inside of him.

"Smells like shit in here," Bobby said, which was the only line he really had so he repeated it daily.

"So close your mouth," Flynn said.

Bobby's jaw hung open. He couldn't believe this. It was like trying to kick a mangy dog and getting kicked back. That's not how it worked. That's not how the game was played. Shit-sniffers like Flynn needed to know their place. He only wished he had the intellectual tools to out-smartass him, but as it was he could only stand there, shocked and unamused, a pimple-faced muscle sculpture with all the cunning of a dirty diaper.

The defiance, in fact, locked Norm up, too, only for a second or two, but dear God, how delicious those few fleeting moments were. Flynn felt like he was tap-dancing on top of their heads. Then he came down to Earth and came down hard. Because when the shock faded, the fists came. Norm punched Flynn in the stomach and landed a few good ones on top of his head that drove him into the floor like a tent spike. And Bobby, not to be outdone, gave him a good, swift punter's kick in the ass that drove him into the lockers.

"See you after school, homo," Bobby told him.

Dozens of kids witnessed the confrontation, of course, but not a one came forward to finger the perpetrators. They didn't need that kind of trouble. And, besides, in their immature little brains it all was kind of funny. Funny because Flynn was this weirdo from another school who landed at Compton, head held high and chest puffed out like he was really something when he was nothing at all. He should've known his place and gradually worked his way up the ladder, rung by rung; it was how it was done. But that little jack-off thought he was too good for that. He wanted to swim with the big fish in clear, blue waters at the top of the food chain instead of accepting his lowly rank as a mud guppy, a bottom-feeder, a sludge puppy. But Norm and Bobby sure showed him, all right. You just had to laugh because Flynn had it coming.

Boy, did he ever.

And to those kids who watched it happen—two big guys against one smaller guy, tsk, tsk—or looked away and pretended they didn't see it at all or smiled uncomfortably because they dared *not* smile with those two apes and incur their wrath—they were just thankful it wasn't them. They *thanked God* it wasn't them. Because at Compton High the last thing you needed were those two apes exposing you as the stuck-up/selfish/vacuous princess you indeed were or the gutless/cowardly/weak-kneed yes-man you were becoming and would be the rest of your narrow little life as a hamster on the wheel.

Flynn breezed through the rest of the day, thinking, brooding, and scheming, coming up with elaborate revenge plans that were ridiculous and mostly copied from Chuck Norris movies he'd seen. Bottom line was, he didn't know kung fu, this was not the movies, and he couldn't blow them away without blowing away his entire life in the process—so it was time to take a good beating.

He knew he didn't stand a chance against those goons. All day long kids were eyeing him up, waiting for him to crack and go to the principal. It was like High Noon all over again. But he wasn't going to back down. Maybe they would hurt him, but he would make damn sure they paid for that privilege in blood and loose teeth. That was important. Not only for himself but for the rest of those wet ends that watched him get bullied and had done nothing about it.

Sixth hour came, world history, and before Flynn even got through the door he felt a warm paw on his shoulder. He spun, ready for action, but it was only Chad.

"You know it doesn't have to be this way," he said.

Flynn swallowed. The entire school must have known about it by now, the beat-down of the century, the blue ribbon ass-kicking they would be talking about for years to come. "I don't see much of a way out."

"You're wrong. There is a way." He pulled Flynn aside and said, "Last year, I was you. Those pricks fucked with me constantly. I was ready to come into school with my old man's twelve-gauge and straighten some asses out. Then...well, let's just say divine intervention shone down upon me. I hooked up with some guys. They took care of my business and they'll take care of yours."

Flynn was suspicious. "Like...what? Some hoods? Some bikers? What are you talking about?"

"I'm talking about giving to those most in need, about straightening out your mess, about friends who will make your enemies their own. And when that happens...God help little Bobby and Norm and the rest of the Compton High varsity turds."

Flynn liked the idea as much as he feared it. But services like that couldn't be free and that was what really scared him. Who were these people? Some kind of gang or professional thugs? Whoever they were, they must have been some real ringers. Bobby and Norm were big guys, both built like brick shithouses. They weren't the sort you wanted to take on if you could avoid it. Still, Flynn knew there were some real animals in this world, cold-blooded monsters that would make the biggest, meanest jock piss their pants...but did he really want to be in debt to people like that?

"I'll handle it myself," he finally said.

"Ah, poor Flynn. I knew him well," Chad said.

Though it didn't occur to him at the time, later when Flynn thought about it, it seemed that his refusal somehow relieved Chad as much as it made him nervous. It was hard to understand such conflicting emotions at the time, but later it made all the sense in the world.

Sixth hour ground to a halt and Flynn went to his locker to put his stuff away. He neither rushed from the school like the others or unnecessarily loitered. He tried to be cool and laid-back. They would be waiting for him, so let them get anxious, let them worry that he had gone to the principal or something because they knew as he did that if they got busted bullying and beating another kid, they would be barred from sports.

So Flynn took his time.

He had already refused Chad, so he was definitely on his own. Nobody would help him. He began to feel more and more like Marshal Kane in High Noon. It was showdown time and it could not be avoided. He always exited the school through the entrance in the west wing, so that's what he did today. He would do nothing differently. He would not give them the satisfaction of thinking they had spooked him. He would walk out the doors and let them see no fear.

At first, he didn't see them because they were hiding around the side of the building, carefully cloaked in the bushes. Despite their size and strength advantage, they still wanted to get the jump on him, big tough guys that they were.

They rushed out and Flynn felt his stomach drop into his shoes. And then they were on him.

Bobby reached him first, grabbing for him with big meaty hands and Flynn did the only thing he could do—he brought the massive tome of his world history text to bear. He had it cradled in his left arm and flung it right at Bobby's face like a discus and had the pleasure of seeing Bobby cry out and stagger backward as it was right on target.

By then Norm had him, screaming, "YOU'LL PAY FOR THAT, YOU LITTLE FUCKING FAGGOT!"

Then Flynn was going at it with Norm, ducking two of his punches and taking a third that glanced off his cheekbone and nearly tore his ear off. But he got in one good punch, smashing his fist into Norm's left eye before taking a shot to the forehead that made his skull explode with stars. He kicked Norm in the shins, stomped on his foot with everything he had, took another shot, and landed a good one to Norm's jaw that made his head fly back.

Then Bobby hit him from behind and he nearly went out cold. He slumped over and Norm got him in a headlock while Bobby punched him in the stomach, doubling him over and knocking the wind—and fight—right out of him. The only good thing was that Bobby's lip was torn open, his chin wet with blood and his teeth pink.

But that was all she wrote because as Norm held him, Bobby pounded him mercilessly. Flynn took two good shots to the face, and three more to the top of the head that dropped him to the sidewalk—and then they were kicking the stuffing out of him.

Broken, beaten, and humiliated, he lay there, refusing to cry but feeling the tears washing the blood down his face. At which point, Mr. Martin, the geography teacher, showed up and helped him over to a bench to sit down.

"Who did this to you?" he asked.

And it was at that moment, doubled-over with pain that he had an epiphany as he stared up at Mr. Martin's face. He knows who did it. He fucking watched it happen. He didn't want to believe it, yet he knew it was true. Mr. Martin had seen it happen and only charged out to help once the dust had settled.

"Flynn…you have to tell me who did this to you."

"That's my business and…I'll handle it in my own way," he told him, spitting out blood.

Mr. Martin looked relieved, didn't he? Oh yes, he certainly did.

"This needs to be handled," he said, nearly choking on the froth of his own regurgitative bullshit. "You can't let people get away with this."

"They already did." He paused. "And you saw it."

"I did nothing of the kind!"

"Yes, you did."

While Mr. Martin stammered and stumbled over his words, Flynn, threaded with aches and pains, wondered why he hadn't broken it up. Was he afraid of them? No, he didn't think it was that. There was only one thing it could be—Mr. Martin was a big booster of the Compton Leopards football team. He'd played for them himself back in the '50s and everyone in his classes had to hear about it again and again. He announced the games on fall nights over at the athletic field and if you drove past his house over on

Pine, he had Leopards pennants and flags flying high and proud. You'd have thought they'd won the Super Bowl the way he carried on. He's protecting those idiots because they're good athletes. Bobby is the star running back and Norm is the best wide receiver this school ever saw. Yeah, that was it. They were both assholes with kitty litter for brains but they were good with a ball and that's all that counted.

Flynn knew he was expendable.

Bobby and Norm were not.

As Mr. Martin went on and on, assuring him of his complete innocence in the matter and vowing to punish the guilty parties—yeah, and turtles can fucking fly and submarines have screen doors and cows have kickstands—to the full extent of the law, what old shit-for-brains alumni extraordinaire and president of the Leopards fan club was really saying was, Sure, they're wild boys but we need 'em to make the plays and give us the numbers, so let's just keep quiet about this, shall we? He went on and on and Flynn, despite his pain, wanted to laugh. Mr. Martin was a real clown. He wondered if he performed at faculty meetings, riding around on a unicycle, pumping a horn, and shaking a rubber chicken.

Finally, Flynn got up, refusing to be brought to the school nurse. "I'm all right. But next time you see those fucking monkeys beating a kid, you might want to intervene."

He left Mr. Martin there trying to assure him that he would never allow such a thing to happen…even though he most surely had.

5

As he walked home, Flynn knew there was no way in hell he could let his mom and dad see him like this. His mom would flip out and have the state police, county sheriff, and the FBI involved before she was through and that would barely stem her rage. She was a great mom and Flynn knew it, but you didn't want to cross her. His dad was just the opposite—laid-back and easygoing, always had that, Aw, shucks, what can you do about it? look on his face.

But Mom was different. Mom was a missile out in a silo in Nebraska waiting to reign hell down on the Ruskies. She was canned heat. She was Godzilla itching to stomp Tokyo. She was potential energy ready to go kinetic and God help any that were in her path. By the time she was done threatening, rallying her forces, and suing the ever living balls off the school district, Mr. Martin would no longer have a job and Compton High wouldn't be able to afford a football team.

Flynn knew she loved him and she was a real mother bear protecting her cubs when it came to her children, but…well, despite the beating he'd taken, it just didn't look right for a guy to have his mother fighting his battles.

No, there had to be another way.

Regardless, he couldn't let her see him like that or she'd go up like the bomb that fell on Hiroshima. He had to come up with something. As he walked…well, limped…home, he kept turning it around in his mind. In his desperation, he even thought of throwing himself out in front of a moving car, but that was definitely adding insult to injury and he wasn't about to drag some innocent driver down with him.

Dad would still be at work at the license bureau for several hours, but Mom would be home. She worked mornings at State Farm, but her afternoons were free. Ever since Bethany went away to college to study marketing and Flynn had reached the age where he could look after himself, she had a lot of time on her hands. She didn't like crafts or soap operas like other moms and crossword puzzles pissed her off, so she had taken up watercolor painting.

She went to the arts center twice a week for instruction. At first, she had sucked at it but she was gradually getting better. Her choice of subject matter left a little something to be desired—kitschy clowns of all things. Clowns with balloons. Clowns walking tight wires with little umbrellas in their hands. Clowns laughing. Clowns crying. Clowns riding on the backs of horses (he never understood that at all). He had always wondered who painted those awful clown paintings you see in peoples' houses—usually your cat-loving great aunt Tilly or Granny Mircella, who wasn't quite right in the head—but now he knew.

The problem with Mom's clowns (besides the obvious) were that they always looked angry. It was something Flynn and his dad giggled over. They always looked like they'd walked the hard road and maybe done a little time for simple larceny. Chuckles ain't in the mood for your shit today, kiddies, so fuck off. He had a hard night with his pal Johnny Walker, capisce?

Mom would no doubt be home rendering another disenfranchised clown.

What to do about that?

Flynn thought it over and over and the answer came to him unbidden: his motorcycle. He had a Suzuki 125 out in the garage that his old man had gotten for him and his mother was vehemently opposed to. She called it a death trap and an accident waiting to happen.

Sure enough, her car was in the driveway.

It wasn't unusual for him to hop on the bike for a spin after school so he did just that. Riding hurt like hell but it would all be worth it, he thought—if it worked. He came back an hour later having spent most of his time lying in the grass beneath an oak. He walked into the house, bruised and banged-up.

"Had a little spill," he said.

Mom's paintbrush went airborne, she rushed over to him, and he let the wheels spin and propel him along. He had to go to the clinic, of course, and get checked out. No broken bones, thank God, lacerations and contusions aplenty but nothing serious. When he got home, he was tucked in bed and he did little but eat steaming cups of Mug-O-Lunch, ice cream, and Pop-Tarts. His dad came home with the new issue of Cream and brought him some cheeseburgers from Burger Chef. It almost seemed that all was right in the world.

But it wasn't.

As he watched Magnum, P.I. and then Barney Miller, he kept thinking about Mr. Martin and particularly Norm and Bobby. They were probably having a real hoot over the whole thing and that's what bothered Flynn the most.

That they were going to get away with it.

That they weren't going to get punished.

And that they knew this and gloated over the fact. That's what really turned the screw in his belly and made him hunger for revenge. Some accounts just had to be settled. As he drifted off that night, he thought real hard about what Chad had said.

6

His mom insisted he take the rest of the week off from school and he was okay with that. By Monday, he was feeling pretty good, but the knowing leers and mocking smiles he got from people nearly turned his stomach. Got yours, didn't you, Flynn? He was called into the principal's office during second hour. Mr. Martin, of course, had done his teacherly duty and reported what happened last week. Flynn was grilled by Mr. Russel in the presence of Mr. Martin, but he wouldn't give any names.

"I just can't understand why you're being so difficult about this, Flynn. This kind of thing can't go unpunished."

"You wouldn't do anything about it anyway," he told him.

And there was no mistaking the fact that Mr. Martin flushed and had to look away.

Mr. Russel kept at it. He wanted names and he wanted witnesses. Flynn would not cooperate. He knew then, deep in his heart, that accounts would be settled but not by a couple pecksniffs like Russel and Martin that were waving the Compton Leopards flag. Their brains had long since stopped functioning.

The interrogation ended there with Mr. Russel at his wit's end. Flynn had a strong desire to say, if you want to know who did it, ask Mr. Martin. But he didn't. Maybe he should have, but something in him—pride? Self-respect?—wouldn't let him sink to that. Mr. Martin knew and he had to live with that knowledge. Flynn hoped it gave him a fucking aneurism.

For three days, it was quiet. He did not see Bobby or Norm and the looks from the other students began to fade. He saw Mr. Martin a few times, but he refused to meet the accusatory look in Flynn's eyes. That was okay. That was just fine. Sooner or later, he was going to regret what he did. That's what Flynn kept telling himself. That in the end, shitheads like Martin always got what they deserved. He honestly didn't believe it, but it made him feel better to think so.

Then on Thursday, things started to heat up again. He walked the halls between classes feeling like the lone man who had dared stand up to the system, meeting every look with one of his own. Before he got to bio that day, he ran into Norm and Bobby. He took pleasure in the fact that Bobby had a good shiner that was just beginning to fade and Norm had a nasty-looking scar on his lip that continued up an inch toward his nose.

"You think this is done, don't you?" Norm said.

"No, it's not done. Not by a long shot."

"Oh, you hear that, Bobby? Piss-boy is threatening us. I guess we'll see you after school again, pussy."

"You can count on it."

But they didn't see him after school. It was all bluff and bravado. He would have liked nothing better than to give Norm a matching set of shiners, but he didn't feel like taking a beating again. Frustrated and angry, he walked right out of school that day and went straight home, telling his mom he was coming down with something. He spent a good hour in his room, sobbing and punching his pillow, thinking about it all and hating them and maybe hating himself a little bit more. It had all gone too far and he couldn't live like that anymore. He just couldn't. But what could he do? What could he really do?

Then the phone rang.

"Hey, Flynn," the voice said. "You know who this is?"

Flynn did. Chad. Chad again.

Like he knew. He knew I was at the end of my rope and he knew just when to call, Flynn thought.

"Yeah. What do you want?"

Chad laughed. "Oh, don't play dumb. Don't be a whipping boy your entire life. It's not about what I want, it's about what you want. Are you sick of that shit yet?"

Flynn swallowed, his mouth betraying him: "Yeah...I can't take it anymore."

"Okay...then what you need are the right friends."

Flynn sat there. Who were they? A gang? But by that point, he honestly didn't give a rat's ass. He wanted payback in the worst possible way. He wanted blood and he intended on having it one way or another. "Yeah, that's what I want. Can you recommend some?"

"I can if you're sure it's what you want," Chad said. And was there something in his voice? A hesitation? An undercurrent of dread? Something Chad didn't dare put into words, but one that clearly said, You sure, Flynn? You sure you want to go this far?

But Flynn said, "It's what I want."

"Okay," Chad sighed. "Okay. You know the alley behind the National Fruit building off Main?"

"Yeah."

"Be there in an hour."

"Why?"

Chad chuckled in a cool voice. "Because…because we'll have a present for you."

The line went dead. Flynn sat there a long time, staring at the phone before placing it back on its cradle. Here was a way out being offered to him, yet…yet, he couldn't shake a feeling of apprehension about it all. Like maybe he'd just made the worst mistake of his life.

We'll have a present for you.

7

Mistake or not, ten minutes later he was on Main, passing all the storefronts with their cardboard Halloween cutouts taped to the windows—witches peering over cauldrons, pumpkin-headed jesters, crepe-paper skeletons—just rushing along, his heart pounding and nerves jangling. The A&P had hamburger on sale and you could bowl two games for the price of one at Taplinger Lanes, take advantage of the Spooktacular Savings at Lauerman's Department Store and get half-off rubber masks at Rexall Drugs. Flynn turned the corner past Clyde's Barbershop and nearly ran into a guy dressed like a ghost. He had a red bucket in one hand, collecting for Unicef's Halloween drive.

"Boo," he said.

Flynn nearly had a heart attack. It was Halloween tomorrow for godsake; people running around in sheets was hardly a novelty… yet, a fear that was formless and nameless got under his skin and stayed there, refusing to leave. It haunted his bones like a ghost clinging to the rafters of a deserted house. He couldn't explain it or rationalize it; it was simply there. Only later did he understand that it was a foreboding of the worst possible type.

As he walked, a voice in the back of his head said, It's not too late, you know. You can turn back and call all this off before it gets out of hand. It's never too late for that.

But it was.

Because certain things set into action cannot be recalled and certain forces once called up cannot be put down.

He kept going until he spotted the National Fruit building dead center of a row of warehouses. It was a grimy, industrial area of machine shops and freight depots, the train yards down the way. The air smelled like rust and machine oil. Flynn cut into the alley alongside National Fruit and there, just beyond a loading dock, was a little grassy courtyard flanked by a boarded-up railroad hotel. Chad was there.

"Hey, Flynn, what took ya?"

"Got here as quick as I could."

The first thing he saw was a long, sleek black Cadillac. With its rising tailfins it looked like a missile. He had poured over enough of his dad's classic car magazines by that point to know a 1959 El Dorado when he saw one. The second thing he saw were two guys standing behind it. Tall, hard-looking guys with flat-top crewcuts, white T-shirts, cuffed jeans, and scuffed black leather engineer's boots with buckles on them. One was blond and the other was dark. They were both pale as ghosts. They looked like a couple hoods from the 1950s, the sort that show up in black-and-white AIP movies at three in the morning.

Flynn looked at them and felt a chill run down his spine, dread opening up in his belly like a buzzard stretching its wings. They looked older, like they'd been around awhile. Experience and rough living had lined their faces, given them old scars and wounds that had never healed probably, both of which twisted their features into sardonic death masks.

Chad introduced them. The blond guy was Bones; the dark-haired guy was Toddy. Their eyes were filled with acid. It bubbled and simmered, looking as if it could have eaten holes in sheet metal.

Here they are, Flynn thought, his knees badly needing to knock together like a schmuck in a cartoon. These are your patron saints. These are the devils that are coming to your aid. Take a good look.

Facedown in the curled autumn leaves, there was another in attendance. He was wearing a purple-and-white Compton High Leopards letter jacket. He was shaking and groaning. Chad didn't bother introducing him, but then he didn't really need to.

Oh Christ, what have they done? What have they done?

Toddy smiled at Flynn, his eyes black as chips of flint. "See, Bones? Flynn came. I told you he'd come."

Bones did not smile; the cruel slash of his mouth seemed incapable of anything but a sardonic smirk. "Sure, that's what you said."

The kid on the ground struggled and every time he tried to pull himself up, Bones stomped his boot down on his spine, flattening him. That made him smile. Pain and suffering got him off and all you had to do was look into the black fathomless wells of his eyes to know that. He was a hood, a tough guy, a real dyed-in-the-wool fucking meat-eater, but he was not stupid. Flynn saw that right off. There was a black, simmering intelligence in his eyes that would make your heart pound with terror if he looked at you. He stood there, boot on his victim's back, pulling long and slow off a cigarette. His arms were flexing with thick cords of muscle, the hands heavy and callused, the wrists thick, the forearms bulging, the biceps massive and straining beneath the skin like he had softballs in there. There was a skull-and-crossbones tattoo on his left forearm, a scorpion on the right.

Chad said, "Look what we got for you, Flynn."

Toddy laughed with a sound like a shovel scraped over a tomb lid and nodded to his friend. Bones stepped back and let the guy on the ground roll over. It was Bobby Swinn. Big shit on campus, star running back, and all-around jackass. He was moaning, his left eye stark and petrified like a deer waiting for a hunter's bullet, the right swollen purple and nearly closed. Leaves were stuck in his hair and there was blood all over his face. In fact, it had run like a red creek, turning the large C on his letter jacket from pristine white to a dirty pink. Bits of leaves, twigs, and dirt were caught in the livid purple bloodstains on his face.

He was sobbing.

Actually sobbing.

He looked at Flynn with that wide, tormented eye. "Flynn," he said, spitting out a wad of blood and maybe a tooth or two. "Tell 'em it was all a joke! I'm your friend, you know I'm your friend! Tell 'em it was a joke, all a stupid fucking joke—"

Bones chuckled and stomped his boot on Bobby's left hand. There must have been cleats on the bottom, because the skin from his wrist to his knuckles was peeled back right to the meat. Bobby screamed, writhing on the ground, vomiting out a pink clot.

"Call 'em off," he groaned in a snotty, phlegmy voice. "Oh, please, Flynn, call 'em off! Tell 'em it was a joke! Tell 'em I'm your friend! Please! You gotta tell 'em you don't want this! You don't know what they'll do, what—"

"Shut the fuck up," Toddy told him.

Bones kicked him in the face. Something glanced off the tin skirting of National Fruit and Flynn realized they were teeth. Goddamn teeth. Bobby was lying on the ground, a bloody mess. He was making a mumbling/gobbling sound, out of his head with pain and fear.

Toddy walked over. He walked past Chad and Chad shook like somebody had walked over his grave. Toddy grinned like a skull and put those flat black and somehow reptilian eyes on Flynn. Something in that gaze was so intense that Flynn felt his stomach roll over.

"See, Flynn?" he said. "We do you favors, you do us favors. That's how it works, see? You do see that, don't you?"

Flynn had to drag his voice up from the cellar of his throat. "Sure. Sure, I get it."

Toddy put a hand on his shoulder and even through his windbreaker, that hand was as cold as defrosting meat. "See? Flynn's our friend, Bones. Didn't I tell you that he was gonna be our friend?"

Bones nodded, his huge arms folded across his chest. The scorpion tattoo on his forearm—lethal and blood-red—looked like it was going to crawl off at any moment.

"Yeah, that's what you said."

Toddy turned back to Flynn, giving him a gentle little slap on the cheek. There was a Waffen SS death's head symbol tattooed to the back of his hand. "From now on, Flynn, you're with us. Somebody fucks with you, they fuck with us."

"These guys'll be your best friends," Chad said.

Or your worst enemies, a voice in Flynn's head echoed. He knew right then and there that he had just signed his name on the dotted line, signed it in blood and the devil would collect, given time. But for all that, seeing Bobby Swinn writhing on the ground like a worm made him feel good inside—and more like a man than he had in many weeks. Here was power. Here was vengeance. Here was the boot that crushed toads like Bobby Swinn.

"You wanna watch us work on him, Flynn?" Toddy asked him, his face in too close; his breath like moldering canvas. "You wanna watch how these fucks cry for their mamas? Because, trust me, they always do. In the end, they always cry like babies."

But Flynn had had enough.

He hated Bobby with every ounce of venom in his soul. Bobby was the sort of guy who waltzed through school, year by year, immediately accepted. Just because he could run fast and catch a ball, people fawned over him. Though he was not particularly bright and his personality was shit, all the kids admired and respected him. They laughed at every stupid, insipid joke he made, hung on his every word like he was Gandhi and not some idiot who could barely string a sentence together and was squeaking by in remedial English.

In the real world, he was a zero; in the convoluted, fantasy world of high school, a prodigy. He got the prettiest girls, got invited to the best parties, and drove a brand-new Camaro. A gift from his old man who, like everyone else, was simply enamored of his son. Not realizing that after graduation, that if those sports scholarships didn't come through, old Bobby would be real challenged just handling the deep-fryer at A&W or figuring out which end of the broom to use when he swept up over at Woolworths.

So, yeah, Flynn hated Bobby and anyone like him. Anyone with all the free passes and good luck who decided it wasn't enough, that they had to be Class-A, prime-cut assholes to boot. Guys who had to take others down so they could rise up and feel better about themselves because inside they were miserable, small, crawling worms and they were terrified people would find out. But as much as he hated Bobby, what was happening now was plain wrong. This was not just a beating; this was an atrocity.

But a voice in the back of his head tried to set him straight: Did Bobby show you any mercy when he and Norm jumped you? If the tables were turned, do you think he'd show you one ounce of fucking compassion?

Still, Flynn didn't like it. This was wrong, it was criminal. "Maybe…maybe he's had enough," he said, honestly afraid that if Toddy turned Bones loose, he would kill Bobby, actually kill him.

Toddy turned on him, eyes seeping with blackness. He grabbed Flynn by the shirt. "Hell's wrong with you, man? You think that puke would ever back off on you? You think him and Normie Kinder and the rest of those dipfucks would ever show you mercy?"

It was as if he had read his thoughts.

Flynn was breathing hard. "No...no they wouldn't."

Toddy didn't release him. He pulled him closer, so close he could see into his eyes, see what was behind them and it looked like a graveyard waiting to be filled.

"Listen to me, man," Toddy said. "We're doing this for you! For you! I gotta know right fucking now if you're with us or against us. What's it gonna be? Because you look like a smart boy and I'm thinking you don't want to be against us...you don't want that, do you?"

Flynn shook his head.

"Good. Good boy. You're gonna work out. I can see that. And once you're our friend, Flynn, you're always our friend. We'll always be looking out for you. A year, ten, twenty...don't make no difference, once you're in, you're in, and there's no walking away."

"What...what are you gonna do with him?"

"We're gonna wait for midnight," Toddy said. "Then it'll be Halloween. Then this fucking piece of shit is going trick-or-treating."

Bones giggled.

Chad came over and led Flynn out of the alley as Bones dragged Bobby toward the El Dorado as if he weighed about ten pounds. Bobby was indeed crying for his mother and Flynn knew without a doubt that he would never see her again. He felt hollow inside as he heard the grating laughter of Bones and Toddy. He looked back once and he saw the trunk of the Caddy open, making a smacking sound like parting wet lips.

"No," Chad said, turning him away from it. "It's better not to see certain things."

Then the courtyard was well behind them and the sun was sinking behind the rooftops. Night was coming on, cool and insistent and forever.

Neither said anything until they got to Main Street. By then, Flynn could barely hold it in any longer. "Who are those guys?" he asked.

But Chad shook his head. "I gave you a choice on the phone, Flynn. You could have walked away from this, no harm done."

"What do you mean?"

Chad looked around, a scared look in his eyes. "Just don't hold it against me, all right?"

"Hold what against you?"

But Chad was gone.

Flynn stood there, all by his lonesome on the corner. He felt somehow confused, exhilarated, and sick to his stomach, knowing he had made a choice in something and wondering if there honestly had been a choice at all. The leaves blew up the walks with a scratching sound and for some reason, he thought that's how they would sound blowing over the mouth of a tomb in a windy graveyard.

8

He couldn't get it out of his mind. He tried to justify it all by telling himself that Bobby Swinn was nothing but a big, greasy sack of shit and that sooner or later somebody was going flush him. There was truth to that just as there was truth to the fact that Bobby was a bully and an asshole and an all-around waste of living, breathing flesh. Those were immutable, incontrovertible facts. If you put those before a jury, you would certainly win your case. But the only jury that was trying this case was his own conscience and it was telling him flat out that, yes, Bobby was indeed a steaming, stinking overfilled diaper but that it was not his place nor was it his job to play judge, jury, and executioner. Those sorts of things had to be left to a higher authority.

These were the things that went through Flynn's mind for days after the National Fruit Incident (as it came to be known). His days were tormented, his nights generally sleepless. What shut-eye he did get was usually bad as the fate of Bobby Swinn invaded his dreams and informed his nightmares, turning them into real horrors in which Toddy and Bones were not human at all but night-winged vultures that picked the flesh from Bobby's bones with hooked, scabrous beaks.

On Friday, Halloween, Bobby was not in school.

Flynn saw Norm Kinder walking the halls alone or sometimes with some other guys wearing the obligatory Leopards letter jackets. Norm never met his eyes. Something had gone wrong in his world and he looked, if anything, despondent. Flynn wondered if there was more going on there than just Bobby's absence; if maybe Toddy and Bones were trolling for Norm, too, and Norm felt it.

The day finally ended and Flynn went home.

All the way he felt haunted, his heart pounding and his temples throbbing at the carved pumpkins on porches, the scarecrows and Halloween decorations in windows. So many sneering witches and grinning skulls. He had never stopped to realize in his short life that Halloween was essentially about death. Maybe it had become a fun, silly lark by 1980, a night for dressing up and begging candy, going to parties and pranking...but at its roots it was all about death, a memory of dark sacrificial rites performed in sacred groves to keep the dead in their graves and the ghosts from scratching at your windows long past midnight. He learned that in U.S. history in seventh grade, but it wasn't until now that he actually thought much about it.

Sacrifice.

You make a sacrifice for good luck.

You make a sacrifice so the dark gods will favor you.

You make a sacrifice, a blood offering, to better your life and appease supernatural forces so that they'll look kindly upon you, removing obstacles from your path.

You make a sacrifice because—

We do you favors, you do us favors.

Oh, Jesus, what had he gotten himself into now?

At home, Mom had the house decorated and never, ever in his life had Flynn been so utterly disturbed by something as innocuous as jack-o'-lanterns and crepe paper skeletons. He handed out candy to trick-or-treaters, Snickers and Clark bars, Zagnuts and Pixy Stix, because he really had nothing better to do. The little kids made him smile more often than not, but once, just after dark, when he found a lone skeleton standing out there, he felt something cold gather at his spine. It was nothing but a stray reveler grabbing a last few treats before making his way to the night's parties, but in Flynn's mind it was something else entirely—a goblin come begging for an offering. He stuffed candy into the skeleton's bag, but still the skeleton stood there. Give him more, he thought. Give him whatever it takes to get him off the porch. So he did, a cold fear settling into him that if he didn't, the skeleton would take off its plastic skull mask and beneath it he would see Bobby Swinn's bird-pecked face.

It was not a good night.

He had nothing really to do, nothing to distract himself with.

He wasn't the most popular guy at Compton High so it wasn't like he was the belle of the ball with dozens of party invitations. His lone invitation was from Daryl Smite, whose father was loading up neighborhood kids in his station wagon and taking them out to the Riverhill drive-in for an all-night horror fest.

"Oh, you gotta come! My dad's nuts! He's a real mental case!" Daryl insisted. "We stuff ourselves on candy and hot dogs and pizza, then about three in the morning, we go pranking and knock on people's doors and stuff."

"With your dad?"

"He organizes the whole thing! I told you he's nuts! He's a real gas," Daryl said, which reminded Flynn again of those old 1950s AIP movies that were shown at three a.m. It was the only place you could realistically hear anyone say the word "gas" as a cool thing.

In the end, Flynn declined and it wasn't because of the social ostracizing that was connected to anything Daryl was involved in, but because he just wasn't in the mood for anything remotely approaching fun.

He spent the rest of the night watching horror movies with his mom, pretending to enjoy himself as he stared blankly at old black-and-white spook shows like Terror in the Crypt, The Spider, and Blood of Dracula. Fifteen minutes into the latter, his mom fell asleep on the couch and he found himself staring not at the TV but at the darkness creeping around the edges of the drawn drapes at the living room window. The wind was kicking up and he could hear leaves blowing up the street. For some reason, this gave him a cold chill.

Seconds after he shut off Blood of Dracula, he heard a car drive by very slowly, its engine hopped up and rumbling. His stomach rolled over at the sound of it and for a few desperate moments he thought he might vomit out of pure, unadulterated terror. He waited there in the darkness for five, then ten minutes, listening for the return of the car, which he knew without a doubt would be a 1959 Cadillac El Dorado. He was terrified it would stop out front and he would hear the clumping of boots as Toddy and Bones came calling.

But it didn't happen.

It was probably some teenagers out fooling around. This is what he told himself. He almost believed it. Maybe it wasn't the El

Dorado. Maybe. Yet, he knew it was out there. He could feel it like a swimmer can feel a shark circling them. It was out there, all right, a black-finned predator cruising the streets in search of meat.

On Saturday, after a sleepless night, he couldn't seem to relax. He kept waiting for the El Dorado to pull into the driveway or for the phone to ring, Chad summoning him to another meeting with Bones and Toddy where they would demand payment for services rendered. But neither happened. All in all, it was a boring day.

Around five, his mom took a break from her latest clown painting—another clown on a horse, this one balancing on one foot and holding up a tiny umbrella—and found him sprawled on the couch. "Are you just going to sit around all day and watch Godzilla movies?"

"I don't know."

"Who should I ask?"

"I just don't feel like anything."

"Well, if you need suggestions, the front yard could use some raking."

"It always comes down to things like that with you."

"That's the way I am," she admitted. "I'm pushing fifty and my bones are getting creaky and I'm waiting for my change of life so I can turn into a real moody freak, shivering one minute and sweating the next. Then I look at you and you're sixteen and you sit around and do nothing. It irks me. I want to trade lives with you. It bothers me to see you wasting your good years like this."

"What should I be doing?"

"Having friends, chasing girls, getting into trouble...anything but oozing on my sofa like a pile of slag."

He laughed. She always could get him to smile. And she was right. But how could he admit to her that his life had gone to shit since moving to Compton? How could he make her understand the depth of his pain and the terror that was growing in him day by day? He couldn't. There were some things adults could understand and other things that were simply beyond them. They saw only youth not being put to good use many years after theirs had faded. Like it's the answer to everything, he thought. Like it makes anything better. I'd give it up in a minute to be old and safe. Being young and in danger sucks. But she wouldn't understand that any more than he really did himself. And what if he told her about Toddy and Bones? Would she laugh? Would she shake her head at him and call the whole thing absurd? Or would she drag him down to the police station and make him confess the entire sordid business? Probably all three. And going to the police would be the worst mistake he had ever made. They wouldn't stand for it and you know it. Maybe you don't understand everything here, maybe you only have the sketchiest idea of what's going on, but you know damn well that what's been transacted between you and Bones and Toddy is above all TOP SECRET. It's not something to be repeated in mixed company. If you let the cat out of the bag, it'll be you going into the trunk of the El Dorado instead of Bobby. You'll be the one going trick-or-treating next. You'll hear the '59 Caddy one night and the clump-clump sound of boots and they'll be knocking at the door. You won't want to open it, but you won't have a choice. And when you do, you'll see them out there, waiting for you, grinning with faces like rotten black toadstools, all teeth and eyes like shining ball bearings. They will demand payment and you won't have anything to give them but yourself. No, he could not repeat the dark truths he knew because it probably wouldn't just be him they would come for. The idea of something happening to his mother was more than his mind could take. Way much more.

Mom sat down on the couch by him and put his feet up on her lap. She played with his toes as she had when he was little. There was a warm softness around her mouth while she did so. She looked so fragile for a moment or two that it made him feel moist and weak inside.

"You don't like it here, do you?"

Don't hurt her feelings. Lie! Lie! But he couldn't. "It's…I don't know…it's not that I don't like it, it's just that everything is different and I don't know anyone."

"Sure. But that'll change. Things like that always change."

"I guess so."

"They do. One of these days you'll connect with one person and through them you'll have a dozen more friends. Trust me. It always works that way."

He shrugged.

She sighed. "So you're just going to sit here and brood all day long? Waste a perfectly good Saturday night?"

"Well, there's a kung fu movie on channel ten tonight."

"Wow, you are a thrill a minute."

He scowled at her and she scowled right back, which was traditionally a declaration of war between them. She jumped at him and started mercilessly tickling him. "No! No, Mom, no!" he cried out, trying to be offended and act too grown up for such things but she did not relent. She knew his weak spots, having located and exploited them when he was a baby. They wrestled, but she immobilized him quickly and he couldn't help but squirm and laugh.

Finally, she broke it off.

He straightened his shirt. "You know, if somebody saw that, they'd think we were weird. I'm sixteen for godsake."

"Yeah, you're sixteen and weird. What about it?" She grabbed up the newspaper from the coffee table. "Your dad's working late again…he's probably got a couple blondes stashed away at the office. Oh, well. They got a double-feature horror flick downtown. Let's go see it. What do you say?"

"I can't be seen in public with my mother."

"Oh, don't be such a drip, Flynn. We'll have fun. They got two new ones—Friday the 13th and The Children. One's about a guy with a mask cutting up teenagers and the other's about radioactive tots or something—and not the tater variety. Let's do this."

"Can I get two boxes of candy?"

"Only if they're not Boston Baked Beans. I'm not having you throw up all night."

"Mom, I was like, five, when I did that."

She shook her finger at him. "Mommy knows best."

He didn't think he'd have any fun at all, but he was wrong. At the Rialto on Main, they glutted themselves on buttered popcorn, Cokes, Red Hots, Bonkers, and Wacky Wafers. By the time they left, they were practically hypoglycemic. The movies turned out to be pretty good. Not great, of course, but a good way to spend a night. Afterward, his mom wanted to know what cool people did on Saturday nights so he took her to the arcade and introduced her to Asteroids and Pac-Man, the latter of which she got into right away.

They played until closing time, listening to Blondie, Queen, and Adam Ant on the jukebox. Then they went over to Shakey's Pizza Parlor and ate yet again. It was a good night, a fun night, and one he would remember for a long time.

By the time they got home, he was starting to wonder if any of that crazy shit with Toddy and Bones had even really happened. It all seemed so absurd that it couldn't be true. He nearly called Bobby Swinn's house just to hear his voice because surely he would; surely this whole thing was some kind of sick joke and he was the fall guy. That was food for thought. What did he really know about Chad? It could have been a gag. Nothing but a fucking gag.

You saw Bobby. That was no joke. That was real. That was serious as death. And you're responsible.

And that haunted him more than anything else: his responsibility, his culpability. He couldn't get it off his mind all weekend. It didn't matter what he was doing or what he was thinking, it was always there just beneath his thoughts, the idea that he had sentenced Bobby Swinn to death. No, Flynn had not wanted him killed, but, then again, he hadn't done a damn thing to stop it either. That was the worst part of it. He knew damn well what those animals were going to do to Bobby but he hadn't raised a finger to stop the proceedings. No doubt, he would have been killed, too, but somehow that didn't seem as bad as living with the knowledge that he had signed Bobby's death warrant. It was absolutely insane that he could feel any compassion for that drooling, brain-dead ape…yet he did and that in itself had a lot to say about the capricious nature of humanity.

By Sunday night, he began to feel numb about it all. The rioting emotions in his head had finally played themselves out and he was beyond really feeling anything. Some purely selfish psychological survival mechanism had kicked in and he began blaming everyone but himself. It was Bobby's fault because Bobby was a lumbering, idiotic bully. He got what he deserved. The old adage was that if you lived by the sword, you died by it, but in Bobby's case it was more along the lines that he was a bully who was offed by worse bullies. There was karmic justice in that. So, yes, it was Bobby's fault. In fact, it was probably his parents' fault for bringing a beast like him into being in the first place and not noticing his aggressive asshole nature and nipping it in the bud. Now they would be crying over the body of their son in a coffin (if any remains were even found) and they had no one to blame but themselves.

That went through Flynn's head until it made him feel even more guilty, so that selfish survival mechanism found another target: his father. Sure, it was Dad's fault. Dad had moved them from goddamn Chicago to this goddamn pissant little town and that had brought all this goddamn mess into being. If Dad hadn't taken the job, they would still have been safely ensconced in Chicago and Flynn's life would be intact and he would have been popular and had friends and been dating girls and playing sports and hanging out with his crew playing Space Invaders and Missile Command on Atari. Life would have been good. But no. The old man moved them here and threw a colossal monkey wrench into the works. If it hadn't been for him and his stupid idea to move to this shitty little nothing town, then Flynn's social life wouldn't have imploded and he wouldn't have been the wingnut he now was. He wouldn't have been singled out with a target on his fucking back and took more shit than your average toilet. And if that hadn't have happened, he would have never come into contact with Chad and been seduced into cheap revenge by Toddy and Bones and Bobby would still be alive and everyone would be happy.

But, of course, that was all bullshit.

It wasn't Dad's fault. Dad was doing what he thought was best for everyone. What it came down to was choices. Dad had made what he thought was the right one and his son had definitely made the wrong one.

Only one to blame is you, Flynn thought. You could have said no. You could have walked away from it. You could have listened to what Daryl said and you wouldn't be going through this fucking torture.

True, true, and true.

But as he considered that and accepted the truth of it (much as he hated to), he started thinking deeply about how it had come to be. There had been no single incident at Compton High that had marked him as a loser and a doofus; it had been a cumulative thing. And that was the crazy part about it all. He'd always had it so together in Chicago. He had friends. He was popular. He was good at sports. He was smart in school. He was liked and respected. But at Compton, for whatever reason, he had been laboring under a black cloud of bad luck from day one. Fate had it out for him.

Unless it hadn't been bad luck.

And it hadn't been fate.

What if you were selected? What if Chad targeted you from day one because Toddy and Bones were looking for a certain type to bring into the fold? And since they couldn't find what they were looking for, they manufactured it in you.

That was nuts. That was paranoid thinking. That would mean that Toddy and Bones were not just your average thugs but entities capable of bending destiny and fate to their will to achieve a desired effect.

You're losing it. They're just hoods. That's all they are. That's all they can be.

Still, he was not so sure of that. There were too many coincidences at play here that if strung together did not seem coincidental at all. And in Flynn's paranoia, it made sense. There was a logic at work here. He was a new kid adrift at a new school. No friends, no backup, no support system. If he'd had any of that, what had happened and what he feared was still happening would not have been so easy. He was the perfect candidate. Toddy and Bones couldn't have asked for a guy more in need of their services. It was as if he had been groomed to that end from day one.

He knew if he kept thinking that way he was going to come apart at the seams. His self-confidence and self-esteem were already in the gutter and paranoia would only make it worse.

But what if…what if?

Sunday night, his mom told him to take out the trash and he, as usual, grumbled about it. He bagged everything up and brought it out to the can in the alley. As he was crossing the yard, he was seized by an overwhelming sense of menace. It crawled right under his skin and stopped him dead, left him trembling in the shadows. His skin was beaded with gooseflesh, his guts rolling over themselves. Something in his chest tightened. It felt like a cold finger was moving just behind his heart.

He heard a rumbling and this time it was no perfectly innocent scenario that his fear pumped into something terrible. No, it was the El Dorado. It cruised slowly up the alley; midnight black, sleek and deadly. Flynn did everything he could do not to cry out in sheer terror. Five minutes later, he forced himself to move, to bring the Hefty bag out to the trash. And as he dropped it into the banged-up metal garbage can, he had the worst feeling that it wasn't just the trash he was dumping in there but his life.

9

NOW

When October rolled around, the dread set into him, making him feel his age, making the blood run cold and slow in his veins and filling him with an ominous sense of expectation. As the weather turned, so did his heart. He could feel it creeping into him when the colors started changing and the leaves started falling, cardboard witches and skeletons appearing in windows and pumpkins sprouting on porches. He began to fear the shadows, the moan of the wind, steps coming up the walk or tree branches creaking overhead. It was the irrational terror a man feels when the sins of his youth have returned to haunt him.

But how could you explain that to your wife?

To anyone?

How could you make them realize what it was like when you were fifty-two years old and the coming of Halloween made you feel like you were a scared kid of sixteen again? How could you put it into words so that they would understand? All they saw when they looked at him was a successful accountant who'd made a killing in real estate, had retired before his fortieth birthday, had a daughter who had just graduated with honors from medical school and a son who was a contract lawyer, a great wife and a great house, timeshare in Tahiti and a summer house in the Keys...yeah, they saw all the peripheral stuff, but had no idea what crawled in his soul and kept him awake at night.

"Oh, for godsake, Flynn," Marjorie said as she came through the door. "You still don't have the Halloween decorations up? Are you going to be a complete Scrooge again this year?"

And what could he say to that? What could he really say? Honey, listen to me, okay? Something strange and terrible and frightening happened to me when I was sixteen. See, I was unpopular, picked on, bullied, then this kid named Chad gave me a way out and—

Marjorie stepped out of her shoes and came over to him, trying to carry two pumpkins that were large and orange and uniformly round. The perfect Halloween gourds. She was scowling at Flynn because she was a small woman—small and petite and pretty, oh yes—and those pumpkins probably weighed as much as she did.

Flynn set aside his remote control and Wall Street Journal, and said, "You need help, dear?"

Marjorie wrestled the pumpkins onto the dining room table. "No, Flynn," she said, panting, "whatever gave you that idea? I like trying to balance two fifty-pound pumpkins while my husband sits on his ass and reads the paper."

But the sarcasm was lost on him.

Maybe had this been July or February or March, he would have come right back at her the way he sometimes did. Injecting her sarcastic invective with all the comic absurdity he could muster until they were both trading lines like a couple in a screwball comedy, laughing their collective asses off.

But this was October.

And things can happen in October. Perfectly awful things.

He didn't have much in the way of a sense of humor in October. It was not a time for harvest celebration or football games or reflection on the success of the past year. No, it was a time for brooding and depression and silent agony. A time for sleepless nights and guilt and a whole basket of aberrant psychological goodies that would have raised a lot of therapeutic eyebrows…had he dared speak of them. Yes, October. A time to stare dumbly into the looking glass of his soul and shiver at what he saw there.

Marjorie fixed him with those dark eyes of hers. When she was in the proper mood, dear God, those eyes were luscious and sensuous, could make something run hot as tallow inside him…but when she was angry, those eyes were just black.

"Every year it's this way with you, Flynn. Every damn year since I met you. You're an outgoing, wonderful man eleven months of the year, but when October rolls around, you're moody and weird and damn unpleasant," she said to him. "It's getting old. No, in fact, it was old twenty years ago, now it's just fucking annoying."

Flynn swallowed. "I can't stand Halloween."

"Oh really? I wouldn't have known."

"I think it's silly."

She rolled her eyes as she did every year. "Jesus, Flynn. It's one day a year. One day. Why do you get so damn strange about it?"

But he couldn't tell her because he couldn't even tell himself sometimes. Marjorie and he rarely fought, in fact almost never. But when October rolled around, well, things got tense and sometimes ugly. It had been hard on Joey and Lisa growing up with a father who absolutely and categorically refused to take part in trick-or-treating, Halloween carnivals, or the rest of it. It made no sense to them. Particularly when their father loved every other holiday.

"Just this once," Marjorie said to him. "Try not to be an ass."

Looking at her, he realized then that she was like so many things in his life: perfect. A small, shapely brunette, drop-dead gorgeous even though she was two years shy of fifty herself. He'd met her when he was twenty-two. He was working at Schulman and Rhodes, another accountant lost in a sea of number-crunchers. But one that would rise effortlessly through the ranks and become full partner within five years. Barney Shipp, another bean counter at the firm and Flynn's best friend at the time, had said, "Hey, Janie's got this friend you gotta meet. Name's Marjorie. Great ass, great tits, leggy and pretty and dark, you know? Just the way you like 'em, old man. She's a real catch, so get out your net." Barney went on to say that Marjorie had those dark eyes, looked like she could be a real spitfire. But the meaner they were, the better they were in bed, he'd joked. Flynn met her, dated her, bedded and wed her. She gave him two exceptional kids. And while she was doing that, opportunity after opportunity fell into his lap. He made a killing in the tech sector, snared all the big accounts for the firm, and invested ten grand in a series of housing developments and strolled away in the end with upward of twenty million dollars.

A Cinderella story.

But it had been that way for more years than he cared to remember, the old Midas touch turning everything to gold. Many people were successful in life and that was usually a combination of drive, hard work, talent, and plain old luck. But for Flynn there had been none of the above, save awfully good luck. He was not especially driven nor hardworking and was certainly no more talented than any other accountant. Yet, things had worked out for him, time and time again. His luck was not merely good, it was epic.

Sitting there, thinking about it, it was almost scary how things tended to work in his favor. Not only the financial and professional success, the perfect wife and kids, but silly things, too. When colds or flu passed around, he never caught them. He always made green lights, drove like a maniac but was never pulled over. He never cut himself shaving or had indigestion or ingrown toenails. He subsisted on a cholesterol-rich diet, yet his blood levels were lower than Marjorie's, who dieted and exercised compulsively. He smoked two packs a day and could jog a mile without getting out of breath. Some people found pennies in the streets, but he always found twenties and fifties. If he entered a football or baseball pool, he always won. He was fifty-two years old, but his hair had not thinned and there was not a speck of gray to be found. And despite his diet, he was thin and firm and couldn't ever remember having so much as an ache or a pain.

He could have sat there all day, created an endless laundry list of the things that worked entirely in his favor, because everything did. And that wasn't just good luck, that was positively fated luck, supernatural luck.

Luck that was absolutely frightening if you spent any time thinking about it.

And Flynn did not like to.

Because when he did, his mind invariably went back to his sixteenth year, when his old man moved them north to Compton. He'd been a fairly popular kid, a normal kid, liked and maybe even admired by a few. Schoolwork wasn't easy, but doable. His grades were good, his social life fine, his athletic abilities above average. Then they'd moved to Compton, where he'd proceeded to fall apart and live the neurotic existence of an unpopular, despised, much-bullied teen. And then he'd met Chad and Chad had introduced him to Toddy and Bones and—

And it all changed, didn't it? The good luck came to you, but none of it was without a price. But ever since, nothing but one good thing after another.

"Can you at least give me a hand, Mr. Scrooge?" Marjorie asked him.

She was over at the picture window of their big Cape Cod on Candlelight Lane, hanging a jointed skeleton in the window…or trying to. The damn thing was taller than she was. He went over there and held it up while she taped it in place. Next came the jack-o'-lantern and the ghost and the green-faced witch.

"There," Marjorie said. "That's better. Now we don't look like a bunch of crabby old Scrooges. I hope we get lots of trick-or-treaters."

And they would. Flynn knew they would. They'd all be nice kids, too. And that wasn't because of the affluent neighborhood they lived in, but because that's the way things worked for him. No toilet paper or soaped windows, smashed pumpkins or doors knocked on in the dead of night. No, sir. Just bright-eyed, respectful, happy children, smiling up at the beautiful woman and the handsome man in their lovely house.

"You're worse this year, you know," Marjorie said to him.

"Yeah, I suppose I am."

"Is it the town? Is it Compton? Would you rather go back to Chicago?"

Flynn couldn't tell her the truth. If it wouldn't have broken her heart, he would have run back to the Windy City. But Marjorie loved Compton. She'd been infatuated the moment she'd seen the town, telling him with glee that it looked like something out of a Thomas Kinkade print. That was reaching, he thought at the time…and yet there was something lost in time about Compton, something charming and comfy and Mayberry-esque to it as if it had been placed under a glass dome forty years before to protect it from the onslaught of progress.

She found it lovely; Flynn found it creepy as all hell.

After he'd left, he had never come back. Not until two months ago. There had been no point. Mom and Dad were long dead; no relatives, no nothing. Then Marjorie had suggested visiting the town he generally refused to talk about and had fallen in love.

But, hell, what wasn't there to love? A picture-perfect Normal Rockwell midwestern little town. All those fine old brick buildings on Main, the big Victorians down by the park, the friendly people, the clean air…yeah, it was hard not to like a town that looked like it had been snipped from a postcard or stolen from an old movie. She loved it. Absolutely. So they'd found a nice house and moved. It seemed like fate in retrospect. The stars had been right, in perfect alignment. The house had been waiting for them, no business obligations left in Chicago; kids long gone. It was waiting to happen. And right away, Flynn had started having bad dreams, bad feelings, the sense that Compton was a booby trap waiting to spring shut on him in the darkness.

"Lot of old memories here, I guess," he said.

"Your mom and dad?"

"Yeah."

It was bullshit, but she bought it.

It had occurred to him around the time of his fiftieth birthday that a big part of life was the ability to bullshit and bullshit effectively. Anybody could get off a few little white lies from time to time, but those who were truly successful had an almost instinctive ability to spread manure thickly and seamlessly while never getting so much as a drop on their shoes. They could toss around the shit with both hands but the stink never stuck to them. In fact, it generally stuck to others.

Marjorie gave him a hug and a peck on the cheek, and told him how it would get better. He thought about his mom and dad. They'd been killed out on the interstate in a five-car accident when he was seventeen. It was probably the only truly bad thing that had ever happened to him since he was sixteen. Bad luck, sure, but it had all worked out in his favor, hadn't it? Dad had a ton of life insurance and that put Flynn through college, got him out of Compton. Without the money, he'd probably be working in a factory or selling vacuum cleaners. Mom and Dad dying had been terrible. But their deaths had been…well, advantageous to his future. Things always worked out for him and that tragedy was certainly no different—it made the wheels of fate spin in his direction.

Thinking that, he felt morose beyond belief. Mom and Dad had been so good, such kind and supportive people. Golden right to the core. He looked around at the trappings of his good fortune and grimaced. I'd throw it away, I'd throw it all fucking away for another week with them. To go fishing with Dad one more time. To hang out with Mom for even a couple hours. Oh Jesus, Jesus… He steeled himself. His eyes misted and he blinked before any tears gathered. The crazy, incomprehensible thing was that despite all the money, the success, the material wealth, the great kids, the perfect wife… despite all that (which was much, much more than most people ever had), he realized that he had never truly felt whole since his parents died. That part of him had always been lonely. And maybe, just maybe, that wasn't really crazy or incomprehensible at all.

I haven't been living a lie exactly, he told himself, but there's been so much good luck that I can't really appreciate it because I've got nothing bad to compare it to.

Which was true and also false. When things had been shit when he was sixteen—and the jury was still out as to whether that was fate or careful engineering by certain dark forces—he'd wanted them to get better. He'd wanted things to change and they had. And the deaths of his parents had been the terrible price he'd paid for it.

Marjorie went to snare some more Halloween decorations. One of the many things they had not gotten around to unpacking yet. Flynn stood there by the window, staring out at his adopted hometown. The sun was setting over the trees, painting rooftops orange and copper. It was a pretty little town. It had grown since he was last there, of course, but not in an ugly way. New neighborhoods and businesses, but the new Compton coexisted with the old Compton symbiotically. They complemented one another. There was not so much new that it canceled out the old. The town had a strong sense of itself, its history. Its memories lived unimpeded and its future moved subtly forward, so that you didn't even see it coming, but were comfortable when it arrived.

Yes, pretty on the surface, Flynn thought to himself, but if you flipped it over like a pretty rock, there were slimy and squirming things on the other side. And it became most noticeable to him after sundown when darkness threaded the streets and avenues. There was a sense of some ancient and brooding malignancy out there waiting in the shadows. A puppet master that worked lives and engineered destinies, slowly tightening its strings, pulling you into places you did not want to go and making you dance to obscene melodies best left forgotten.

Sighing, he watched the sun sink away, extinguished like a cigarette dropped in a dark puddle. The darkness spread over the town and the wind moaned, trees shook, and leaves blew up the streets. As he watched, a black cat crossed the walk in front of the house. It meant nothing, of course, but the idea of it left a bitter taste in his mouth. And for one moment, just one disturbing moment, he thought he saw two figures out there watching him from the trees across the road.

He quickly shut the drapes. Breathing fast and hard, he poured himself a whiskey and gunned it down. He lit a cigarette and tried to steady his nerves.

10

By seven that night, Flynn's cell had rung no less than five times. It started right after he thought he saw those people across the street that he was certain couldn't have been there in the first place. It was nerves. It was anxiety. It was bad memories roosting in the dark corners of his mind suddenly taking wing. He had nearly talked himself out of it when the phone rang. No big deal. But as he reached for his cell, something inside him went white with fear, with dismay, with an apprehension that made his hand shake so badly he could barely hold the phone.

Thank God Marjorie wasn't in the room.

The look on his face would have no doubt petrified her. As he glanced at the screen on his Nokia and saw the words Private Caller, his heart jumped in his chest and he had the most disconcerting need to scream.

Jesus Christ, Connors, what's your fucking problem?

It was probably nothing. Who doesn't get a few mystery private callers from time to time? Yet, despite cold, hard logic and razor-edged common sense, he was scared. He was terrified as he hadn't been since he was a teenager. Which wasn't acceptable. He poured himself a few fingers of Weller 90-proof and followed it with a few more until he had pretty much drank the whole hand. He had a cigarette, a few more sips, and by then he was feeling cool and mellow.

No worries.

Then the phone ran again.

Private Caller.

He ignored it and killed the ringtone. Over the next thirty minutes, it rang two more times. That's when he shut the damn thing off and put it in a drawer, telling himself, I don't deal with private fucking callers. You don't have the decency to tell me who you are, fuck you. That made him feel better. Much better, in fact. Fueled by the Weller, charged with nicotine, he felt more like a man and less like some cowering worm.

Fifteen minutes later, the cordless rang and he jumped. In his mind he could see two faces he hadn't seen since he was a teenager, both of them grinning like desert skulls, reminding him only too well of the many nightmares that had crawled through his dreams when he was sixteen.

He snatched it from its cradle and listened. He didn't speak, he just listened. What he heard was the wind, a moaning, distant gust of wind blowing through empty places and deserted spaces. It blew down back alleys and across weedy vacant lots, groaning among leaning headstones in lonely country cemeteries and skimming the surface of black lakes. It rose up and up, then died out, fading away into piping laughter that existed mainly in the dark environs of his imagination.

Terror exploding in him like the flapping of dozens of black wings, he hung up before he heard a voice calling him into the past.

Five minutes later, it rang again and this time Marjorie heard it.

"Oh, could you get it, honey?" she called from the den. "I've got my hands full. If it's Carolyn, tell her I'll call her back."

"Sure," he called out, his voice almost a squeak.

He picked up the phone, the feel of it warm and breathing in his hand like something hideously alive. "Hello?" he said.

A crackle of static. "Hey, Flynn, welcome home. I knew you'd come back, sooner or later."

Welcome home—?

See, Bones? Flynn came. I told you he would.

"Who is this?" he asked, trying to keep the fear from his words. Because he knew that voice; he had been expecting it ever since he got back to town. He cleared his throat. "I'm afraid you have me at a disadvantage, I…uh…"

"Oh, you know who this is, Flynn. Don't play stupid. I don't like stupid people and you know it."

"Listen, I'm not playing games here. Tell me who you are and what you want."

There was a shrill, tinny tittering from the other end that became a steady humming of the lines. "You know who I am, Flynn. He knows who we are, don't he, Bones?"

And from a distant, windy place, another voice said, "Yeah, he knows who we are all right."

"Is this a prank? Because if it is, I'm hanging up now."

"That's not very friendly, Flynn. I don't like it. We been good to you, haven't we? You've had the good life, haven't you?" that voice said to him, turning him back thirty-five years. "Remember what I said, Flynn: once you're our friend, you're always our friend."

Flynn felt like something inside him was melting, running like wax. The fear he felt was not just psychological, but physical. It took everything he had not to fall to his knees or pass right out. "I'm calling the police," he said.

"No, you won't," the voice told him. "You know better than that. You know a lot better than that. You don't want us taking your pretty wife trick-or-treating, do you?"

"If this is a threat—"

"It's way beyond that, Flynn. You wanted and you got. Now we want and we're gonna get."

"Listen, that was a long time ago, another life."

The voice laughed with a cruel, grating sound. "It was fucking yesterday. Everything was yesterday. A year, ten, twenty, thirty… don't make no difference, once you're in, you're in, and there's no walking away."

"What…what do you want?"

But the only answer to that was a peal of horrid laughter like the rattling of dry bones.

11

1981

Funny thing was, after he started hanging with Chad and Bones and Toddy, not only did he feel different, he was different. He had confidence, attitude and swagger. The girls did not laugh when he passed. The boys looked at the floor. Even the greasebag toughies and asshole jocks wouldn't hold his burning gaze for more than a second or two. He even had the feeling that he made some of the teachers nervous. But how? Why? Because of who his friends were? The things they had done, or people suspected them of doing? Or was it something chemical? A smell, a scent, a signature?

Flynn didn't know.

Maybe he didn't want to know.

A week after he'd met Bones and Toddy in that alley, he'd taken Chad aside at school and said, "Bobby Swinn hasn't been back to school. People are saying he ran away or disappeared or something. What's going on?"

But Chad just shook his head. "Shit happens, that's all. People live and then they die. You hear about Mr. Martin?"

That sonofabitch.

Flynn was almost afraid to ask, but he did.

"They found him dead in bed. Had a heart attack, I guess. Another piece of shit gets flushed."

"Did…did Toddy and Bones—"

"Things are getting better for you, aren't they, Flynn?"

"Yeah, but that don't answer—"

"Do yourself a favor. Just take the good they give you, okay? Don't ask questions. Just don't ask questions."

So he didn't.

He didn't even ask about Norm Kinder, who had become a blank-eyed, broken wretch who stared at the floor whenever Flynn passed him. He looked like he was barely alive. Over the next three months, he would attempt suicide twice. Flynn was certain that Toddy and Bones were behind it, but he never mentioned the fact.

They were scary. There was no getting around that unpleasant little point. And it wasn't just their dead eyes or violence or antisocial attitudes, it was something more. Something you felt when you were around them, something you felt in your marrow and deep down in the pit of your stomach. There was something dangerous and... wrong about them.

One of the scariest things about them was that they seemed to be...rejuvenating. The first time he'd seen them they had looked like a couple hard-hitters in their thirties maybe, a couple of aging hoods, ex-cons and bad-asses that had made a career out of hurting people. But now they had ditched the 1950s crewcuts and grown their hair out and they looked...younger. The sort of guys that had dropped out of high school and hung around on street corners itching for action—petty criminals on the fast track to state prison.

Regardless, they were younger.

There was no getting past that disturbing little point.

But how? Flynn asked himself. How could such a thing be?

He tried not to think about it much. Like Chad said, it was better not to ask questions. The last thing he wanted was to get on their bad side because that was a sure ride straight to hell. Sometimes when he looked into their coal-black eyes—something he didn't like to do much because it made his guts roll up like a rug—he got the sense that there was something ancient and malefic staring back out at him. That there was an inhuman darkness there, cold and lifeless like the deepest abyssal depths of the sea.

But, even with that, they were good to Flynn.

They took care of him and watched his back and they really didn't ask much in return, just that he hang out with them. So he started wearing jeans with holes in the knees and got himself a leather jacket. He began to grow his hair out and smoked cigarettes, got drunk with them and toked some grass. They hung around behind the bleachers at football games and called out obscene things to the girls and taunted the boys. Now and then, they asked simple things from him. If Toddy wanted some cigarettes, a bottle of booze, or just about anything else under the sun, Flynn would go into King Liquor Party Store or Safeway and steal what he needed. It had to be stolen; Toddy didn't believe in paying for things. If Bones wanted to take a ride in a stolen car, Chad and Flynn went and borrowed some wheels for the night. Yes, criminal, illegal things, but it never seemed that much to ask because he always knew there was a dark protective magic with those two and he'd never, ever get busted or rousted by the cops. That's not how things worked in the orbit of Toddy and Bones.

Every time he did these things, they were pleased.

Real pleased.

Toddy would say, "See, Bones? Flynn's one of us…didn't I say he'd be one of us?"

"Yeah, that's what you said."

Flynn did these things to prove he was tough, had some balls, was worth hanging around with. To them, he knew, these were little tests. He was proving himself to them. So he always went along with anything they said, anything they wanted to do. Mostly it was joyriding in Toddy's street-mean 1959 El Dorado, harassing women walking alone, throwing empty beer bottles at pedestrians, clipping off mailboxes and running down stray dogs. Nothing too heavy. But sometimes it elevated, got maybe a little dangerous, a little sick.

When Cassidy Holmes, a hot senior cheerleader, had laughed at Chad when he'd asked her out, they'd had to pay her back. Bones snatched her cat, a fluffy tiger-striped female. And then, as Flynn looked on in horror, he'd snapped its neck with a deft twist of his wrist. Then Bones took the cat and a ball of twine, tied the cat by the neck and hung it right in front of Cassidy's door. Then he knocked and ran like a kid leaving a bag of burning shit on the doorstep.

When the door opened, you could hear Cassidy's scream a block away. Toddy and Bones boomed with laughter. Chad just laughed along, though his eyes were scared. Flynn didn't know what to do. At least, until Chad elbowed him in the back of the Caddy and then he got it: he'd better laugh. He'd better fucking laugh like dead cats were the funniest thing he'd ever heard of. So he did. Just the four of them in that evil street machine that was black and glossy laughing themselves silly. But sometimes it was better to laugh than to scream.

One night, maybe two days before Halloween, Toddy wanted to smash pumpkins. They were just hanging out, looking for trouble, and this was what he wanted to do. Chad had giggled, saying that smashing pumpkins was stupid kid's stuff and the look he'd gotten from Toddy was bad, real bad. Bad enough that in the darkness, leaning up against the black shell of the '59 Cadillac, Chad went white as spilled milk.

"What'd you say?" Toddy asked him.

Bones folded his arms. "Yeah, what was that you said, fuckface?"

"Nothing…I…nothing."

"I think he said he wanted to go trick-or-treating. Ain't that right, Mr. Hot Shit with the big yapping fucking mouth?"

"No, no…please. I'm sorry, man."

Bones laughed but his cruel, crooked mouth did not change from a permanent frown. "I like it when he begs, when he crawls like the fucking slug he is."

Toddy shrugged. "That's good, Chaddy. You shut your mouth and you'll live longer. Besides, I like acting like a kid sometimes. It's been a long time. A real long time. Maybe never."

Which made the both of them laugh in throaty, bestial chuckles. Chad and Flynn stood there, trying to catch their breath now that a possibly nasty scenario had been avoided.

They shut off the Caddy and went pumpkin-hunting. A time-honored Halloween tradition, right up there with tipping over outhouses and tossing dead cats on porches. Except with Toddy and Bones there was something positively vindictive about it. It wasn't enough to simply smash them out on the sidewalk or toss them in the road, these guys smashed them on the roofs of cars and against the sides of houses and sometimes right on the porches. Toddy threw one right through a screen door and Bones knocked a dog that barked at him senseless with another.

And after the ritual smashing, Chad and Flynn ran; but Bones and Toddy liked to linger, maybe hoping someone would accost them. Thankfully, no one did…save for a young woman who stomped out on her porch and threatened to call the police. But one look at Bones standing at the bottom of the steps sent her right back in. And Flynn figured that was a good thing, because if they'd gotten their hands on her…well, her family would have needed a real small box at the funeral because there wouldn't have been much left.

What stayed with him about that night was when they came upon a porch festively decorated with scarecrows, corn shocks, and dozens of carved and uncarved pumpkins. Toddy was first up there and he grabbed a fine, fat gourd and then instantly dropped it with a little cry, stood there staring at his palms. Then he started to laugh.

"Booby-trapped," he said. "Fucking thing was booby-trapped."

Flynn saw what he meant. It was ingenious, really. Apparently this particular family had gotten sick and tired of teenage punks smashing their pumpkins, so they'd come up with a devilish little way to fight back: razor blades. They'd cut perfect little slits in this particular pumpkin, dozens of them, and inserted razor blades so that only about a quarter-inch of blade was showing. You would not see it unless the streetlight caught it just so. Toddy had picked up the pumpkin firmly and quickly like any other prankster and the blades had slit his hands open.

And he thought it was funny.

He roared with hysterical laughter, holding up his hands for all to see. His palms were gashed right open. And not only his palms, but the heel of his hand right up to his fingertips was laid right open, the flesh hanging like confetti. It was bad, sure. Certainly nothing to be cackling about. But the real horror of it was that he did not bleed.

Flynn saw it and would never forget it.

Toddy did not bleed at all, not so much as a drop.

Bones started laughing, too, and then he picked up a sizable and uncarved pumpkin and threw it right through a window. Then they all ran, laughing and hopping fences and reveling in the act of destruction. Well, at least Toddy and Bones laughed, but they would laugh at the damnedest things. Flynn had been coming home from school one day and witnessed a grisly sight. A dog had been struck by a car and dragged down the street. There was blood and fur and entrails everywhere, a ragged red smear that smelled ripe and metallic. It was a terrible thing…but it got worse. He heard a rumbling and the El Dorado pulled up, Toddy and Bones hopping out.

They both looked at the dog, then started laughing their asses off, laughing so hard they could barely breathe.

"That's five bucks you owe me," Toddy said. "Told you I could drag that sucker for an easy city block."

Flynn felt his heart sink low inside him. Such a thing was terrible in and of itself, but here in the middle of the day with the bright afternoon sun shining down…it was an atrocity.

"I think…I think Lassie's trying to tell us something," Toddy giggled. "What's that, girl? You don't like having your brains squirting out your asshole?"

Bones laughed without ever smiling. "Sure, I like that. Hey, fucking Lassie, fetch a bone! Fetch a bone! How about that one sticking out your belly!"

Flynn had been forced to stand there with them, his guts in his throat, and laugh along. It was a real delightful scene. But people started paying attention to them, looking real angry about it all, so he suggested they better get out of there but Toddy and Bones wouldn't have it.

"Don't be a pussy," Toddy told him.

They kept on laughing and he had to laugh along with them even though his guts were trying to crawl up the back of his throat with a greasy peristaltic motion. And, sure enough, some guy came out of a house down the way and found them laughing. He breezed right past Toddy and Bones and grabbed Flynn by the shirt, nearly hoisting him off his feet. "You think this is funny, you sick sonofabitch? You think that poor animal is something to laugh about?"

Flynn tried to explain to him that he didn't understand, he didn't understand at all. He wanted the guy to leave before it was too late but there was no way he could make him realize that with Toddy and Bones there.

"They ought to fucking lock up animals like you!" the guy said and slapped Flynn across the face. "Sick, fucked-up punk! Goddamn useless waste of flesh!"

He slapped him again and by then, Toddy and Bones were no longer laughing. They were glaring at Mr. Upright Concerned Citizen with death-stares and Flynn knew right then and there that this guy was fucking toast. He made to slap Flynn again, changed his mind and shoved him on his ass, again breezing right past Toddy and Bones like they weren't even there and that was because—

He don't see them. They're standing right there and he don't see them. Only I can see 'em.

Toddy and Bones came over and helped him to his feet, brushing him off.

"That prick is really asking for it," Toddy said. "Who the hell's he think he is treating our friend like that?"

Bones was breathing hard, his teeth clenched. "I'm guessing he's going trick-or-treating."

And maybe Flynn had suspected it before, but at that moment he knew that there really were such things as ghosts and two of them were evil things, sadistic monsters hungry for death and Mr. Upright Concerned Citizen was going to find out all about that.

Not two days later, the guy was the victim of a hit-and-run. He had gone out to check the mail, the newspaper said, and was run down. But rumor had it that he was not just run down but driven over again and again and again.

Flynn wasn't surprised when he read about it.

He was pained and felt guilty as hell, but he certainly wasn't surprised. He only wished he could have adequately warned Mr. Upright Concerned Citizen that there were some things in this world—and out of it—that you just didn't fuck with.

12

He had been afraid of them before that little incident, but after that, they terrified him. He kept telling himself that it didn't happen the way he remembered it, that maybe the guy had purposefully avoided Toddy and Bones because they were bad news, that he went for someone he could handle, that being Flynn himself. That's not true, a little annoying voice in his head said. He went straight for you. He didn't even look at them or the car. They didn't exist. You know damn well for him they didn't exist. But as the days passed, he began to doubt that any of it had happened the way he remembered. He purposely deluded himself, gave his mind something it could handle and his mind went for it, accepting it gladly.

Ghosts, he said to himself more than once, that's fucking silly. Ghosts, my ass.

Yet, certain things would not leave him alone. Little voices in his head would mock him by saying, Riddle me this, dumbass. What does not bleed, gets younger instead of older, and cannot be seen?

That was the riddle he could not bear to think about.

Regardless, Toddy and Bones scared him even if he refused to admit it openly and he couldn't get past the fact that there was something exceptionally evil and twisted about them. If he hadn't believed it before, two things then happened that made him sure of it: The first was that old Bullet-Head, Mr. Russel, the principal of Compton High had suspended Chad for skipping classes. Chad had asked Flynn not to mention it to Bones and Toddy; he was afraid of what might happen if they found out. But they found out as they always found things out. You didn't need to tell them: they knew.

Not three days after the suspension, they grabbed Russel's ten-year-old son out of the backyard and dragged him into a thicket behind his house. They tied a noose around his ankles and hung him upside down from a tree limb, about three feet off the ground. Then they swung him back and forth, laughing the whole while.

"Hey, I got me an idea," Bones said. "Let's do like in them cowboy pictures, eh?"

"The swinging?"

"Yeah, the Indians catch some cowboy and they swing him through the fire."

Flynn hoped to God they were kidding, but he could tell by the yellow, sickly color of Chad's face that they were not. Bones gathered up tree branches and sticks and leaves and heaped it under the kid's head. If it hadn't been for some lady walking her dog, who knows how far it would have gone. Flynn knew he wouldn't have been able to watch that. He would have had to intervene and if he did, he figured that kid would not have swung alone. But the lady came and they ran off. Russel's son never identified any of them. Maybe he was afraid to.

That was the first thing.

The second was that Flynn himself got in trouble. As a gag, he swiped Mr. Costigan's lunch from second-hour American lit and tossed it out the third-floor window. The kids all laughed. All except one: Daniel Harms.

Daniel Harms was a straight-A student with few friends, the butt of every joke, a tormented boy who was exactly what Flynn would have been had Chad not intervened. Harms was a legendary tattler and it was only a matter of time before he dropped a dime.

Of course, he never got the chance.

After school one day, the black Caddy pulled into the lot, mean and hungry. Toddy hopped out and showed Flynn what was on the floor in the back—Daniel Harms, bound and gagged—and terrified.

Somebody fucks with you, they fuck with us.

"We got you a little present, Flynn," he said.

Right about then, Flynn got about as scared as he'd ever been. Jesus, this was kidnapping and you name it. This was no prank. This was criminal and deviant and goddamn fucked-up. It was Bobby Swinn all over again. He knew the right thing to do was to tell an adult and bring the police in on it…but he knew he'd never do that. If he involved his mom or dad, there would be a funeral in the family and he knew it. And the police? What good would that do? Toddy and Bones were beyond the reach of the law.

There were things he could have done, proper and ethical things, but he was too afraid. And not just for himself but for his family. So, looking down at Harms, he said, "Good for that little squealer. Good for that little narc, fucking teacher's pet, fucking dick-sucker." This made Toddy and Bones laugh. "What...what you gonna do with him?" he asked.

Toddy grinned with all those narrow teeth. "We're gonna take him for a ride, take him trick-or-treating, fuck with his head. Then we'll let him go."

"Sure," Bones said. "Then we'll let him go."

But they never did let him go. Flynn did not know what happened and he did not ask. What it came down to was that there was another empty seat at Compton High.

13

NOW

Three days before Halloween, Flynn started his day like this: he stepped out of his big brass bed, promptly slipped on one of his socks, skidded on the polished hardwood floor and fell on his ass.

"Nice going, swift," Marjorie said to him, seeing that he was uninjured and thinking that it was very funny.

"Shit," Flynn said.

"I'm sorry," she told him, "but…well, honestly, it was funny. Especially for you. I don't think I've ever seen you trip or stumble the whole time I've known you."

He went into the bathroom and it didn't get any better. Old Mister Winky didn't want to relax and Flynn pissed on the floor. He dropped the soap in the shower and bumped his head on the washcloth rack when he tried to retrieve it. He cut himself shaving and then stubbed his toe on the doorjamb. Maybe some people were clumsy and accident-prone, but Flynn was not one of them. His luck was good, always good.

But today was starting out badly and he accepted it for what it was: an omen.

And it kept right on rolling. He got a call from his broker in Chicago and learned that he had lost $50,000 on a restaurant chain he'd invested in. A pipe burst in the basement and spewed filthy brown water all over an antique dresser Marjorie was refinishing. Her luck, it seemed, was no better. She cut her finger making a salad for lunch and when they sat down to eat, she choked on a piece of chicken and was nearly blue by the time Flynn forced it out of her with the Heimlich maneuver. Something he had learned in health class in high school but had never used before.

But it worked.

They didn't have much appetite after that. They decided a cuddle on the couch and a bottle of wine was more to their liking. Flynn let her choose because he knew nothing about wine. She always told him there was a good wine for every mood and every meal. She chose a bottle of 2006 Spottswoode Cabernet Sauvignon and he had to admit, despite his limited palate, it was very good. But even the trip to the cellar was not without its mishaps. She nearly fell on the stairs on the way down and then almost dropped the bottle on the way back up.

As they sipped their wine, she said, "What's happening to us today, Flynn? Good God, we're a disaster. They say bad luck comes in threes...but sixes and sevens and eights? I was going to go pick up a couple Cornish hens and some good bread for supper, but I'm not so sure I should be behind the wheel."

"Oh, we're having one of those days. Everyone gets them sooner or later."

Marjorie did not look as if she really believed that. There was a darkness around her eyes and a grim set to her mouth. "Seems like we're getting more than our share, don't you think?"

Of course we are, my love, and it's because we came to this fucking shithole town. Whatever was active when I was sixteen is still active. Don't ask me how or why or what it really is because I don't know. But as soon as we came back, I sensed it—a sort of slow-simmering evil that was about to come to a boil.

Of course, he couldn't say that because she would think he was nuts and he would be inclined to agree. "Well, it'll pass. It always does."

Again, she was not buying into that. She was an intuitive and perceptive woman. She had sensed something here, something that was not right and it was bothering her. "Has it ever occurred to you that we have frighteningly good luck?"

He was feeling uneasy. Very uneasy. He didn't sip his wine now, he gulped it. "It's that way with some people. We just...we just have the touch, you know? The stars were right when we were born."

"I'm serious."

"Baby, I don't know what to say to that. Yes, we've had amazingly good luck. But shit has to happen sooner or later, doesn't it? If all we have to deal with are some leaky pipes and crappy investments and—"

"And me almost choking to death?"

She was making him nervous now. "What I mean is, things are bound to go bad now and then. It's the law of averages at work."

She finished her wine. "Sometimes I wonder."

"What do you mean?"

"Our luck. It's been fantastic. What if it starts to run out? Most people get a little bad luck on a weekly or monthly basis. They get it a little at a time. You can suck that up…but what if it were to all go to shit at the same time?"

"Luck isn't real, dear. It's just a word people use to frame coincidence or make sense of it. That's all it is."

That seemed to relax her somewhat. "I suppose."

Slowly, he managed to talk her away from all that and direct her toward their upcoming vacation down in the Keys. They would be leaving in a week. He only had to make it that long and once they were out of this town, they would never come back. He would explain it to her and maybe with their run of bad luck she might just believe it. Maybe. But telling her would mean admitting to things that he hadn't even admitted to himself since he left this goddamn place when he was seventeen. He wondered what she would think of him when she knew.

There were no other major incidents that afternoon.

That was something. Marjorie lost herself in her Halloween decorating and he was forced to lend a hand from time to time. She made him nervous when she climbed up ladders to hang crepe paper spiders from the ceiling, but she never fell or even tottered.

Just before five, he announced that he was going for a drive. Something was building in him—terror, apprehension, too many things—and he knew damn well that he'd never be able to keep it bottled up if he didn't get out of the house. So he took a ride and was not in the least surprised when he pulled up before an austere brick building on Main that housed the offices of Haglish, Monroe, Penning, and Reese.

It was time to renew an old acquaintance.

It was time to visit Chad.

14

Finding the building was the easy part, getting out of the SUV and actually going through with it was quite another. Flynn sat there behind the wheel for the longest time, hemming and hawing, worrying and chain-smoking. If he'd had any nails left by that time, he would have probably chewed them off. The truth was that he really didn't want to see Chad, let alone speak with him. Good God, he hadn't seen him since he was seventeen at his parents' funeral, before he left Compton for good. Since then, no calls or cards, not so much as an email. Seeing him again after so many years was not only going to be uncomfortable but damned awkward.

And maybe even frightening.

It would be reconnecting with his high school years, rekindling a fire that he wanted to believe had long ago burned out, and that truly scared the shit out of him. He was probably being ridiculous and overly dramatic, but the very idea left him cold inside. The idea of renewing their association (friendship was too strong a word) was like prying open some dark Pandora's box and setting his teenage demons free.

As the clock crept closer to 5:30 and people began to file out of the building, he knew it was time to act. He either did this or he went home and cowered. So, nervous as a kitten, he jogged up the steps, sucked in a deep breath, and opened the heavy oak door (being very careful not to smudge the antique brass push plate with his sweaty hand).

He saw a stoop-shouldered old man sweeping up and as he passed him, Flynn was struck by the idea that he was familiar somehow. It took him a moment or two to realize that the old man was Norm Kinder. Not just aged by life, but worn out, broken and sucked dry. Hey, Normie, a teenaged voice in his head chuckled.

You run any touchdowns lately? He didn't recognize Flynn at all. In fact, Flynn was certain his mind was gone, that he had become a mental defective of sorts.

And you brought that about. Maybe you didn't mean for it to happen, but you're ultimately responsible.

For a few moments, he stood there watching Norm sweeping, the guilt inside him rising to levels that were nearly painful. He wanted to do something for him but there was really nothing he could do. Sighing, he went over to the elevator.

He knew instinctively that Haglish, Monroe, Penning, and Reese would be on the top floor and his instincts were correct.

He rode the elevator up alone, the closeness of the walls making him feel claustrophobic and uneasy for some reason. He had ridden what seemed hundreds of elevators in his time and had never before realized how coffin-like they were. Once that grim image was established in his imagination, he began wondering what it might be like to be trapped between floors, alone in the dark. But you wouldn't be alone, now would you? And in his mind he saw the grinning cadaverous faces of Toddy and Bones—

Then the elevator doors slid open, startling him.

Sighing, Flynn wiped a few beads of sweat from his brow and stepped into a spacious lobby. The hardwood floors gleamed. The walnut paneling was polished to a fine dark luster. There were tasteful, soothing prints by Monet and Heighton in gilt frames on the walls and expensive Italian furniture below. The entire place positively stank of money and reeked of success.

Of course it does, he thought. Chad paid his dues like you did. Did you think he would be any less successful?

No, of course not.

There was a protective magic shielding their lives; an enchanted barrier that deflected bad luck onto the poor, miserable wretches outside their circle.

He stepped farther into the lobby in the direction of the receptionist's desk. He saw a tall, distinguished man hovering over a model-pretty blue-eyed brunette whose short black skirt was hiked up to mid-thigh, giving him a full view of her long, tanned, exquisitely sexy legs. It was the sort of eyeful that could launch a hundred middle-aged fantasies. She suddenly noticed that Flynn was there, offering him a world-beating smile of dazzling white teeth that was the perfect combination of regal charm and girl-next-door seduction.

He almost laughed because…well, because she was simply too perfect. She had stepped out of a magazine. Women like that didn't really exist except in the fantasies of men. But here she was, looking exactly as every man expected his secretary to look but so few ever did. He had a mad desire to touch her to see if she was real.

But then his eyes drifted to the man.

Tall, distinguished, broad-shouldered and well-tanned. He could have been a well-preserved fifty, but looked more like forty or maybe even thirty-five. He reminded Flynn of a doctor from a soap opera—rugged good looks and a square, dimpled jaw, dark coiffed hair feathered with silver. He was the epitome of masculine virility and confidence.

That's Chad.

That's fucking Chad.

The pimply, fat, ugly duckling had found himself a magical cocoon and emerged as a beautiful butterfly with perfect looks, charm, and bearing. Flynn had a pretty good idea that he had just interrupted an offer of drinks and dinner at some discrete location. Chad was pouring it on; a fifty-something old man effortlessly seducing a twenty-five year-old woman. He would have no doubt bagged—and bedded—his prey if it had not been for a certain interloper arriving on the scene.

Chad looked at him, turned away from the receptionist, and went into his office. Flynn knew he was supposed to follow—and he did—planting himself on a leather sofa.

"I'd start this off by saying you might not remember me, but I can see that you remember me just fine," he said. "And I have to wonder if that's a good thing or a bad thing."

Chad stared at him the way he probably stared at clients who were guilty of heinous crimes. There was no friendship or warmth in his eyes, just careful scrutiny. "Of course I remember you, Flynn. The old days are hard to forget."

Yes, aren't they? Flynn thought. He chose his next words carefully. "The funny thing is, Chad, that you really don't look surprised to see me at all."

"Why should I be? I've been expecting you. I knew you'd be back sooner or later. I knew you wouldn't have a choice. I've dreaded this day for years."

Flynn felt the spit in his mouth dry up. His hands began to shake so he pressed them flat against his legs. What he wanted was for Chad to dismiss the old days and the old nightmares. But he hadn't done that. With a look and a few words he had confirmed their awful reality.

Flynn cleared his throat. "It looks like you've done well for yourself."

Chad smiled thinly and sat down behind his desk. "Yes, I have. And I'm willing to bet you have, too."

Flynn nodded. "Oh yes, I've had good luck, Chad. Unbelievably good luck. Year after year after year. Everything I touched turned to gold. I sometimes thought I could have pissed platinum if I really put my mind to it. I could do no wrong. That was, up until this morning."

Chad kept watching him. He knew, all right. He knew exactly what his old friend was going to say.

"Until this morning," Flynn went on, "I don't think I ever tripped over a curb or spilled a beer, stubbed my toe or dripped gravy on my tie. I never lost a dime in the markets or ever had a woman shoot me down. What I wanted, I got. That's the way it always was."

"Then you came back to Compton and things started to turn, eh? Things started to sour. But it wasn't until this morning that your luck seemed to have totally run out. Is that it?" Chad nodded because he knew how it worked. He knew quite well. "Nothing you can say would surprise me. Nothing at all."

After that, there was silence. For maybe an easy three or four minutes, a dreadful and uncomfortable silence. Flynn knew that Chad was wondering the very thing he was wondering: did they dare go any further with this? Did they dare toy with those forces that had made their lives so good by trying to dissect them and holding their inner workings out in plain sight?

No, as far as Flynn was concerned, they did not. Not just yet.

"Tell me about your life, Chad. Tell me how good it's been."

This didn't elicit so much as a smile. But Chad rolled with it and told him it was as golden as he suspected. "I was a loser, Flynn. You know that. I know that. Then when I was a senior in high school, everything changed. It had been getting good for some time, but when I was a senior, it really clicked. I aced everything. I maintained a 4.0 GPA and made the honor roll. Pretty amazing for a guy who hung around out in the parking lot smoking dope and cutting class. You left at the beginning of the year so you never saw just how right things went for me. How popular I became. The money that fell into my lap. The friends I had and the hot cars I drove and the hotter girls I banged." He laughed at that because it was probably a word he hadn't used in thirty-odd years. "I walked tall and I walked proud. People feared me. They respected me. They wanted to be me. Whenever I was around…heh, heh…those tight-assed varsity cheerleaders who had once looked at me like a fly-specked turd couldn't drop their short skirts fast enough.

"After graduation I went to Duke on a full scholarship, pre-law. I was a member of Sigma Chi and I won three student leadership awards. Me of all people. I graduated in the top five percent of my class. Same for law school. And you know what? I never studied, never cracked a book…yet, I'd wake up in the morning with an encyclopedic knowledge of whatever exams I had that day. I always had the answers. All the answers. Now and again I'd fudge a few so it didn't look like I was cheating. I lived a dream life. Jesus Christ, I dated Brooke Patterson, who went on to become Miss North Carolina. I had it all. Anything I wanted. That was my life, Flynn. I lived like a fucking rock star. I mean for godsake you know what I did the night before I took the bar exam? While all my friends were cramming and beating their brains out, I spent the night in bed with a Brazilian swimsuit model and a bag of primo blow. How do you like that? The next day, I breezed the exam. No problem."

But that, of course, was only the beginning.

"What I dreaded most was coming back to Compton, but I didn't have a choice. I had family. I had responsibilities." He laughed at this with a manic, edgy sort of sound. "I knew if I didn't come back, my mom and dad were going to suffer for it. I was expected. And I don't think I need to elucidate on who and what were expecting me…"

No, he didn't need to do that.

Chad's fantastic, near supernatural luck kept right on rolling. He won twelve million dollars in the state lottery. Seed money. Because what he wanted most of all was to become a full partner in an established law firm, something unheard of for a kid fresh out of law school, even one with his impressive credentials. To pull that off he needed connections. And, of course, they fell right into his lap. The firm of Haglish,, Monroe, and Penning was in trouble. Some bad investments had put them in enormous debt and they were failing fast. Chad bought his way in as a full partner. He stepped through the door, bright, confident, aggressive, and extremely ambitious. Within a year, Haglish, Monroe, Penning, and Reese were in the black. Within five they were pulling in high-dollar clients that the white-shoe firms in Chicago couldn't even touch.

Chad smiled. "What do you think the chances of that are? That a small partnership in a shithole town like Compton with a population of less than twenty thousand could beat the big boys and multinationals at their own game?"

"Infinitesimal," Flynn said.

"At the very least. Hell, we had firms in Chicago and New York trying to buy us out—and our impressive clientele and lucrative contracts—for ten times what I won in that lottery."

Had Flynn been listening to anyone else he would have thought that here was a man that was very pleased with himself— and rightly so—but he knew better. Chad wasn't celebrating his achievements. No, this was a confession of sorts, a prologue leading up to something much darker, and that's what scared him.

"Did you ever marry?"

Chad nodded. "Yes, I did. Helena died five years ago."

"I'm sorry."

"Not as sorry as I was."

Flynn didn't say anything. He just waited because he knew it was coming, those things he did not want to hear. Chad sat there behind his antique executive desk, steepling his fingers and manicured nails. His healthy tan was fading. He looked pallid as a corpse. "Yes, everything has gone my way. But it wasn't free. Nothing is free in this life. I've had to pay for every drop of success. I've had to pay in flesh and blood and sanity. I've bartered off my soul inch by inch. While you were living the good life far away from this terrible place, I was paying the price, Flynn. I was greasing the wheels of perdition with human blood—"

"Chad...don't do this."

Chad laughed at him with a strident, near hysterical sound. "You got out, Flynn, and you stayed out. But I knew you'd be back. You'd have to come back and when you did, you'd have to play the game or suffer the consequences. You bought your way out once with the lives of your mother and father but there's no way out this time."

Flynn felt his face getting hot. "Stop it, Chad. You're being irrational."

"You sold them, Flynn, and we both know it."

"You better shut up right now," Flynn warned him and meant it.

Because it wasn't true; not really. He had not sold them. He had not told Toddy and Bones to take them. If they had taken them, if they were truly responsible for their deaths out on the interstate, then it was not an offering—it was punishment. Because Toddy and Bones had wanted something and they had wanted Flynn to give it to them but he wouldn't. He refused. So they took something else.

"See, Flynn," Chad said, "they engineered that. They took their pound of flesh. It bought your way out because it was really out of your hands. You had to move to Chicago to be with your sister while she finished school. But they knew you'd come back. Even then they had it planned. You would come back to town sooner or later and bring them the thing they wanted most, the thing you loved best. And you would offer it with your own hands. And what's her name? Marjorie, is it?"

Flynn stood up. This had gone far enough.

"Oh, Jesus, don't act so high and mighty," Chad told him. He shook his head, his eyes full of tears. "It's never easy. It's not meant to be. All of this costs. When Helena was six months pregnant, they told me they wanted her. I refused. So they took the baby. Stillborn. A few years later I gave her to them."

Flynn felt like a great hollow had just been dug inside him, leaving an echoing void that could never be filled. His heart began to pound and his palms were greasy with sweat. I didn't come back for that. I didn't come back to sacrifice Marjorie to them. He tried to say that to Chad but his tongue was stuck to the roof of his mouth. He couldn't so much as blink. It felt like his eyes were painted on.

Chad chuckled with a wounded voice. "Oh...dear God, Flynn...

how I rooted for you! You were my saving grace! You were evidence that they could be beaten and that their power only extended so far! You were like my hero! You gave me fucking hope!" He broke up into laughter as tears ran down his face and his entire body shook. "I thought, Look, look, look! Flynn got out and he'll never come back and there isn't a fucking thing they can do about it! Ha! Ha! He beat them! He really fucking beat them!" He wiped his eyes with a tissue, trying to control the whimpering in his throat. "Then...then you came back. They pulled you back and here you are pretending that it was your idea to come home when it wasn't your idea at all. You've brought them what they want and now you must offer it to them with your own hands..."

Filled with seams of hot and cold anger and recrimination, Flynn left then. He stormed out because he didn't want to hear anymore. He was sick to his stomach and it felt like his mind was going to fly apart inside his head. He made it out to the SUV and sat behind the wheel, fumbling a cigarette into his mouth. He finally lit it after dropping his Bic three times.

We do you favors, you do us favors.

No, no, he didn't want to hear those voices. It was all bullshit. It was teenage fantasy. It was absurdity. There couldn't possibly be any basis in fact...yet, he knew there was. He kept thinking about what Chad had said about his unborn baby and his wife. And that's not all, oh no, it wouldn't be the first time for him. He gave them more. It was fucking madness. But it was real.

He tried to tell himself that he had not come back because they summoned him and that he hadn't come back to give them Marjorie...but he couldn't be sure. He just couldn't remember what had made him come back in the first place. Had it been his idea? Marjorie's?

His cell rang and he answered it, dearly needing to hear his wife's voice. He would tell her to pack up, that they had to leave in a hurry.

But it wasn't Marjorie, of course.

"Hey, Flynn," Toddy said. "See you're visiting old friends. We like that. It warms the cockles of our hearts. There's two other friends, real good, good friends who did a lot for you, that you've been avoiding. We can't have that. There's a debt that's overdue."

"What do you want?" he said. "Is it money? Is it—"

Toddy laughed. It was practically a screeching. "Ain't no banks where we come from, son. We want something else. Something you love. Something that's gonna be real expensive to your heart and soul and I think you know what that is."

Flynn wanted to scream, he wanted to shout, but he was practically in shock. His mouth opened and closed, aping speech, but no sounds came out. He sat there, trembling, moaning deep in his throat like a pain-wracked old man on his deathbed.

"Now, you do the right thing, Flynn. You bring her to us. Wish I could say we're gonna make it fast, but you're long overdue and we got to apply a late charge, which means your beloved is gonna scream for fucking days. Bring her, Flynn. If you don't, we'll come for her on Halloween and you don't want that. You don't want that at all."

He tossed the cell and turned over the SUV, throwing it in drive. He squealed away down Main Street, desperate now to get home to Marjorie before those monsters got to her. He drove like a maniac in his panic, but finally he mellowed slightly and slowed down. He lit another cigarette and tried to think. Tried to reason. There had to be a way out of this.

There had to be something he could do.

They would not get Marjorie.

He would not allow it.

15

That night, the dream came for him.

It was not of his making like an ordinary dream—his subconscious mind sweeping up the refuse of the day—but a full-fledged nightmare sent into his head to torment him, to turn his sleep into a twisted, skin-crawling delirium.

It started on a dark, empty street.

There was a growling sound of a hungry beast sliding through the shadows, sniffing for meat. It was big, it was mean, it was voracious. Flynn stood there, rooted in place, his mouth opening and closing. He wanted to cry out for help but he had no voice. He knew he had to get out of there before the beast reached him, but his feet were heavy, lumbering things. Moving them even a few inches was impossibly difficult.

Too late.

The beast was coming.

He could see it now emerging from the shadows: a dark, fluid shape, an immense black rocket-shaped shark swimming through the air with its mouth open and dozens of gleaming interlocked teeth on display. When it reached him, those teeth would part as the jaws opened and then it would bite him in half. There was no escape.

The growling got louder.

It was no shark. It was the '59 Caddy El Dorado eating up the night. Still, it was a shark. It had the sleek fins of a guided missile, gleaming bone-white trim, and a glistening black hide. Its bullet taillights were the color of blood, its headlights lit like glowing baleful eyes, its chrome grill morphing into the fang-filled mouth of some primeval nightmare from the dawn of the world.

As it came closer, Flynn realized the growling was the sound of its engine—the triple-carb V8 that could bite down with 345 horsepower when the mood struck and launch it forward at 130 miles an hour.

It would have him.

It would feed on him.

Its jaws would crunch his bones to splinters.

Crying out silently, he kept trying to move, dragging his feet as the growling of the Caddy got closer and closer and he could feel the heat of its engine and the sweet, clean smell of the oil pumping through it.

Its front bumper nudged him and he went loose and greasy with abject terror. He looked back one last time as its mouth opened to swallow him whole and he saw two grotesque forms sitting in the front seat. He didn't know what they were, but they certainly weren't Toddy or Bones.

In fact, they weren't even human.

He came out of it, shaking, sweating, not screaming like a character in a B-movie, but with a much deeper and silent terror that was formless and stark. Perspiration was running down his face and he couldn't seem to stop the convulsive waves of shudders that passed through his body. He shook uncontrollably like he had a good case of the flu.

It was enough to wake up Marjorie next to him. She placed a hand on his arm. "Are you all right?" she asked.

He couldn't seem to answer her. His mouth wouldn't work and his thoughts were wild and disordered. He lay there, staring into the darkness as the sweat cooled on him, wondering if he had suffered a stroke.

"Flynn? Flynn?" Marjorie said with a rising note of panic in her voice. She turned on the light and put both of her hands on him. "Flynn, please, what is it?"

"A dream, a nightmare," he managed. "It was bad. Real bad."

"Christ, you scared the hell out of me."

It was still there, fresh in his mind. The car was a monster and it was going to eat him. He wanted to tell her about it…but how could he? The idea of being eaten by a car was absurd and she would have laughed. How could she not? To understand his horror, she would have had to know everything, what that car symbolized, what it had been in his teenage years and what it was now.

No, no, I can't. I can't tell her.

"What the heck was it about?"

The question, of course, was raised. Would an answer be forthcoming? No, of course not. "I'm not sure. It was bad, whatever the hell it was."

"I've never known you to have dreams like that. Are you feeling all right?"

"Yeah, it was just a dream. It's nothing to fret about."

"Who's fretting?"

He could see that she wasn't happy. Her eyes had narrowed and she was suspicious. She knew him as well as he knew himself. She knew he was lying but what really troubled her, he figured, is that she didn't know why.

She turned off the light and settled back onto her pillow. He could hear her breathing evenly. She wasn't sleeping. He knew she wasn't sleeping. She was doing what wives did when they sensed trouble stirring the calm waters of their pond: she was biding her time, considering things. When the time was right and his guard was sufficiently down, she would leap.

After a time, knowing he'd get no sleep until this was done with, he said, "Well, go ahead. Ask your question."

"What makes you think I have one?"

He sighed. "Experience."

"Okay. You've been acting weird ever since we came to Compton, Flynn. You're touchy, you're moody, you're crabby. You fly off the handle. You brood. You peer out the curtains like you're in the Witness Protection Program or something and the bad guys have finally tracked you down." She paused and he could hear her lick her lips in the darkness. A sound he found unbearably exciting. "I don't know what your thing is, Flynn. I mean, I'd be the first to admit you can be a real pain in the ass sometimes, but it's brief. You act weird, you get tense, you mouth off to me, then you apologize. No harm done. But lately...I know you have some bad memories here but for godsake, are they this bad?"

Despite himself, he smiled at her intuition and spot-on appraisal of the situation. He couldn't fool her; she read him too easily. This was the perfect opportunity to spill his guts and tell her everything.

Maybe she'd suggest therapy, but he didn't think so. She would not believe what he told her, not really, but she would accept some underlying cause: That something, perhaps, traumatic had happened when he was a kid and the town was bringing it all back to him. He had no idea what she would make of his conversation with Chad. Internally, he shook his head. No, no goddamn way. He was not going to tell her.

What would she fucking think of me if she learned the truth? If she found out about Toddy and Bones and the fact that I knew they had murdered several people but I did nothing about it? What would she think?

He knew and knew very well. She would think of him the way he thought of himself all these years—with complete loathing. If she accepted any of it at all, which she probably wouldn't.

But she could check. It's all a matter of public record—the disappearances of Bobby Swinn and Daniel Harms… and all the rest of it.

He sighed, preparing a lie that wasn't exactly a lie. "It's this town, baby. I fucking hate it here. I hated it when I was sixteen and I hate it now. I know you like it here. Hell, I know you love it here… but for me, I don't know, it's always going to be a bad place with bad memories."

"Do you want to tell me what those memories are?"

"No. No, I don't. That wound has scabbed over and I'm not about to make it bleed again."

She didn't like that and he sensed as much. He had put a wall between them and she wasn't comfortable with the idea. But at the same time, she knew Flynn. She knew how pigheadly stubborn he could be. Until he chose to tell her, she could not make him.

All she said was, "So where does all this leave us?"

"I don't know."

More silence. Then: "Flynn, if this town makes you miserable, I'm all for getting out. We can find another place. I like this house and I like this town. But I'm not in love with them. I'm in love with you. And if you're not going to be happy, then I won't be either. If it makes you feel better, we can pack up in the morning and get the hell out. But before we do that, you're going to tell me why. You're going to tell me everything and until you do, we're not going anywhere."

With that, she rolled over and said no more.

He spent the next couple of hours lying there and staring into the darkness. The rational part of his brain told him that none of this could be true. That none of it had happened the way he remembered it. But the irrational—and intuitive—part of his brain told him that he was in denial, dangerous denial. Because it was true, it was happening, and if he needed evidence of that, his chat with Chad and the phone call from Toddy gave him all he needed.

It was happening.

And he was scared to death.

16

Things were tense for the next couple of days. Marjorie did not bring up their late night conversation and, at first, Flynn was okay with that. Hell, he was grateful for that. It was the last thing in the world he wanted to talk about. Regardless, it was there all the time. He could see it in her eyes that she had put a question to him and expected an answer. Unfortunately, he didn't have the guts to give her one. He tried hard not to see that question steadily becoming a look of disappointment. It was there and it hurt him. He also tried hard not to think of the past and what Chad had said or that goddamn phone call, but there was no getting away from any of it. He was a satellite caught in the awful, malefic pull of the dark star that was Toddy and Bones and he could escape it no more than a moon can escape its own orbit.

He spent a lot of time working out in the yard raking leaves. It was wonderfully simple, mind-numbing work that kept his muscles busy, put calluses on his hands, and kept his mind from indulging into too many morbid fantasies. They were there, of course. He could only suppress them so much, but they became skewed and ridiculous as he processed them through his machismo. He was going to toss the rake aside, climb into his SUV, and drive over to Haglish, Monroe, Penning, and Reese with a full head of steam. Then he was going to take the elevator to the top floor, find Chad, and proceed to slap the shit out of him in full view of not only his clients but his office staff. That was a good one. In reality, regardless of how good it might feel, it would only land him in jail. And as he was whiling away his nights in the Graybar Hotel, Toddy and Bones (and possibly good old Chad himself) would come after Marjorie and take their pound of flesh, their offering, their fucking sacrifice.

As he bagged up leaves out on the boulevard, he looked around the neighborhood at all the gaudy, mass-produced McMansions squeezed onto small elaborately landscaped lots, garish monstrosities with faux brick siding, cathedral windows, and pillared porches. Symbols of excess and unnecessary extravagance for yuppies in debt up to their necks who would never be rich but wanted others to think they were. His own house was no exception. He watched people raking and trimming bushes and covering shrubs with sackcloth for the coming winter.

It's so normal, it's all so typically Middle American…how can things like Toddy and Bones exist against a backdrop like this?

That was one of the most disconcerting things about all this; its paradoxical nature. It was all so conflicting and incongruous. Things like them belonged in a fog-bound village or some murky European castle, but not here, not in Compton, and definitely not on Candlelight Lane with its assortment of perfectly tasteless, pompous, and utterly pretentious factory-made copies of real mansions and its nouveau riche wannabes with their high-end SUVs, convertibles, and pimped-up trucks.

Flynn finished up the leaves, offering obligatory waves to neighbors, and thinking. When he was a teenager, there was no Candlelight Lane. Back then it was simply ordinary Norton Avenue, which circled around the eastern edge of town. There was little out here but rows of tract houses, a few odd spillovers from Main Street—the Dairy-Flo, a roller rink, and a Shakey's Pizza Parlor—a ball field, a little park, and the Riverhill drive-in theater. All of that was gone now. Even the hills had been bulldozed flat. All to make way for urban sprawl and the expansion of subdivisions and greater yuppiedom that would be known by the lofty, utterly synthetic title of Candlelight Lane.

Candlelight Lane, my white ass, he thought as he piled green Hefty bags for a trip to the compost site. Everywhere else in town, leaves were heaped at the curbs for pickup by the street sweeper, but not here. Not on Candlelight Lane.

He was disgusted by where he was and what he was in danger of becoming, by what had been done to the only part of town he ever really liked, and mostly by the fact that while reality existed for his many fine upstanding neighbors, it was steadily crumbling away for him. The foundation of his life was showing some terrible cracks and it was only a matter of time before the floor collapsed and he was plunged headlong into the darkness of the cellar.

The days passed and he waited for the phone to ring, waited for that '59 Caddy to come prowling through the neighborhood, and mostly he waited for the bloated parasite known as Chad Reese to re-insinuate himself in his life.

None of which happened.

Things were quiet.

They were calm.

Yet, the tension held because Flynn could feel forces building around him. It sounded like something from a cheap 1970s made-for-TV movie, but that's how it felt to him. Dark forces were gathering their strength, charging their batteries, and when the time came to come out of dormancy, it would be absolute hell on earth for Flynn Connors and his wife.

The tension also held because there were unspoken things between Marjorie and him. It was not their way. They had always been good together. They supported one another and together made a whole of two promising pieces. But now that bond was fractured and Flynn didn't know what to do to cement it back together. He still refused to tell her about any of it and that was the barrier that kept them apart. Day by day, he could sense the growing disappointment in her and it hurt, it really hurt.

Finally, three days since the night of their midnight conversation, she said, "You probably haven't noticed, but ever since we've moved here we've had absolutely no sex life. We did at first, but it's gradually tapered down to nothing."

"I noticed."

"And?"

He shrugged. "This town is eating me alive." It was true. It was absolutely true, but he immediately wished he hadn't said it.

"Hmm," she said. "I was looking at myself in the mirror after I got out of the shower yesterday and you know, I'm not nineteen anymore, but I still consider myself eminently fuckable."

Flynn started laughing. "You do have a way with words."

"Flynn..."

"This town is turning me into shit. I knew it would the first day we visited, but you liked it so much. I wanted you to be happy. I wanted you to live in a nice place and this is the place you chose." He leaned back and lit a cigarette, knowing with a pang of guilt that he was smoking way too much these days. "I was hoping that by coming here I could…I don't know…exorcize my own demons, but you know what? They're too strong. They're just too strong."

"They're not going to get any weaker if you avoid them," she said. "Bring them out into the open, face them, let me face them with you."

No, no, dear God, baby, you don't want that.

"I can't."

"Please, Flynn. Please."

She was nearly begging. This is what he was doing to her. The proud, intelligent, wonderful woman he loved was begging to be let into his life. Her lips were mashed together, her eyes misting.

"I'm not ready yet."

"Flynn…Jesus Christ, don't do this to me. I'm scared to death for you. Please don't make it worse. Please don't make me grovel."

The tears were coming from her eyes now and she was not one to cry unless she was entirely emotionally wrecked. But here they were, splashing down her cheeks. When he tried to wipe them away, she slapped his hand aside. "Please," she sobbed, "Tell me what's going on."

He felt great pain and great sympathy for her at that moment. His heart was heavy in his chest and it hurt with each beat, a dull bottoming-out sort of pain. But there was also anger—not only at himself for his weakness, at what he had done, and what he still might do, but at Marjorie for finally locating his soft white underbelly and twisting the knife that protruded from it. There were some things…some things that simply had to be left alone.

"You have no idea what you're asking," he said to her, feeling the hate come boiling out of him, black with venom. "This isn't the sort of thing you're thinking. It's not some half-assed teenage drama I can't get over, it's way beyond that. It's big. It's ugly. It's fucking dangerous. If you toy with it, you'll find out how dangerous. Please, Marjorie, for your own sake, stay out of this. At least for now. Let me work through this…then later maybe we can sort it out together."

"And maybe we won't be able to."

"Baby—"

"It's about trust, Flynn. It's all about trust."

No it's not. It never has been. It's about ethics and morals and making the right choice or making the worst one imaginable.

He stomped away and went outside, searching for stray leaves on the lawn. There were none. The only ones were in the street and as he watched, they blew away, scattering like the years.

He lit another cigarette, standing there by the hedges. He saw a young couple walking down the sidewalk across the street. The boy was tall and blonde, the girl buxom and dark. They were holding hands. They were laughing. They were nuzzling and pressing up against each other. Neither of them realized that they would probably never feel that alive again in their entire life. That age wiped away not only the years but your youth and your hope and your optimism. It made your heart beat slower and your blood run that much colder. They paused at the corner, making out. He felt an ache in his chest. There was nothing better than your girl's hot tongue in your mouth on a chilly day. The feel of her pert breasts pressed up against you, the globes of her ass beneath your clutching hand. The closeness. The connection. The intimacy. They crossed the street, cutting through the vacant lot at the end and making for the last struggling stand of woods beyond that would no doubt soon fall victim to the blade of the bulldozer for more neighborhoods of architectural nightmares. But for now those woods were there. They would seek a sheltered, secret place and their tongues would dance hotly in each other's mouths. His hand would slide up her shirt and explore the firm cones of her breasts. Maybe she would let him investigate the heat between her legs, that godhead of natural mystery and sweet seduction, the cosmic all of the human condition. Maybe she would stroke him with her hand or, if it was truly a lucky day, maybe she'd take him in her mouth and give him a hot-blooded memory that would still haunt him in middle age. And maybe, just maybe, despite the chill in the air, he'd lay her down in the leaves and let the primeval beasts run unfettered. They would never be more in love than they were today.

Flynn, feeling his age, his sins coming back to torment him, collapsed in a redwood chair back by the garage. Teenage years were considered the best years of your life. And to some, they were.

But to the majority, they were a season of pain and doubt; a gangly and awkward time when your body matured faster than your mind, leaving you uncertain and confused with threadbare self-confidence and shaky self-esteem. You always expected them to be better than they really were. Where was your perfect girlfriend/boyfriend? Your perfect car? Your perfect friends and perfect life? This was the time when you realized how hard those things were to come by and you joined group after group in an eternal grasp for something you could never hold in your hand. People said the media was to blame. That movies, books, and TV shows set a high standard that could never be achieved unless you were really lucky, really good-looking, or really rich…even then, it was mostly out of reach.

The stereotypes of the carefree, joyous teenage existence were created by writers and directors anxious to give their audience what they expected and give themselves something they never had but wanted dearly. They were trying to fill a hollow in themselves and give those fleeting teenage years a cultural identity that never really existed in the first place.

Flynn lit another cigarette off the butt of the last. His heart fluttered in his chest from the massive onslaught of nicotine. He barely noticed. He was thinking that being a teenager was the greatest blessing in the world and the most horrendous curse imaginable. All his life, he'd had to sit around in offices and break rooms, bars and restaurants, listening to people talking up their teenage years, reliving their glory days and never once touching upon the misery and heartbreak of it all. As he heard the stories, he always wondered why the hell his had been so awful. Was it him? Was he that fucked up to begin with? But no, it wasn't him, not entirely, it was only his expectations that were fucked up. He aimed too high and crawled too low. Maybe those people he'd listened to all those years were the ones who were fucked up—he was able to admit that he'd been a screwed-up teenager but they never could, they would never look at the reality of those waning long-gone years and see the desperation and tragedy of it all.

And maybe you're just getting old and you don't have the guts to face what you soon must. You don't have your youth to support you. All you have is age and experience and those things aren't enough to hold up a feather.

What he had to do now was to wipe the slate clean and quit bemoaning and dissecting the teenage Flynn Connors, who invariably made the wrong choice at the wrong time again and again. That was done. That was the past. Mistakes and poor choices were made by a boy with no confidence looking for a way out in his desperation. Now, that same boy as a man had to correct all that. He had to think his way out of it. He would have to be cunning and brutal if it came to it. He would need to be ready to fight.

Toddy and Bones aren't going to go away. They've given you a reprieve for a few days because a few days mean nothing to them. No more than thirty-five years does. Maybe you haven't really seen them face-to-face yet, but you know that when you do, they are going to look exactly as they did in 1980 and 1981. They will still be hot-blooded teenage toughs while you are now a middle-aged man. They will still be monstrous death-parasites and, inside, you will still be a frightened teenager. They want something from you and it's the one thing you can never give them.

So be prepared to fight.

To outthink them.

They were arrogant then, they'll be arrogant now. Keep that in mind. That's their Achilles' heel. They expect fear, they expect groveling, they expect panic—but what they don't expect is out and out defiance. Don't forget how they reacted that day long ago when you came after their car with a baseball bat.

With that in mind, he began to make plans.

Just like back in high school, it was High Noon and he was Marshal Kane, scared white inside, but rising to the occasion because there wasn't a damn person he could depend on but himself. There was always Marjorie, of course, but there was no way in hell he was putting her in the line of fire.

17

That night after Marjorie went to bed, Flynn sat there, smoking and drinking straight from a bottle of Weller bourbon. It was crass and unthinkable, but he was beyond such trifling things by that point. He was waiting. He was standing guard. Whatever was building around him was getting stronger and stronger. He could feel it gathering like static electricity. What was going to happen was going to happen soon. Marjorie was not talking to him at all. Things were going to hell on every front and there was no getting past that.

Then, just before midnight, his cell rang.

Here it is. This is it and you know it.

"Yes?" he said.

"Flynn." It was Chad. He sounded oddly out of breath as if he had been running. "You can't keep avoiding this. It's only going to make things harder on both of us."

Flynn wanted to hang up, but he didn't. "You're out of your mind, Chad. You know that, don't you?"

"I'm hardly interested in your appraisal of my mental health. If I'm a little around the bend, then no one has more right. You think I sleep well at night knowing what I've done? You think a moment of the day goes by that I'm not scared they'll come for me? That they'll demand something else?"

"You made your choices. Don't drag me into it."

Chad started laughing, but it was a cold, derisive laughter. "You're already into it. Don't be an ass."

"I'm hanging up now, Chad. Don't call this number again."

"Wait!" he cried, breathing hard again. His voice not only sounded breathless but frantic. "Flynn, you don't have a choice. You have to do what they want. If you don't, they'll come for both of you...don't you see that? Then they'll come for me."

Ah, now they were getting to the meat of the matter.

"That's your problem, Chad."

"My problem? My problem? Goddamn right it's my problem. It's yours, too. C'mon, Flynn. You knew this was coming. You've had everything a man could want same as me, but it all comes with a price, don't you see that? The better you do in life, the more you have to pay in the end. Your account's overdue." He swallowed a couple times, his voice dry, cracking, and wizened. "You know what you have to do. They'll be waiting at the place you first met them tomorrow or the day after. They're expecting you. If you don't bring them what they want, they'll come and take it."

Flynn's entire body was tense like a fist that wanted to strike. "I don't know what you did or what you promised, Chad. That's not my problem."

"It is, you fucking idiot!" Chad cried over the line. "You have to pay! Bring her to them! Do you hear me! Bring your wife to them!"

"Go to hell, Chad."

On the other end, Chad's breathing continued to escalate, though he calmed considerably. "I'm trying to keep us both from going to hell. Don't you see that? I've been where you are. I know exactly what you're thinking, that you can stand up against them, that you can fight them. But you can't. They're beyond anything you can imagine. They'll do things to you. They'll send…others to torment you. In the end, you'll give them what they want."

"No way in hell."

"Bring her to them, Flynn. It's the only way. Do it before it's too late."

"No."

"Then you doom both of us. And I can't have that. You either offer her or I'll do it myself. Either way she's going—"

Flynn broke the connection.

It was enough.

More than enough.

He sat there, sweating and shaking, sick to his stomach. There had to be a way out. There just had to be. Regardless, from now on he couldn't let Marjorie out of his sight.

18

1981

In retrospect, maybe he could have stopped it, maybe he could have slammed the gates of hell shut before he completely damned himself.

Maybe.

But he didn't want to. That was the sad fact of the matter. He got off on the power and celebrity of it all. He was drunk with it. The evil at hand seduced him effortlessly and he was an oh-so-willing pawn in a game that was, perhaps, much larger than anything he could have imagined. He knew things were going from bad to worse, that something truly horrible was in the works. He could feel critical mass building but he was too afraid—and maybe too exhilarated—to stop it.

He liked how people in school and on the streets went out of their way to make him happy. He liked how everybody wanted to be his friend. How the popular kids respected him and the prettiest girls fawned over him. Even the teachers didn't fuck with him. There was an aura around him and it was as if everyone he encountered could feel its power, its promise, and its menace.

And if sometimes his conscience got in the way, telling him that who and what he was becoming were going to turn his soul black like a rotten apple core, he would simply say to himself, You really haven't done anything. You've stolen some cars and ripped off some booze and fingered some assholes that needed to be taught a lesson, but you haven't harmed anyone directly. Toddy and Bones will move on eventually and you'll be a nothing again so enjoy it while you have it.

And he did, even though he was haunted by guilt and

near-petrified to be in the company of them and terrified of not pleasing them. They were always watching him. It was as if they could look right inside him, peer deep into him and pick away at his subconscious like buzzards eager to strip a meaty carcass. Maybe that was imagination, but it seemed like every time he was with him he lost more of himself. He had the worst feeling that they could have torn his soul out by the bloody roots and fed upon it anytime they chose. Sometimes he could even see them in his dreams, eyes gleaming a chromium yellow and grinning lips pulled back from the narrow teeth of rodents.

As the year ended and spring blended into the green of high summer, it got so he simply couldn't take it anymore.

Chad and he had taken to chumming around even though they really didn't like each other. Like two criminals brooding over a common crime and sharing the same lockup, they were thrown together.

One afternoon after a wild night spent riding hell-for-leather in the '59 El Dorado, he went to see Chad. The Reeses lived in a plain, squat little frame house with an obligatory white picket fence around it. Flynn had been there before. Chad's parents were basically two mannequins with haunted eyes, two pale living husks that rarely spoke. Chad said it was because his kid brother, Donny, had drowned in Squaw Lake the summer before and they had never gotten over it. Maybe that was part of it. But Flynn figured it had a little more to do with their other son, who scared the shit out of them. Chad bullied them constantly and they cowered every time he entered the room. His father looked perpetually stunned and his mother whimpered whenever Chad raised his voice to her.

"Don't pay her any mind," Chad said one time. "She's been like that ever since Dicky, her Pekinese, burned up."

"Burned up?"

"Sure. She kept nosing around in my room when I wasn't there. Bitch found my dope and had a cow. She sent old Father Wendt from St. Paul's to have a talk with me. Heart to heart and all." He laughed. "Well, I showed him a few things and he went fast. Get it?"

"What about the dog?"

"Ah, I told the old lady to stay out of my business or she was going to lose something real dear to her. But she didn't. She kept pawing through my stuff so…heh, heh…one night little Dicky burst into flames while they were watching T.J. fucking Hooker. Christ, the stink, man. Took a month to get the smell of deep-fried Pekinese out of the house."

Flynn didn't ask how it happened and he didn't listen when Chad went through the statistical possibilities of spontaneous combustion. That was the last time he'd been there.

Then a few days before the Fourth of July, he stopped by. When they were up in Chad's room pulling off a doobie, he said, "I want to know what they are."

Chad didn't bother pretending ignorance of the question. "I don't know. I never asked and I don't plan on starting."

Flynn didn't necessarily believe that. He had a feeling there was something Chad wanted to tell him but was afraid to put into words.

"Are they ghosts?"

Chad laughed. "Ghosts, he says."

"I'm serious."

And he was. He couldn't stop thinking about the dog Toddy and Bones had pasted with the Caddy and how Mr. Upright Concerned Citizen—now deceased—had not seen them standing there. He couldn't get past that.

"Not ghosts, dickhead. Not in the way you think."

Chad told him they hadn't come up out of any graves and they weren't some toughs that had died in a '59 Cadillac and decided to haunt the streets or any of that cheap movie-of-the-week shit. All he could say was that his life before them was crap. He was tormented continually by the popular pricks at school and he couldn't take it anymore. One day, on his way home from school, he got roughed up pretty bad by some wet ends from the football team who had a special hatred for him. They had beaten him down and he was on the ground in an alley. Every time he tried to get up, they kicked him. They—and particularly a real meat-eater named Ritchie Arcano— told him he wasn't allowed to stand. He had to crawl home on his belly like the fucking worm he was.

"I remember…I don't know…just crying out for help, for somebody to help me."

That's when Toddy showed.

Chad had never seen him before. He stepped out of nowhere, a mean-looking sonofabitch with motorcycle boots on and his thumbs hooked into the pockets of his oily jeans. He had a crew cut, an acid leer in his eyes, and he grinned like a dead snake.

"This ain't for you, old man," Ritchie told him. "Get out of here while you still can."

"Old?" Flynn asked.

Chad swallowed. "He looked older, I guess. I thought he was maybe in his forties or around fifty. There were gray streaks in his hair…but, man, he was one badass motherfucker and you could see it."

"But that old?" Flynn said. "How come he looked that old? He and Bones were like in their thirties when I first met them and when they creamed that dog they looked like they were in their twenties."

Chad wasn't interested in that; he wanted to go on with his story so Flynn let him.

He said that the air had gotten real cold in the alley as if somebody had opened the door of a deep freeze. Ritchie's friends were shivering and it wasn't just because the temperature had dipped. They were scared shitless.

"And I didn't blame them, man," Chad admitted. "Toddy was like the Angel of fucking Death or something. And you want to hear something really weird?"

"What?"

"It was the middle of the afternoon. A bright sunny day. I was on the ground. I could see the shadows of Ritchie and the boys just fine…but not Toddy. He didn't cast a shadow."

Chad gulped dryly a few times and went on with his tale.

Toddy stood there, staring at the boys with hot black eyes, something under his skin tensing like it wanted to leap out and slash open their bellies, stuff itself with what fell out. He told Ritchie and his followers to piss off and go home, that their mommies needed a good fingering. Two of the meatheads took offense to that and made a terrible mistake: they made a grab for Toddy. Toddy laughed and his arm flexed twice, his fist smashing into their faces in a blur. Both of them were on the ground bleeding. One of them was whimpering. Toddy turned toward the other two and they ran like they were eating yardage under the Friday night lights.

But not Ritchie.

He couldn't back down. His walnut-size brain insisted he do something. He charged Toddy and Chad heard an awful meaty thudding sound like a sledge hammer hitting a gourd again and again (as he put it) and big tough guy, superstar defensive end Ritchie Arcano was down on the pavement, minus three teeth, gagging blood. All 6'4", 280 pounds of him was quivering, soft white meat.

Toddy wasn't done, however.

He stomped his leather motorcycle boot down on Ritchie's left hand and Chad clearly heard the bones snapping like green twigs. Poor old Ritchie screamed like a ten-year-old girl. But even that wasn't enough for Toddy. He smashed his boot down with incredible pressure, grinding Ritchie's hand between it and the pavement.

Chad was sweating as he remembered it. "Jesus...the fucking sound of it. Gah. Ritchie went out cold. I mean dead fucking cold."

Later, Chad heard that every bone was broken in Ritchie's hand. It took seven months and half a dozen reconstructive surgeries before he could hold a pencil let alone a football.

"Shit," was all Flynn could say.

"Shit is right. Ritchie and his family moved away." Chad grinned now like a monkey with a tin cup. "Rumor had it a muscle car kept pulling into their driveway around midnight every night and gunning its engine. Whenever the cops showed, the car wasn't there." Chad shrugged, roached the doob and lit a cigarette. "All I know is that I've been with Toddy and Bones ever since. They want something? They get it, no matter what it is. My life is good now and I'm not about to bite the hand that feeds. You better think about that. Think about it real hard."

Flynn nodded. "That still don't tell me what they are."

"You gotta quit with that. Keep your nose clean."

"I don't want to be part of this anymore."

There. It was said. No more bullshitting around.

Chad stared at him for the longest time, the cigarette hanging from his mouth, a ribbon of blue smoke rising from it like an exclamation point. "I never thought you were stupid, Flynn. I thought you were a smart guy. But if you think you can walk away from this, then you're a fucking idiot. You're in too far. Man. They own you like they own me. You wanted help and you got it. You got everything you wanted. You think it was all free? That there was no obligation? Dumbass. Maybe you didn't sign your name in blood, but you might as well have."

"Fuck that."

"No, Flynn. Fuck you. Because they will. They'll fuck you in ways you can't imagine. And they'll fuck your family, too. They'll cut your mother into pieces and make you watch. They'll peel the skin off your sister and—"

Flynn hit him.

He knocked him right off his chair to the floor and Chad laughed with an evil mocking sound. "You stupid little pissbag. You fucking brain-dead squirt of shit." He wiped blood from his mouth, slowly standing up. "Don't you get it? They gave and you took. They asked for little things and you provided them. Now you're in deep and they're going to want something bigger, something real, something more personal. Maybe your mom and maybe your sister…and you know what? You're going to give them what they ask for. They're gonna want an offering and if they don't get it…if they don't get it, they'll come for you."

Flynn grabbed him and slammed him up against the wall, hard enough to knock books off a shelf and his telescope from its stand. "I won't! You hear me? I won't give them a goddamn thing! I won't—"

Now Chad—with surprising strength—slammed him up against the wall. "YES, YOU WILL, YOU FUCKING ASSHOLE!" he screamed, red in the face and frothing white foam at the mouth. "YOU WON'T HAVE A CHOICE! IF YOU DON'T, WE'RE BOTH SCREWED AND I'M NOT GOING DOWN FOR A PIECE OF SHIT LIKE YOU! THEY'LL ASK AND YOU'LL GIVE THEM WHAT THEY WANT!"

Then he got in real close, so close his hot, sour breath was in Flynn's face, his eyes bulging white and red-rimmed. "Do you think I wanted to do what they asked? Do you think I enjoyed it? Do you think for one moment I liked holding my kid brother under the water while he kicked and thrashed and died in my arms? Do you think I got off on that?"

There it was.

The bomb was dropped.

Whatever vague, macabre suspicions Flynn had before were now confirmed. Chad had been part of whatever Toddy and Bones were for much longer than he so was it really that surprising that the stakes had been upped and the demands were higher? No, not really. What was surprising was that Chad complied; that he more or less sacrificed his kid brother to those fucking monsters.

After Chad dropped his not-so-little bomb, there was really nothing to say. Flynn stood there, staring at him, making no attempt to hide the contempt he felt. Chad pulled away from him, collapsing in the corner, his head pressed down between his knees. He was sobbing and blubbering. His dark, unforgivable secret was out and the pain was running from him in rivers of poison. The unspeakable deed had been spoken and there was no going back.

"Don't look at me," he said. "Please don't fucking look at me."

But Flynn couldn't help himself.

This was it, this was the foul depths that stark terror could sink the human animal to. This was how low it could take you; down into a bottomless black pit of self-loathing and self-degradation. It would make you do anything to save your own skin. It wasn't enough for Toddy and Bones to perpetrate the horrors themselves. No, when the time came and payment was due, they wanted you to destroy yourself and all that you held sacred. They wanted you to swim in your own piss and wallow in your own shit, to drink yourself full of your own bile. They demanded expiation by your own hand. That was true evil, true corruption, the ultimate in self-defilement. They wanted you to rip out your own soul and place it bleeding at their feet.

"You wait," Chad sobbed. "You just fucking wait. When the times comes, you'll do it, too. You won't have a choice."

"The hell I won't," Flynn told him.

19

The summer passed and he saw nothing of Chad. As far as he knew, he might have been dead. He saw Toddy and Bones only once. They passed him on Main and Toddy waved, but that was it. Day after day, he kept expecting to hear the Caddy rumbling up the street, but it never came. By the time August ended and September brought the chill nights, he began to feel not only safe but confident that he was out of the loop, that it was all behind him.

Yet, he wasn't 100% convinced.

That nagging, haunting voice in his head kept saying, It's the calm before the storm. They're toying with you. They're letting you relax, letting you think you're off the hook. But you're not and you know it. They're only backing off because Chad spilled the beans and they don't want to spook you.

Maybe that was true. The bottom line was that Chad had spilled the beans about what had happened to his brother out at Squaw Lake. Flynn wanted to believe it was bullshit. He told himself again and again it was, but he couldn't convince himself. Three times he had picked up the phone to call the police only to set it back down. Would it do any good at this juncture to involve the cops? To tear Chad's family apart even more? What good could come of his parents knowing that their youngest was not only dead but murdered by the hand of their oldest?

No, he couldn't go to the authorities.

He just couldn't.

By October he was bothered a bit less by his conscience and that's when the El Dorado showed up again. As he walked out of school the first week in October, there it was and there were Toddy and Bones. He felt the old familiar fear knot up his belly.

"Long time no see," he said, falling back into it smooth and easy so as not to arouse suspicion.

"Sometimes we need to recharge our batteries," Toddy told him, smiling his usual death-grin.

"But don't worry," Bones said. "We were keeping an eye out, making sure you were safe and sound."

Flynn just stood there, smiling, his heart pounding in his throat. They had regenerated again. The last time he had seen them up close—the incident of the dog and Mr. Upright Concerned Citizen— they had looked so much younger like they were in their twenties… now they looked like teenagers. The deep-etched lines of hard living had been smoothed from their faces. Even the knife cut that ran from Bones' nose to his left ear was a barely noticeable pink weal that was fading fast. Their skin was clear and unblemished.

They could have walked right into the school and fit in.

Flynn was reminded of American Lit last year when they'd read Stoker's Dracula. In the novel, the infamous count rejuvenated himself on blood. At the opening of the book he was an old man with a white mustache and by the end, a young man. Is that it? he thought. Are they vampires? Parasites that feed on death and violence? Do they drink themselves full with it, fatten themselves up like spiders sipping the life from juicy flies? It was insane, but he was almost sure he was onto something.

"How they been hanging?" Toddy asked.

"High and dry."

"That a boy."

It was at that moment as the three of them stood there next to the purring beast of the '59 El Dorado that Daryl Smite happened by. Good old Daryl. He had a stack of college texts in his arms and he was singing "Whip It" by Devo, much to the annoyance of the cool kids who passed by him.

Then he saw Flynn. He stopped, looked at him, then his eyes roamed beyond and glanced at Toddy, Bones, and the car. There was no mistaking it. He saw them. He fucking saw them. Daryl moved off then, his pace increased, his singing voice carrying a high-pitched note of anxiety.

Flynn thought: If he saw them, that means he—

"Let's take a ride," Toddy said.

When Flynn jumped into the backseat, Chad was there. He was

pale and shaking as if he had a good fever going. There was a glazed look in his eyes as if he had looked through a window into hell and something had looked back at him. He was out of it. He didn't even seem to recognize Flynn. There were bright pink welts on his face that looked like cigarette burns.

What have they done to him?

As Toddy squealed away from the curb, Bones hooked a heavy, tattooed arm over the seat. "He ain't saying much, Flynn. See, we been good to old Chaddywhacker. Real good. But he ain't been so good to us. Not so good at all."

"Chaddy Von Pimpledick has been saying shit he shouldn't be saying," Toddy explained.

"Talking about stuff that don't concern him."

"Stuff that pisses us off."

"Makes us real fucking angry."

"Makes us want to hurt people. Hurt 'em real bad."

Flynn said nothing. It felt like his stomach was lodged in his esophagus. Out of the corner of his eye he was watching Chad. He was staring into space with those dead eyes. He looked like someone that had just undergone shock treatment.

Toddy lit a cigarette. "See, Flynn. It's all about trust. You trust us, we trust you. You're good to us, we're better to you. You want something, we get it for you. We want something, you do the same. Friends take care of friends. But if you fuck with us—" and here he turned from the wheel and stabbed a finger in Chad's direction "—and we're your worst enemy."

"We'll fucking eat you alive," Bones grumbled.

It seemed that with each word they spoke, Chad reeled as if he was being hit. He cringed and kept cringing as they talked about how they took care of their friends and all they asked in return was loyalty. What they did, they did out of friendship and friends didn't betray that loyalty, they didn't make up bullshit stories and spread them around. That was a big no-no.

Except it wasn't a bullshit story, Flynn thought. You wanted his brother and he gave him to you.

Toddy pulled off his cigarette, shrugged. "Things got ugly there for awhile, didn't they, Chad? But it's all cool now because we straightened our little Chaddywhacker out. Didn't we, Bones?"

"We sure did."

"We took him places, Flynn. We took him places and we showed him the sights. We took him trick-or-treating."

Chad made a whimpering sound at this.

"And now Chad's real sorry. Ain't that right, Chad?"

Chad swallowed a couple of times.

"I said," Toddy growled with more insistence, "ain't that right, Chad?"

"Yeah. I'm real sorry. Real, real sorry that I fucked up," he said, his voice dry and wizened as if the places they had taken him and the sights they showed him had taken years off his life.

Bones chuckled with a dry, rasping sound. "He's so sorry, Flynn, that he brought us a little peace offering."

It was then that Flynn heard a thumping sound. At first, he couldn't place it. He thought maybe they had run over something. But that wasn't it at all. When he heard it again, he knew it had come from the trunk. Thump-thump, thump-thump. Somebody was in there. Somebody that wanted out badly.

They kidnapped somebody, he thought, feeling cold inside. And Chad arranged it for them the same way he arranged his brother's death.

"Sure," Bones said in a playful sort of tone. "He brought us something special to play with during our long, lonely nights."

Toddy pulled the Caddy to a halt at the curb. "And ain't that just the way a friend treats his friends? By giving them a gift?"

Flynn wanted to scream, but he didn't dare. He knew he had to play it cool or he'd be going into the trunk next. "Yeah, it's only right," he said. "You gotta take care of your friends."

Toddy smiled and looked over at Bones. "Didn't I tell you Flynn was our kind?"

"You sure did."

Toddy opened the door. "We'll see you around, man. We got things to do and long distances to travel…don't we, Chad?"

As Flynn climbed out, Chad looked over at him with complete desperation. But there was nothing he could do for him. As the Caddy roared away, he ran. He made it almost a block before he fell into some bushes and threw up.

20

TWO DAYS LATER.

Sociology and You.

Flynn was waiting in his usual seat by the window trying to avoid the attention of the beautiful, popular kids who were now a permanent part of his orbit. When they finally quit buzzing around him like flies sharing a common turd and Mrs. Bruez had gotten through with morning attendance and had assigned a chapter in their texts—"The Origins of Intolerance"—he turned around in his seat and gave his full attention to Daryl Smite.

Daryl was no fool, of course. "Well, I was wondering when you were going to get around to it," he said.

"I bet you were. You saw them, didn't you?"

Daryl smiled, showing his bad teeth and what seemed like about an inch of gums. "Whom are you referring to, Flynn old boy?"

"Listen, goddammit. I'm not in the mood so don't mess with me."

Daryl's laughter turned more than a few heads. The other students—the ones that mattered—looked at Flynn in amazement that he was associating with a complete loser like Daryl Smite. My God, what was he thinking? The sad part of it all was that Flynn was very much part of their world now and his face actually reddened as if he had been caught doing something unpleasant. Infected by the same snobby virus as they, he reacted in kind. You can't be seen talking to this zero, an elitist voice in his head reprimanded him. Are you out of your mind? Are you trying to tear down everything we've built?

And recognizing his own snobbery and hating it, he refused to back down. Daryl Smite had been a friend of sorts once. Maybe, he still was. And quite possibly the only real friend he had.

"I need your help, Daryl. I really do."

"That much is obvious. The problem here, Flynn, is that ever since you've climbed the golden ladder of popularity here at Compton, you can't be bothered to talk to people like me or even acknowledge our lowly presence. You've become as synthetic as your newfound friends."

Flynn felt his shoulders slump because he was right, he was absolutely right. He had become just as judgmental, immature, and plastic as the others. He shared their intolerances and prejudices, flaunting them like a battle standard. Now he was being called on it and rightly so.

"I deserve that."

"You deserve a lot more."

"Daryl…please."

He sighed. "All right, all right. Let it not be said that I am no friend of poor, dumb animals even if they walk on two feet or wear letters on their jackets."

"Tell me how you saw them."

Daryl shrugged. "Once they've entered your life, you can always see them, and they can always see you. You can't hide from them and they can't hide from you."

"Then you've—"

"No, Flynn. Not at all. I never sunk that low. Not as low as you and definitely not as low as Chad Reese, who crawls on the ground like a reptile because he's their favorite pet."

"But…"

"But nothing," Daryl said, eyes intense and voice sharp. "I know what you went through last year, Flynn. I know how hard it was. I know how worthless it makes you feel when everyone else has to put you down and step on you to lift themselves up so they don't feel so insecure about their own fragile identities. Those two creatures—we'll call them Bones and Toddy, shall we?—look for the weak and bullied, those with two left feet and targets on their backs. They look for the downtrodden and abused, those that can't handle rejection, square pegs that can't fit into the round, well-plumbed, oily holes of the popular crowd. They instinctively find them, help them, lift them up and make them invincible, golden and untouchable…then they drain them dry."

Yes, like parasites, like vampires, like fucking leeches. That's exactly what they do.

Flynn said, "Is that what they did to you?" He envisioned Daryl as some big he-man about campus that had been drained and reduced to the apex nerd before him.

"No. They tried to step in and help, but I sent them packing. I didn't want their help. Not then, not now."

Flynn shook his head. "It's not that easy."

"Of course it is. Right and wrong are always perfectly black and white. Their power you fear so much is your own need. You made them monsters by accepting what they offered. I refused, so they have no power over me. I'm incorruptible. That scares them."

He explained that the proof of that was that he knew about them, could see them, yet they did nothing about him and that was because there was nothing they could do. He wasn't stupid enough to rant and rave about their existence and get himself locked up. And definitely not suicidal enough to interfere with their plans. And certainly not weak enough to accept what they offered.

"So they can't touch me."

Flynn was floored.

It was easy enough when you were one of the chosen ones and ran with the in-crowd to marginalize people like Daryl. He was the ultimate nerd, a shunned entity, a walking social disease, a scab that needed picking. He stumbled daily through Compton High with his heaps of college textbooks, flaunting his memberships in the Computer Club and Chess Society, smiling his crooked smile and laughing at his own bad jokes, always pouring over a Star Trek novelization or a novel by Isaac Asimov or Frank Herbert, oblivious to the laughter and sneering he created, mumbling to himself and tripping over his own feet, a loser, a zero, an outcast that seemed overjoyed with his lack of status.

But that was a mistake.

He was brilliant in math, physics, chemistry, and electronics. He had plans for his life—his real life, not the escapist fantasy of high school—and he was not about to allow the cheap thrills and shallow self-gratification of Toddy and Bones to interfere with that. His ethics, morality, and sharp mind would ensure him an enormously successful future. The cool guys who belittled him and knocked the books from his arms would probably work for him some day. And all the princesses with the big eyes, perky tits, and long legs that laughed at him now would no doubt tear out each other's throats one day for the chance to share his bed because he was going places and he would succeed in a big way.

Flynn figured that was the way of the world: the nothings always became something and the somethings were fated to become nothing.

"What are they?" he finally asked.

Daryl took his time answering. "I don't know. I'd rather not think about it. I doubt they're supernatural or anything. Ghosts and angels and demons are sheer fantasy. Who knows? Maybe they're the sort of things that inspired such stories."

"What can I do?"

"You can say no. You can reject them before you become human garbage like Chad."

"But you can't help me?"

"No, Flynn. Only you can help you. You can't hide from them… then again, they can't hide from you."

21

It was all sage advice and he thought about it hard over the next couple weeks. He'd even gone so far as to tell Daryl about all the dirt in his life from Bobby Swinn to Mr. Upright Concerned Citizen to Daniel Harms, what Chad had supposedly done with his brother to what was in the trunk of the El Dorado. Daryl said he didn't want to know about any of that. His advice did not change. "Say no. Reject them. Nullify their power."

But Flynn wondered if it was too late for that. He'd already accepted more than a few of their gifts and he was not naïve enough to believe he wouldn't have to pay for them. This was the egg of dread that slowly hatched in his head as the days passed and his anxiety increased tenfold. Now and again, he chatted it up with Daryl, searching, ever searching, for some pearl of wisdom that would really put things into perspective. But there was none forthcoming. Daryl was resolute in his advice. It never changed; it never varied.

When another week passed, he began to relax and the same old self-deception took hold of him and told him it was probably all over with and he had nothing to worry about. Down deep, of course, he didn't believe it. But at surface level, yes, he told himself it was true.

Then something started happening.

Something inexplicable.

Something with no apparent cause. It was the most minor of things, at least at first. It was nothing more than a smell. A particularly revolting smell, but still just a smell. It came seemingly out of nowhere—a sweet, sickening odor of decay like the stink of a squirrel rotting in the walls of a deserted house. The first time he smelled it when he was out in the backyard raking leaves, he looked high and low for a source. Five minutes into it, the smell was gone. Then it happened again at school of all places. Two bites into his sloppy joe in the cafeteria and the stench rose up all around him, so unbelievably nauseating he had to dump his tray and get outside in the fresh air. After that, it became more frequent. Still impossibly irregular so that he could never fix a pattern to it, but it happened almost daily. While he was brushing his teeth in the morning or sitting in Intro to Trig in the afternoon or lying in bed at night. If it was possible to be haunted by something as harmless as an odor, he was indeed haunted.

About the same time, he was cozying up to Liz Farrenbach, without a doubt the best-looking girl at Compton. She was a tall, leggy brunette with flawless olive skin, night-black hair down the middle of her back, and huge green eyes that were slightly upturned, giving her an exotic Euro-Asian look that made his heart pound. When she sauntered up the halls of Compton in her short plaid skirts, long legs pumping, boys melted and male teachers stared with their jaws sprung. She was the real thing. There were plenty of cute/pretty/sexy girls in school, but Liz was drop-dead gorgeous like a cover girl and everyone knew it. She hardly dated because no one was good enough for her and she had turned up her perky bosom at Flynn more than once. Then he began to notice she was softening. He asked her if she wanted to do something and she said okay.

They had a great time doing pretty much nothing but walking around and laughing, being young and alive with the first bloom of love in their cheeks. They went over to the Dairy-Flo before it closed for the season and ate chili dogs.

That's when it happened again.

Flynn, giggling with Liz, half daydreaming about getting his hand up her shirt, bit into his chili dog and that rotting stink hit him like a train. It was particularly bad like a dozen graves had burst open at the same time…a green, gassy smell of putrescence. The chili and hot dog in his mouth tasted foul as if he had bitten into maggoty meat.

He stumbled away from the table, his stomach coming right up the back of his throat, and tossed his guts out into the garbage can. When he was done hacking, he looked up and Liz was standing there with her arms crossed and a look of disgust on her perfect face.

"Is there something wrong with you?" she asked.

"No," he gasped, wiping bile from his lips. "It…no, it just comes and goes."

Her jade eyes narrowed. "Vomit. Yuck. It grosses me out."

She stomped away and there was nothing he could say or do to stay her. She passed out of his life and never came back. He was devastated. She would not answer his calls and she refused to even acknowledge him at school. The girl of his dreams had come into his life and exited just as quickly. He shouldn't have been surprised because everything was suddenly going to shit. He started flunking out in classes. He'd been skating through his studies for so long, acing every test without ever studying, the right answer always on the tip of his tongue when he was asked, that when the magic vanished from his life he was far, far behind everyone else and had almost forgotten what it was to study and cram. The popular crowd began to lose interest in him. The girls who'd worshiped him like he was a teenage pop star gracing the cover of Tiger Beat barely looked at him. The boys who'd waited breathlessly for his every word as if he was a sage began to criticize him. He heard laughter behind his back. His teachers gave him shit. One of the toughies that hung around out in the parking lot shoved him out of the way in the cafeteria. His favored status was deteriorating. He was becoming what he'd originally been at Compton—a wingnut, a loser, a nonentity.

In some ways, he found it refreshing. In others, terrifying.

But he knew what was behind it or, rather, who was behind it. If he wanted his luck and charm and popularity back, then he was going to have to ask Toddy and Bones to help him. He might have to beg them. They'd do it, make no mistake about that. And once he was riding high again, they'd want something in return. Something dear to him, something expensive, something that would turn him into a crawling little weasel like Chad, forever under their thumb and forever in their debt.

He refused to do that.

He would rather be a tormented nerd like Daryl. The price of popularity was too high. Say no. Reject them. Nullify their power. That was what he had to do. There was no other way.

22

After Liz dumped him—if you could really be dumped after one date—his heart was broken. That night, he lay in bed and stared blankly at sitcoms. Around nine the phone rang and his youthful optimism combined with his heartbreak made him leap up, thinking, It's Liz and she's sorry she was a bitch and all. But it wasn't her; it was Chad.

"Your time's almost up, man," he said. "You better start thinking about what you're going to do."

Flynn felt his heart plummet and something in his soul crack open. Here it was. He had been expecting it and here it was.

"What are you talking about?"

"You know damn well what I'm talking about, dumbass. You got maybe days before they come for you. Don't bother hiding because you can't. They can find you anywhere. You better start thinking about what you're going to do."

"I'm not going to do anything."

Chad laughed with a dry, crackling sound like the death rattle of an old man gasping for his final breath. "Flynn. Listen to me. Listen good. They're gonna want something and if they don't get it they're gonna take you for a ride, they're gonna take you trick-or-treating just like they did me."

"You're nuts."

But Chad insisted he was anything but. The ride they had taken him on had pushed him as close to the edge as he'd ever been, but it hadn't put him all the way over.

Flynn sighed. He was half-angry and half-scared. Ever since he'd seen Chad in the back of the Caddy that day—dazed, confused, maybe in shock—he'd wanted to know what that was about just as another part of him wanted anything but. "Where did they take you?" he found himself asking even though he knew it was a mistake.

"They took me for a ride," Chad started by saying, his voice oddly modulated and even for someone about to launch into a nightmare. "They took me trick-or-treating to a place that wasn't like this one. Things are different there. It not so…ordered there."

"What are you talking about?"

Chad told him that Toddy and Bones picked him up and he knew he was in the shit right away. He had been dating a girl named Danice McKerran and she, as pretty girls will do, wrapped him quite easily around her finger until he began to change, began to think differently and see things in a whole new way. That's when he realized he was in love. Suddenly, the world didn't seem so gray and other people were not shit he had to step on, use or abuse. He was smiling a lot. He was happy. He spoke kindly to others and he developed something that had always been an alien trait to him— sympathy. He finally gave a damn about somebody besides himself. And it wasn't just Danice—though, God knew, he loved her so much he woke up thinking about her and went to bed dreaming about her, the hours in-between filled with soppy, romantic ideas that made him feel lighter than air…and would have made him sick to his stomach a month before, truth be told—it was others, too. He began to treat his mom and dad with some respect. He stopped yelling at them, belittling them, treating them like servants and punishing them if they got out of line. He started thinking that maybe this was it, maybe this is what had always been lacking, maybe there had been a deep black hole in his heart and Danice had finally filled it as she filled him.

"I found my place, man," Chad said, a rusty edge to his voice that was somewhere between tears and hysteria. "I found my warm place, my sweet spot. I finally found the place I fit."

Flynn had known, of course, that Chad and Danice had become an item. But he'd had no idea that what was between them was running so deep. Danice was a good-looking redhead with a bosom much-envied by other girls and much-desired by other boys. But she wasn't some pretty little wallflower, some handsome accessory, no sir, not Danice. Danice had a feral, black streak running down her middle and if you crossed her, you would find out all about that.

Case in point, Flynn's second week at Compton High he'd been in the commons eating lunch with the rest of the animals and Danice came storming in, blowing steam from both nostrils, her dark eyes practically molten. Apparently a girl named Brittany Clark had been fooling around with Danice's boyfriend (who was Mike LaCosse at the time). Brittany was wearing hoop earrings with feathers on them. Danice grabbed those hoops and yanked them both right through Brittany's earlobes.

That's the kind of girl Danice was. She was good at heart, but you didn't cross her. She had been Chad's true love and probably the only girl that could have kept him under control.

"They wanted her," Chad said.

Flynn swallowed. "Toddy and Bones?"

"Who do you think? She meant nothing to them, but because I was in love with her, they wanted her. They wanted a sacrifice for what they had done for me and it had to be the thing I loved most. Because that's how it works. That's how it always works."

Chad, finally standing up like a man now that true love blushed his heart, told them no. He'd give them anything, but not Danice. They told him he only got Danice in the first place because they made it happen. Anything else, he told them. Anything. He'd give them anything else. He'd lie, cheat, steal, even murder for them… but they could not have Danice. No fucking way.

"What happened?" Flynn asked, though he had a pretty good idea it was nothing good.

Chad said, at first, they just shrugged and said how proud they were of him, that he was a real man and you don't get between a real man and his ladylove. He honestly believed he had called their bluff finally, drawn a line in the sand, and they had backed down. Fear had always been their strength, but since he was showing no fear, they were essentially powerless. He kept thinking that until he left Danice's house late one night and there was the El Dorado waiting for him. Toddy hit him twice, dropping him, then Bones threw him into the back of the car.

"I was defiant, man, and they were going to make me pay. They were going to punish me," Chad said. "So they took me trick-or-treating…"

At least, that's what they liked to call it. Flynn knew damn well that trick-or-treating was the end of the line. No one survived it… yet, Chad had. They had taken him trick-or-treating and he had returned. Maybe he hadn't looked so good—hell, he looked like living death—but he had returned, which meant trick-or-treating wasn't just a death ride, a short trip to a deep hole in the woods, but something else.

And it most certainly was something else.

Chad said they took him out in the country, staying to back roads and county trunks and he was scared shitless. He was certain they were going to pull over in a field somewhere and kill him. But that never happened. After about twenty minutes of driving, they were on a straightaway and Toddy opened up the El Dorado, pushing her for everything she had. Faster and faster they went until the night was a blur and Chad was certain they were going to crash. He kept begging them to stop, to slow down, but they only laughed and went that much faster.

"I looked over the seat and I saw the speedometer and it was pegged at 120," Chad said. "That was the crazy thing, because in any ordinary car of that period 120 would have been the limit but that speedometer registered 120 only halfway across the dial…after that, there were a series of red numbers, P12, P25, P75, P125 and on and on."

As they edged beyond 120, something incredible began to happen. It started with what Chad called a "slingshot effect" in which it felt like the Caddy shot forward with incredible speed.

"You can't imagine what I mean, Flynn," he said, breathing fast and heavy on the other end. "When I was in grade school, I had one of those Wrist Rocket slingshots. You could put a rock right through a tin can with one of those. I put one through a windshield once and right through a metal garbage can another time. That's what it was like—like that car had been fired from a Wrist Rocket. We took off and I was plastered to the backseat. I felt like a toad that had been stepped on. I thought my guts were going to come right out of my mouth…"

The sensation lasted for maybe five seconds, he said, and when it was over, there was a sort of squealing sound like metal grinding on metal, then a flash of light that blinded him for about ten seconds and, finally, a hollow popping sound like the cork blowing off a bottle of champagne, but loud, loud and hollow and echoing, and the weird thing was that it seemed like he could not only hear the sound waves produced by that but feel them, each one thrumming through him. At that point, he became physically ill. It felt like everything inside him had gone to jelly. Out the windows, everything was black, blacker than any night he had ever seen. By that point, he was slumped over against the door with his face pressed against the glass.

"Then…then the stars came out," he said and there was panic in his voice. "But not the right stars, Flynn, not the ones we know… but others." He swallowed a couple times. "I know the stars. I had a telescope. I used to watch them every night before Toddy and Bones set me free…and these were all wrong. I should have been able to see Saturn and Venus, but they weren't there. Andromeda was gone and so was Ursa Major and Pegasus. I couldn't find Draco or the Little Dipper! I couldn't even find Polaris, the fucking North Star!"

He had never seen a night sky like the one he was looking at. It was nothing from the Northern or Southern hemispheres. The stars he saw were huge and bright, almost globular-looking as if they were as close as the moon, like a million pulsating eyes looking down at him. All of them arranged in weird geometrical constellations like spirals and polyhedrons and helixes…but as bright as they were, as big as they were, they didn't seem to throw any light. The sky around them was uniformly black as was the landscape outside his window.

"It didn't make sense. It didn't make any sense at all," he said, trying to control himself. "I couldn't see anything but that blackness out there. Nothing except mountains. I thought they were mountains…they were tall and jagged against the stars…then I saw that they were moving, moving like some giant caterpillar, you know? Sort of inching along. It was insane…but so was I. My skin felt cold to the touch, my fingers numb, my legs filled with pins and needles. But inside, God, I felt hot like I was burning up. Toddy and Bones kept laughing, chatting away. At first, I could understand them—they were making fun of me, of course—but after a time the language was all garbled, guttural, I don't know, just fucked up like they weren't people but frogs croaking…"

Wherever they had taken him, he was still alive. He was still breathing and his heart was still beating, but he couldn't seem to move. Not without great exertion. It was as if the air was heavy and thick. Not like air really, but almost like a liquid, a slow-coagulating, syrupy sort of medium. He felt like a man at the bottom of the sea or like a diver being squeezed in a decompression tank. He was panicking, trying to fight free of it. He remembered trying to scream, except no sounds came out...only rippling sound waves that bounced around in ultra-slow motion. But it passed. And when it did, he found himself gasping for breath. Every inch of his body was sore and aching. It felt like he'd been taken apart and put back together wrong.

But he could move.

Finally, he could move.

Atmospheric pressure had returned to near-normal, he told Flynn. It still felt a little funny, like the air was bouncing off his skin in beads, but other than that, normal. Yet, he noticed that if he moved his hand too quickly, it left a ghostly sort of image behind, a luminous sort of image, like the sort you might see in a strobe light—like a trail of dozens of spectral still photographs in its wake.

"I'd only seen that once before," he admitted, "and I was tripping out on acid. But this was worse. A lot worse. Then I saw the trees."

"Trees?" Flynn was expecting a lot of things by that point, but nothing as commonplace as trees.

Chad said they weren't like normal trees.

Not in the least.

What he saw outside the car were things like gigantic oaks with huge spreading limbs that had been upended. Trees, black and gnarled and weirdly contoured, that were standing on their branches, their trunks high in the air with fine outgrowths of rootlets sprouting from them like hair.

"Those roots were moving, Flynn. I saw it. Kind of...kind of wriggling like waving fingers. And that was bad. That scared the shit out of me. But what was worse was that those things—trees or treelike things a hundred feet high or more—were walking around on the tips of their branches. I'm not kidding you. I saw it," Chad said and Flynn, despite how crazy it all was, believed him. "They saw us or knew we were there and they started pushing in, crowding around us and those voices...Toddy's and Bones's...they were still croaking and groaning, but getting excited, real excited, like they were getting a fucking charge out of how agitated those trees were getting."

Toddy opened up the El Dorado and shot through the darkness and what they found there was not some inverted, lunatic world out of Lovecraft trembling at the edge of the universe, but Compton.

Chad was breathing hard again. "Not the Compton we know, Flynn, but another Compton. An empty Compton. It didn't seem like we were going to it, but it was coming to us."

It looked like Chad's hometown, but, of course, it wasn't. It was a dark place where nothing grew, no trees, no bushes, not so much as a shrub. It sat on a little jagged spit of land that jutted out into the darkness, into some great star-filled void. He had never seen so many stars before, millions of them, it seemed, like tiny shards of broken glass scattered across a field of black silk. The stars were above, to the left and right of the town, and even beneath the spit of land it sat upon. Toddy moved the Caddy up the streets cautiously, carefully. Things were moving out there, but Chad knew they were not people. He saw glimpses of grotesque forms like sacks creeping in the shadows. He had the most disturbing idea that this was Toddy and Bones' hometown, a deranged anti-world jutting into the maw of some vast trans-galactic gulf. A place that conceivably could not exist, but did. It looked like Compton, but the streets were too narrow, the buildings too high, the angles too sharp, the rooflines too steep. It was like some imitation thrown together out of cracking black wood and splintered quartz, similar enough to be recognizable but distorted, crooked, completely lacking in earthly symmetry. Doorways were not perfectly rectangular and windows not squared off, but askew somehow and out-of-sync. Houses leaned out over streets that were cut so deeply they were like channels. Hilltops were sharp as knife blades. Church spires were like skeletal limbs ready to fall. Even the yards and fields were not flat but inclined, some of them falling away into black recesses where you could glimpse the stars pressing in from beneath.

"You know what scared me most?" Chad whispered over the phone. "The idea that they were going to leave me there. That this was the place where they took everybody and I was next in line."

He said just looking out the window practically made his brain hurt. Everything was wrong. The geometry warped and irregular. The human brain was used to a certain equilibrium, Flynn knew, and to be in a place without proportion, where lines were never straight and circles never perfectly round and angles constantly changing would tax the mind. That was, if such a place really existed, and his common sense told him that Chad was out of his fucking head.

"When I was like in second or third grade, we'd watch these old black-and-white cartoons our teacher was into," Chad said, calming a bit. "Crazy shit, surreal shit, man, where clocks had faces and houses were dancing…everything was like that, fucked up and out of sort."

And silent, he said, unbelievably silent. The only noise was a howling, moaning sound in the distance that reminded him of the wind in ghost towns in old movies, rising and falling, never getting any closer but never going away either. Nothing else seemed to make noise.

"It didn't, Flynn. With everything I was seeing and feeling, I wasn't really paying attention to what I was hearing—which was nothing. Nothing in that damn place made any sound. Even the Caddy was silent. All I could hear was that moaning sound of the wind and the weird noises Toddy and Bones were making from time to time," Chad said, no hysteria in his voice now. He was merely a guy describing what he had experienced the best he could.

"Toddy and Bones looked different. You probably won't believe that or the fact that the front seat where they were sitting looked like it was a really long way away. But it's true. What I could see of them made me glad they hadn't turned around for quite a while because they were like those sacks I caught out of the corner of my eye and, Christ, I didn't want to see their faces. I just wanted it to be over with. I wanted them to kill me, do whatever they wanted to do, whatever it would take to end it all because everything inside me was crawling and when I opened my mouth to say something, to cry and plead with them or just to fucking scream my mind away, the sound didn't carry. It was like being in a vacuum. That's what I thought. I remember old tight-ass Mr. Keeling, Physical Science, ninth grade, telling us sound does not carry in a vacuum and I was in a fucking vacuum…"

But what did carry was insects.

And one of them landed on the windshield.

"It looked like a bug but it wasn't a bug, Flynn. Not like the kind we have here. I don't know what the fuck it was. But it was big and it was weird and it wanted in real bad."

He said it was about the size of a collie, maybe a bit bigger. But whereas the bugs we know are solid things like anything else, this creature did not look solid. It was made of some transparent material like one of those ghost shrimp you see in an aquarium. It was flesh and blood like an ordinary bug, but its insides were completely translucent save for a few vague purplish bands in its legs and a pinkish mass in its head. Other than that and the fact that it had nine legs, it looked like a gigantic fly right down to the bulbous eyes and huge spreading wings. It had a ribbed, plunger-like proboscis that was pressed to the windshield, contracting with waves of suction, its many hooked limbs scratching away at the glass, its forelimbs rubbing together.

"I was glad I couldn't hear the sounds it made," he admitted.

It was about that time that he heard Toddy and Bones speaking in ordinary human voices, taunting him. He could make no sounds, but they had no such problem.

"Looks like it wants to come in and meet Chaddywhacker," Toddy said in a low, evil voice. "You ever see one of these suckers grab himself a human being, Bones?"

Bones laughed with a sound like teeth rattling in a cup. "Ugly business, ain't it? Suck the guts right out of 'em, don't they?"

"Sure do, my friend, sure do."

The 1959 El Dorado had power windows, all of which could be controlled by the driver. Giggling, Toddy lowered Chad's window an inch and then two. The fly—or whatever the hell it was—heard it or sensed it and it crawled along the side of the car to investigate. By this point, Chad fully admitted he was screaming (soundlessly) like a little girl. He tried to use his own power button to roll the window back up but it was no good.

The window rolled down another inch.

The laughter of Toddy and Bones echoed through the car with, it seemed, the same tonal quality as shattering glass. Chad pushed himself as far away from the window as possible, which was against the opposite door. The fly was investigating the cracked window with its proboscis, making sluicing, sucking sounds like a backed-up sump pump. Great quantities of gelatinous clear slime oozed down the inside of the glass. Chad said it stank like turpentine. The fly kept working at the window, hooking one transparent, jointed leg around it and pulling. There were vitreous needle-like spines on the leg that quivered as it pulled at the glass.

"What then?" Flynn asked after a few moments of bated silence.

He could hear Chad swallow a few times. "I kept watching that fly. It was like it was made of glass. There were rows and rows of something like plastic beads on its underbelly...I know they weren't beads, but that's how they looked. I was out of my head. I...I...I fucking pissed my pants, Flynn. You would have, too, if that thing had been coming for you and that prick Toddy was slowly lowering the window."

Flynn had no doubt of that...if such a thing were possible which, of course, it wasn't. Chad had been through something, but this? No, this was madness. He was willing to believe that Toddy and Bones had done something to Chad's head, maybe they dosed him with LSD or something, but beyond that he couldn't really believe any of this. His skeptical stance was hard to maintain, though, because Chad sounded so terrified, so traumatized, so convincing.

"Close up to that thing, I could see it pretty good. In the dark, I shouldn't have been able to see it at all, but it was...I don't know...lit by itself. It threw light. It didn't glow like a firefly exactly, but it was lit up somehow from inside." He was breathing fast again. "That's when I saw what was in its head."

Chad said he could see a pinkish shiny mass that he assumed was the creature's brain...but it wasn't. It actually did look like a brain and more specifically like the globular, pulsating mass of a living evil brain in an old sci-fi flick. But as he watched, the brain unfurled itself like a cat stretching and he saw it was a worm, a swollen maggoty form that must have been some kind of parasite to the fly or even its master. He could see it in there and he was sure it saw him. It had two pearly, lucent eyes and they were fixed on him. The window would have given anytime, but Toddy rolled it up, trapping the fly's foreleg, which shattered like a glass rod. Chad said juice squirted from it, something with the consistency of grapefruit pulp. Several drops caught him in the face and they burned like battery acid.

Flynn clearly remembered the pink welts on Chad's face that day they picked him up after school. He'd thought they looked like cigarette burns. The sort tough kids had on their arms sometimes from playing chicken with lit cigarettes.

Chad said that a severed section of leg, maybe twelve or fourteen inches, was lying on the seat and it was not dead. It flexed and skittered about, the spines on it sharp enough to slit open the leather seats.

"Then…then it just died," he said with a sigh. "It went from being clear to kind of brownish, then it just stopped moving. Toddy drove us back and before long we were in Compton. We made a stop to pick up something and then we picked you up at school."

Flynn saw a hole in the story now. A big one. "But you said they picked you up at night, didn't you?"

"Yeah."

"But it was afternoon when you picked me up."

Chad laughed with a tittering sound. "You're still not getting it, dumbass. The space-time thing. It seemed like we were gone trick-or-treating maybe an hour, an hour and a half tops…but here something like eighteen hours had passed. It's not the same there as it is here. Nothing is. Not time. Not matter. Not space. Nothing."

Flynn was pushed closer and closer to belief regardless of how preposterous it all was. He knew Chad pretty well by that point and Chad had all the imagination of a stump. A story like this was simply beyond him. It was the kind of science-fictional scenario that Daryl Smite might have come up with—his head filled with Tolkien and Lovecraft and Asimov, all of it channeled through his love of theoretical physics.

Now, of course, that the story was told, a question had to be asked even though Flynn shrunk from the idea. "When you guys picked me up, there was someone in the trunk. Don't bother denying it. I could hear someone in there. Now who was it, Chad?"

"Who do you think it was?"

He knew, of course, but he had to hear Chad say it. For some reason, that was important. "Tell me."

"It was Danice."

"They took her."

Chad laughed. "Don't be such a fucking Pollyanna, Flynn. They didn't take her, I fucking gave her to them," he said, his final words echoing over the phone with a terrible finality like the last shovelful of earth thrown on a coffin lid.

23

The thing that bothered him in ways he could not properly fathom was that he heard nothing about Danice McKerran disappearing. In a town the size of Compton, a tale of a missing person traveled like wildfire, usually arriving with its bags fully packed with invented, exaggerated back stories cooked up by the local gossips. But there was nothing about Danice. As sick as Chad made him, Flynn had asked him about her and all he would say was that she went trick-or-treating courtesy of Toddy and Bones. Nothing more. Other than pounding it out of him, there was probably no way to get at the answers.

That was troubling.

Chad had gone trick-or-treating—and then some—and he had returned broken, nearly insane, but he had returned. Was that what happened with Danice? Had she gone and come back? And if that was the case, where was she now? In a nut house? Hiding in her closet? Flynn didn't believe for a minute that she could come out of something like that without so much as a psychic scar or a mental contusion. At the very least, she would have been in a similar state to Chad when he got back.

But do you buy that? he kept asking himself in the days following the conversation. Can you really accept what he was saying and what it means in the bigger picture?

Yes and no.

There was no getting beyond the obvious fact that there was something extremely frightening about Toddy and Bones. He was pretty much convinced they weren't exactly human as such, that they were some kind of parasites; but if he were to buy into what Chad was saying, that took it all to another level. Then they weren't just earthbound monsters, but things from another world or another dimension for godsake.

It's not a matter that you don't believe him and you know it. It's that you don't want to believe him because the very idea scares the shit right out of you, it escalates your fear to new heights.

True, true, and true. In his mind, he supposed, the higher Toddy and Bones were elevated on the scale of weirdness meant the more demonic and invincible they became. He feared everything about them, of course, but after Chad's tale of trick-or-treating, what he feared most were those things he did not know about, abilities he could not even fathom.

A week passed and he did not see them.

He saw Chad in the halls but other than a meeting of eyes—haunted eyes filled with dread—few words passed between them. Their relationship seemed to have devolved (happily) into that of a couple schoolmates who had been close once but had long since moved on to other social realms. At least, that's how Flynn saw it. Probably because that's how he wanted to see it. Human optimism, and particularly that of a seventeen-year-old, is a cup that never completely empties. And with each passing day that he was free of Toddy and Bones, it grew that much fuller.

But despite that, things were hardly perfect at Compton High. His social standing continued to plummet and he began to realize just how much he owed his popularity to Toddy and Bones and how little to his own looks and personality. That was painful, but in a way he was almost pleased. He had tasted the high social echelons of the school and walked the lofty paths with the privileged…and now that he had been booted out, he was able to see it all with a crow's-eye view that showed him how superficial and synthetic it all was. The cool kids were the most lonely and stressed of all, because they lived in constant fear of losing their status…which, of course, mainly existed in their own minds to begin with.

His popular "friends" kept their distance and only the ordinary girls paid any attention to him, which, for some reason, he liked very much. Liz, he came to realize as she rolled her pretty green eyes whenever he encountered her, was a vacuous, conceited, narcissistic little bitch with delusions of grandeur. Nobody really liked her. Even her friends looked unhappy around her. Her personality was basically shit. All the boys wanted her, but it was purely sexual, simply the chemical transmissions of their genes screaming out for her physical perfection. She was a living example of the old adage that the more there is on the outside the less there is on the inside. He bumped into her in the cafeteria one day and as she rolled her eyes at him yet again, he saw with perfect clarity the miserable, soulless hag she would be at fifty when her looks had faded. He burst out laughing and she told him in her best catty snarl to go fuck himself, which only made him laugh harder.

Enjoy yourself, princess, because you're never, ever going to be happy. Nothing will ever be good enough and you will die old, unloved, and alone.

Being that he had started out on the bottom at Compton, climbed to the top, and was in the process of sliding back down again gave him omniscient awareness that the other kids totally lacked. He saw his place in the scheme of things and theirs as well. It made him feel like he was in a monkey cage, but unlike the others, he knew he was a monkey and just how big his cage was. If there was anyone at Compton that was well-adjusted, it was probably Daryl Smite and others like him. Sure, he bore the scars of rejection and ostracism, but he bore them well. He liked who he was and what he would some day be. He was comfortable in his own skin and how many high school kids could honestly claim that?

During the many days of calm, Flynn noticed that the mysterious smell of decay that kept coming at odd times had not visited him since that day with Liz. That was another good thing. Yet another was that he got a part-time job at Reissen Recycling, feeding cans into a crusher after school. Now that he was a working man, his dad gave him the keys to his 1977 pea-green Buick Skylark, a nice-looking car with a 305 under the hood that had some balls. The old man upgraded to a 1981 Olds Ninety-Eight that his mom said looked like something a TV cop would drive.

A week before Halloween, Flynn was driving home from school, feeling tense for no particular reason. He killed the FM because he couldn't tolerate hearing "Bette Davis Eyes" one more time and jammed out to a cassette of April Wine's Nature of the Beast for a few blocks. He was barely a minute into "Sign of the Gypsy Queen" when a sense of horror overwhelmed him. It came seemingly for no reason…but there was a reason. In the rearview mirror, he could see the '59 El Dorado dogging him, not closing in but keeping an even pace.

Oh no, oh shit!

The sight of it shocked him so much he nearly drove into a parked car, swerving at the last possible moment. There was no way they could know he was driving the Skylark, not unless Chad found out and told them. Then, as he stared into his sweaty, pale reflection in the rearview mirror, he could clearly hear Daryl's words. Once they've entered your life, you can always see them and they can always see you. You can't hide from them and they can't hide from you. Yes, he was linked to them as he'd always be linked. He could never hide from them.

Despite the overwhelming sense of fear, he refused to panic. He was going to keep his shit together regardless of the consequences. For some reason, he felt it had never been more important. He killed the music and kept driving. Autumn leaves blew in the gutters. People clutching coats tightly to themselves hunkered down in the wind. None of them had the slightest idea of the monsters in their midst. He drove past businesses with Halloween decorations in their windows and bright orange banners proclaiming moonlight madness sales and ghostly savings. He drove past Burger Chef, where you could buy two Big Shefs for the price of one, but food was the last thing on his mind.

The Caddy was getting closer now.

He turned off Main onto Riverview, then 17th Street and over to Norton Ave. The Caddy was still behind him and closing. He picked up speed, flying past the Dairy Flo and Shakey's and cutting back into town, 10th Street, then 11th and 12th, squealing onto Townline Avenue. No dice. The Caddy was moving in for the kill. He thought madly of cutting out of town, maybe hitting the county roads or the highway, but he knew damn well it was a race he'd never win.

The El Dorado was barely three car lengths behind him now. The smell of sweet decay began to fill the Skylark and he quickly rolled down his window, scooping in fresh air to displace the stink. It didn't work; the stench became colder and somehow more dangerous.

The Caddy was tailgating him now.

He could plainly see Toddy and Bones, their pallid faces glowing, their eyes beady, flashing like neon, mouths twisted into grimaces of pure hate. The Skylark's engine began to cough and sputter. Then it conked out. This was it. He would roll to a stop and they would drag him out and beat him silly in the street before they threw him in the trunk for a ride to the other side and some trick-or-treat fun. He pounded his fists against the steering wheel, crying out that the Skylark was a useless piece of shit. He pulled over as it rolled to a stop. The Caddy slowed, pulled in behind him, then at the last second, Toddy gunned it and laid rubber, whipping past the Skylark and disappearing into the distance.

Flynn started breathing again.

They'll come back. They've incapacitated you and now they'll come back for the kill.

Sitting there, breathing hard, he knew he didn't have a chance in hell. All he had for a weapon was a window scraper. There was a tire iron in the trunk but he could just imagine those animals taking it away from him and beating him silly with it right before they jammed it up his ass. No, he had to move. He tried to turn over the Skylark one last time, but the battery was dead. He pulled the keys from the ignition and jumped out. A few cars passed, but no Caddy.

He got out on the sidewalk and jogged through the wind to the end of the block and then across the avenue, moving down an alley at full clip. Nineteenth and King. Yes! Daryl lived not far away. And like it or not, he was about to get a visitor. Through yards, leaping hedges and leaf piles, he was certain he could hear the rumble of the El Dorado closing in on him like a voracious beast on the prowl.

At the Smite house, most of the leaves—save those that had blown back into the yard—were raked out to the curb. There were two stuffed scarecrows sitting in chairs on the wide porch amidst a collection of shiny orange pumpkins. A baseball glove and bat had been abandoned next to them.

Flynn jogged up the steps and pounded on the door none too gently. "Hey, Daryl!" he called. "Daryl!"

The door was opened and Daryl stood there in stocking feet. "As pleased as I might be, I'm also greatly suspicious," he said. "You must want something."

"I do."

"I figured."

"My car died," Flynn told him. "Can I use your phone?"

Daryl looked satisfied at this. It made sense in his world, and Daryl was definitely a guy who liked things to make sense, to be logical, which was one of the many reasons he generally preferred numbers over people. He led his visitor into a nice, neat kitchen that smelled of fresh-baked bread. A wonderful aroma. Daryl explained that his mom and dad were gone and the booze was off limits. One of his little jokes that made him snort with laughter. The phone hung from the wall by the refrigerator. "Avail yourself," he said.

He went back to whatever he had been doing and Flynn breathed in and out a few times to calm himself. Then he picked up the phone and started dialing his number. Mom would be home. She would no doubt be working on her latest clown masterpiece and listening to Peter, Paul, and Mary albums. She would come and get him. She could be here in ten minutes.

He hung up the phone.

No, he wasn't going to endanger her. He could just about imagine the El Dorado coming after the both of them. Her little red Ford Pinto would be no match for the '59 Caddy. No, this was his problem and he would deal with it alone. He went back into the living room, where he found Daryl sitting in a La-Z-Boy with his feet up, a stack of Dr. Who paperbacks on the table next to him, a repeat of Space: 1999 on the TV.

"Nobody home," he said. "Guess I'll have to leg it."

"Or you could stay," Daryl suggested. "I think I can work you into my crowded social schedule. Stay on for supper. My mom is a real whiz with Hamburger Helper."

Flynn sighed, feeling somewhat relieved at Daryl's joyously boring life and self-deprecating humor. He was going to take him up on it. But before supper, they were going to have a chat about certain things.

At least, that was the plan he formulated.

Then he heard a rumbling outside, the roaring of an engine as it was gunned. The picture window rattled. Flynn went to the window and Daryl was right behind him. The '59 El Dorado was in the driveway.

"Shit," Flynn said.

Daryl was beyond himself with a combination of terror and anger. "You...you brought those things to my house! I let you in and you bring these monsters here? What kind of person are you, anyway?"

Which was a question that Flynn had been asking himself a lot lately.

"I didn't mean for them to come here."

"They were following you, weren't they? And you thought you could hide out here. You're an asshole, Flynn. A complete asshole."

And he was at that.

He was so worried about saving his own skin that he had been willing to put Daryl's at risk. Well, this had to end now. He could see Toddy and Bones sitting in the El Dorado, their faces two grinning death's-heads, nothing but gleaming teeth and hollow-socketed eyes. As terrified as he was, he was also angry. In fact, he felt ugly dirt-mean deep inside. He was a sheep and they were wolves, running him, forever running him. It stopped now. It had to stop now.

"Flynn," Daryl said, his face oily with sweat. "I want...I want you out of my house. Do you hear me? I want you out of my house. I want you out of my house right now."

Flynn nodded. "Yes," he said in a dire voice filled with fatalism.

He did not hesitate.

He went to the front door and stepped out onto the porch. The fear had nearly been eclipsed by anger now. If they wanted a willing, cowering victim, they were going to have to look elsewhere. He heard the door shut behind him. He heard locks being thrown. He was completely on his own now and he supposed he always had been. The car rumbled in the driveway.

"I'm coming," Flynn said.

He reached down and grabbed the baseball bat off the porch and the heft of it in his hands made him feel nearly invincible. Toddy and Bones saw what he was doing. They stared, but they no longer grinned. Flynn had the distinct feeling that they did not like the way this was going. What he was doing was suicidal, but it felt...right. Fear was a weapon. You could cripple your enemy with it, you could break him psychologically, take away his will to fight. That was the game Toddy and Bones played. They used fear. It was probably the most powerful weapon in their arsenal. Now Flynn had overcome it.

He was not afraid.

He was not shivering.

He was not pissing himself in their mighty, omnipotent presence.

No, he was pissed off.

As he moved down the steps, he was absolutely blind and utterly mindless with rage. He had gotten into this situation because he had allowed other people to push him around and in his own weakness he had looked for an easy way out. Toddy and Bones had given him that. Now he was going to meet them on their own ground.

They'll kill you. They'll fucking kill you.

But he wasn't going after them, not particularly. He had another target in mind. The one thing in this world they were tied to. He came down the driveway with the bat in both hands like he was ready to knock one out of the park. They watched him and were not remotely amused. Their faces were stark masks, scarred and weathered like the boles of ancient trees, eyes lit with a cold lunar glow. Toddy was revving the Caddy. He wanted Flynn to know that he could run him down anytime he chose.

Flynn closed in on the car.

The engine roared.

He brought the bat up and then brought it back down in a blurring arc with everything he had, striking the hood and leaving a deep dent. He could have sworn he heard a high, piercing scream coming from inside the car. The '59 had no hood ornament as such, just a Cadillac coat of arms and a silver stylized V beneath it and this is what he swung for, hitting it dead on and hearing the pleasant crunch as the left wing of the V broke loose of its housing and fell to the ground.

This time, there was no mistaking the scream.

He could see the faces of Toddy and Bones quite clearly and they were not filled with wrath now, but contorted with pain and maybe even terror. As Flynn brought the bat up again, feeling stronger with every swing, Toddy floored the Caddy and it screeched out of the driveway, laying rubber. It fishtailed out into the road, then roared away up 19th Street.

Flynn stood there for some time with the bat in his hands,

knowing he had made a terrible mistake, but feeling good, really good, for the first time in a very, very long time.

"Well, you really did it now," he heard a voice say behind him.

He turned and Daryl was standing there, shaking his head.

Flynn grunted. "Yes, I have. And I plan on doing it again."

24

Daryl absolutely and unconditionally wanted no part of any of it and Flynn respected that, understood it, and was more than happy to leave him out of the fun and games. That day he walked away from Daryl's house, he never expected to see him again. Resolutely, he walked up 19th Street, not on the sidewalk like any sane person would do, but out on the pavement, almost daring the Caddy to come for him. The very idea was like wading out into a piranha-infested river with raw, bloody meat in your pockets...yet, something inside him informed him that he was about as safe as he could possibly hope to be.

Oh, they'll come for you, man, but not today and not when you're expecting them. You fought back and they don't know how to handle it. You probably shocked them. Their heads are still reeling from not only your disobedience but your boldness. Who the hell do you think you are anyway? No, they drew a line in the sand and you crossed it, swinging a bat in your hands. They're not used to that shit. They're used to people like Chad...crawling, squirming, spineless things who do what they're told. They're not used to open rebellion.

Flynn nearly laughed at that.

Rebellion.

Rebels, he thought, were brave—and possibly suicidal—individuals. He was neither. He wanted to live. He liked his skin and he wanted to keep wearing it. As he walked he was not even sure why he did any of it other than the fact that he was sick of their shit, sick of being bullied in general, and he decided to do something about it. The memory of it left him feeling a little weak in the knees, but he knew it had been the right thing to do. To stand up against Toddy and Bones might be suicide, but giving in to them meant a long, lingering death of self-loathing.

He walked on and there was a little park across from Henry Elementary School and he kicked his way through the autumn leaves until he found a bench. He needed to sit. He needed to think. Feeling low, he sat there with his head hanging. He tried to convince himself that now that he had made a stand, Toddy and Bones would simply go away, seek out easier pickings. But he knew it wasn't true. He had set something into motion today and where it might end terrified him.

After he'd been there fifteen or twenty minutes, he heard somebody trudging through the leaves. It was Daryl. He stood about ten feet away, his eyes appraising, looking nervous and skittish, but curious.

"Tell me what's going on," he said.

Flynn shook his head. "Daryl, just go, will ya? Don't get yourself all wrapped up in this."

"I think I deserve to know what's going on."

"I think I already told you that."

Daryl sighed. "Didn't I tell you to reject them?"

"It's gone too far for that. They did things for me and now I think they want me to do things for them."

"Then you're in as deep as Chad."

Flynn shrugged. "Maybe not that deep. Not yet."

Daryl sat down beside him. "Tell me what's been happening."

There really wasn't much to tell save for how his luck was starting to go to shit and the strange odors of rotting, dead things that seemed to come literally out of nowhere. He told Daryl all about that, then he told him Chad's story about being taken trick-or-treating, and about Danice. It sounded insane coming from his own mouth, but he went through it from beginning to end.

Daryl was speechless for a few moments, shaking his head back and forth, but it wasn't out of disbelief but amazement. "That's... incredible. Like he took a trip to another dimension, an alternate universe. And what did he say about the speedometer?"

Flynn told him what Chad said: that it went to 120 and then beyond with red number/letter combinations—P12, P25, P75 etc. Daryl seemed very excited about that—very, very excited. This piqued his interest more than anything else. "Parsecs," he finally said.

"What?"

"Parsecs."

"And what is that?"

"A parsec is a unit of measurement that astronomers use. If you read any science fiction, you'd probably know that."

He explained that when distances were too vast for traditional computation, astronomers used parsecs. A parsec was equal to 3.26 light years.

"Light travels at something like 186,000 miles per second. The distance it travels in a year is a light year. One parsec equals 3.26 light years or over thirty trillion kilometers. So if those P designations mean parsecs—and I'm just guessing—then P12, P25, and all that would be immense distances at speeds we couldn't even calculate."

Flynn didn't say anything. It was all a little too science fiction-y for him. It meant, essentially, that Toddy and Bones were from beyond the stars, or from another universe—take your pick. He didn't much care for that and he told Daryl so. There was only so much elasticity to his open mind and this stretched it way beyond the breaking point.

"Would you prefer they were devils out of Hell here to harvest your soul?" Daryl asked him.

"Maybe I would."

"Which completely supports my hypothesis that you are certifiable."

"I'm serious. If they're able to travel faster than the speed of light or in parsecs, if they've mastered physics like we can't even guess at...that means they're not only intelligent but super intelligent, am I right?"

"It would follow."

"Then why are they such assholes? Why are they such murdering, fucked-up monsters? They're no different than some of the animals that walk on two legs in this world. They're like nasty, bratty children who've been given great power and they're misusing it."

Daryl lifted an eyebrow. "Well, they're certainly violating the Prime Directive." He shrugged. "Be that as it may, there's no way we can know where they're from or what they're about. Maybe they're tourists. Maybe it's a case of when in Rome do as the Romans. Who knows? One thing is for sure, I think you have it right when you told me they're tied to that car. If you would have attacked them with the baseball bat, they would have knocked the shit out of you or killed you. But when you attacked the car…well, you were attacking the machine that gets them from this place back to where they come from."

At which point, Daryl launched into something of a monologue about the possibilities of such a race—mostly based upon science-fiction novels he'd read, sci-fi movies he'd seen, and his own imagination and powers of speculation—and what their ultimate goal might be:

"I don't think they're here to take over the world," Flynn finally said. "Whatever they're up to, it's nothing like that. Their ambition is smaller, more…intimate, I guess you'd say. Fear is the thing. They feed on it. The more fear you give them, the stronger they are. That's part of it."

Daryl nodded. "I told you that the first time you asked me about them. Chad is their poster boy. He was needy and they helped him and he's been their slave ever since. Hate to tell you this, Flynn, but that's exactly what they have in mind for you. They're going to keep after you until they break you and you make awful choices to keep them happy."

"I won't do that. They can kill me if they want to, but I won't be like Chad, I won't sacrifice people to them. I won't. No fucking way."

"Well, that gives you a very big one-up on Chad. And what gives you another is that you attacked their car." Daryl giggled at that. "I imagine right now they're very confused. I think they'll keep coming after you, but they're going to step lightly and carefully because you're unpredictable."

"Fat lot of good that'll do me if they kill me or send me to Planet X."

Daryl shook his head. "No, no, no, they won't kill you. It would make no sense. They need you or none of this would exist in the first place. They need your fear, your anxiety. They need you to be in thrall to them. Once you say yes to them—and you did that, didn't you?—then you become part of their network. They give you great things but there's a price to be paid. You become an addict for the girls, the popularity, the good life…then they take it away from you bit by bit. By that point, you're nothing but a junkie and you need what they have so you do what they say. You'll do anything to have it all back same way a junkie will do anything to get that lovely fix. Maybe they're psychic vampires or something. Maybe they feed off not just the fear but all the bad, dirty emotions in you when you defile yourself and betray those you love just to get your fix. It's pretty sickening, but that's part of it, I bet."

Flynn figured it was. He'd seen them getting younger and was that because they fed off bad things and negative emotions and fear or was it because of something else?

You're leaving out another possibility. That they do the things they do just for kicks. Maybe they're intelligent and alien and all that but it doesn't mean they have morals of any sort. They might be like sadistic boys torturing puppies or pulling the wings off flies. They do it because they can and it gets them off.

"You better go," he told Daryl. "I don't want you mixed up in this."

"In a way, I already am." Daryl sighed. "Or maybe in some way, I want to be."

"Don't say that."

"You don't understand. All my life I've been into science fiction, speculative fiction, fantasy, you name it…but here, finally, is the real thing. I just can't turn my back on it. I have to know. One way or another, I have to know."

"That's suicide."

"Maybe. But, like I said, I have to know. Regardless of how dangerous it is, I want to know about that car and I want to know about them."

Flynn tried to talk him out of it, but it was pretty pointless as his mind was obviously made up. Daryl pegged him with question after question concerning Toddy and Bones, and Flynn answered what he could—knowing that like Chad he was saying shit he shouldn't be saying and talking about stuff that didn't concern him—because he really didn't know much other than the fact that they were monsters that seemed to regenerate themselves, that they drove a badass '59 Caddy that could burn its way from one universe to the next, and that they liked to enslave people with their own wants and needs and demand a terrible payment for said services. What else was there to say? He told Daryl all that, knowing he was talking out of class and endangering them both, but once he started, he couldn't stop. And all the while in the darkness of his head he was seeing the faces of Toddy and Bones, except they were shriveled, puckered things like heads pickled in alcohol, bleary-eyed and dead.

"I guess what I'm wondering most about is Danice McKerran," he finished by saying.

"That is perplexing," Daryl admitted, raising an eyebrow like Mr. Spock. "She's in my economics class. She's been gone for a while, though."

"That's what worries me."

"I know where she lives."

"Do you?"

Daryl blushed. "Yes."

"Then let's pay her a visit."

Which, as it turned out, was a really stupid thing to do.

25

NOW

The big chill continued for days.

Marjorie would have nothing to do with him. She was peeved. She was pissed. Flynn knew it was a matter of trust just as she said, but he did not want to involve her in any of it and she did not handle it well. She did not speak to him or look at him. She slept on the couch (something that made him nervous because he was always worried that Bones and Toddy would snatch her away in the night), she avoided his very presence, and she made only enough supper for herself as if there was not another mouth to feed in the house. The latter was no big deal as he was a pretty decent cook himself, but he missed being with her, chatting with her, unwinding with her. He missed her sense of humor. Hell, he missed everything about her. There was a way out, but that would mean endangering her and he was not about to do that regardless of how he was hurting inside.

You're doing the right thing, he told himself again and again, even if he didn't believe it. Not really. Not deep inside where he was really hurting.

Three days before Halloween after yet another lonely, depressing night, he went downstairs, attempted conversation with Marjorie, was completely rebuffed, and went outside to see if any more leaves had invaded the yard. The air was crisp and clean. It smelled of autumn and apples. He found a few stray leaves, but it wasn't until he got into the backyard that he discovered roofing tiles scattered over the lawn. They were everywhere; some whole, others torn in half or completely pulverized into fragments. Some were even blown up into the skeletal branches of trees.

Amazing.

Utterly amazing.

He dodged behind the big maple and got a good look at the garage. Yes, all the shingles had been blown free as if a tornado had passed through in the night. Only a few remained, anchored by nails that were nearly pulled free.

Flynn stood there, the mug of coffee in his left hand rapidly cooling and forgotten. He absently fumbled a cigarette into his mouth and lit it with his Bic. He walked out into the alley and studied the other houses and garages.

None had lost so much as a single tile. Even Mrs. Webber's ramshackle potting shed was still standing.

Now how could that be?

He walked back into his yard. If a wind fierce enough to peel shingles and pull nails had swept through, why were there no tree limbs down? The maple had several dead branches. He walked over there and wiggled one of them. It came off in his hand.

Doesn't make sense. Doesn't make a lick of sense.

He set his mug on the picnic table and walked around the garage to the other side where his SUV was parked. The hood was covered in leaves and scraps of roofing tiles. Sighing, he brushed them off, trying not to scrape the paint. He brushed more of them off the windshield. That's when he saw a scrap of paper stuck under the wiper. He pulled it free. He half expected it to be a political flier or religious pamphlet, but it was neither. And in the dark reaches of his soul, he knew somehow it wouldn't be anything that harmless, that general.

This was specific.

This was intended only for him.

It was receipt.

A & PC

OMPTON

THANK YOU!

$01.75--

$01.75--

$00.15 TX

$3.65—

31 OCT 81

The receipt shook in his hand and for one insane moment, he thought it was going to fly right from his fingers. The A&P on Main had been closed for many, many years. In fact, the building wasn't even there anymore. It had burned down (he was told) back in the 1990s. But here was a receipt that looked practically brand-new as if it had been printed yesterday and not well over thirty years ago. It even had that blue ink they used back in the 1960s and '70s.

And how much you want to bet those two items for a buck seventy-five each were six-packs of Bud because that's what you used to drink when you were out cruising in the '59 Caddy.

His throat felt dry, his body was shaking. He had to lean up against the SUV so he didn't swoon and go right over. He knew there was something written on the other side of the receipt but he didn't have the guts to see what it was. Finally, he turned it over and written in a shaky script was the following:

take a look in the garage
a little present from your friends

Yes, yes, of course. They had put something in there and whatever it was, it was lightning in a bottle, it was wrath and force. It had stripped the shingles from the roof. He pulled one last time off his cigarette, then—almost too casually—he strolled around the other side to the door and stood there, summoning the courage to look inside and see what his "friends" had left him. It was going to be good and he knew it. His skin began to crawl and there was a prickly heat at his spine. As he reached for the doorknob, he felt a weird tingling over the back of his hand as if he had stuck it into a field of static electricity.

You sure you want to do this?

And, no, he was not sure at all but he supposed he had no real choice. He gripped the doorknob and felt a hot jolt right up to his elbow. It left his arm feeling numb. He shook it off and seized the doorknob again. This time it wasn't so bad. He turned the knob and as he did so, the door was yanked from his hand. There was a great hollow booming noise like a fuel can popping on a hot day or ductwork contracting…it was like that but loud as a firecracker and followed by a sucking/rushing of air that nearly pulled him off his feet. And he knew what was inside was going to be bad, very bad because he had experienced something like this before when he was a teenager. The dark memory of it lingered about the edges of his subconscious despite all the many years he'd tried to purge it.

Now that the pressure had been equalized, he stepped into the garage and as soon as he did he smelled something awful like rotting fish that was so strong he had to take a step back.

At that moment, on the other side of the garage, all the jars of nails, screws, and bolts on the shelf exploded one after the other and the timbers of the garage itself made a pained groaning sound like the hull of a ship being squeezed by sea ice.

Instinctively, he reached for the light switch and clicked it on. The bulb flickered, the filament glowing weakly, becoming brighter momentarily and then fading to a soft yellow glow.

That's when he saw it.

The garage was big, designed to handle two cars and an assortment of just about everything else. About fifteen feet away, closer to the main door, there was something clinging to the ceiling that at first looked like some oversized shrimp and then maybe a squid and possibly one of those insane-looking phosphorescent deep sea fishes with the gaping mouths. Whatever in the hell it was, it seemed to be crawling across the ceiling, an absolute monstrosity expanding and then deflating like a wrinkly sack.

Flynn gasped and fell back against the doorway, the child inside him wanting to scream in pure terror.

The creature was many things but none of them were from this world. It was ten or twelve feet long, made of glossy pink flesh mottled with yellow protuberances about the size of fifty-cent pieces that opened and closed like tiny sucking mouths. It had a central bulging body and from it jutted a dozen limbs that were not arms and legs any more than they were tentacles. They were misshapen things, some swollen and fleshy, others narrow like baseball bats, but all covered with a complex arrangement of rubbery tendrils like fingers that were constantly in motion, wiggling and curling. It lacked eyes, but it did have a mouth that was big around as a garbage can lid and set with spike-like teeth, row upon row of them, except they didn't seem to be made of bone but of some translucent material. The mouth opened and closed, opened and closed, sometimes hanging slack and wide for three or four seconds before continuing to gulp like a dying fish. Its limbs squirmed over the ceiling, scraping against the rafters like nails. The more he watched it—and he had been staring at it for no more than twenty seconds by that point—the more limbs it seemed to have, all of them asymmetrical to one another, some resembling scythes and others like rakes or the segmented limbs of insects.

He couldn't seem to get a good idea of its body plan because it was forever changing, growing larger then smaller, elongating then narrowing. It was absolutely deranged.

He only knew one thing for sure: it disgusted him on some primal level. It was the sort of thing you wanted to step on, to crush, to eradicate. Without thinking, his right hand searched the bench next to him and gripped the first thing it found—a hammer. With a cry, he threw it at the beast and it went right through it, crashing against the opposite wall.

The thing was a ghost.

Maybe not a spirit or a phantom exactly, but an organism composed of some ethereal material that could not exist naturally on Earth. And that's why it was clinging to the ceiling...it didn't have a choice. It was as weightless as a helium balloon. If the roof had not been there, it would have probably floated right up into the clouds.

He hadn't noticed at first, but now he saw that it had a long, striated tail with more of those finger-like projections rising from it. The tail swept over the rafters, striking a kayak that was suspended by hooks and knocking it to the floor. Maybe it was composed of something like ectoplasm, but that didn't mean it couldn't manipulate its environment.

It had a series of ventral slits on its belly lined with fine, hairy cilia. They expanded and dilated constantly as if they were gills and it was trying desperately to separate some breathable gases from the air. They began to look pouchy as did the entire creature itself. Its limbs began to descend, hanging limply. Long threads of clear goo dripped from it, sizzling on the concrete floor. As he watched, the thing died and began to decompose, shriveling and blackening even as its flesh liquefied. Within five minutes, it was gone, nothing but a puddle of rapidly evaporating slime on the floor and a repulsive, gassy smell in the air like rotten cabbage.

Flynn staggered outside, leaning against the garage and breathing in and out until his head cleared so that he was no longer seeing black dots before his eyes. He fumbled a cigarette into his mouth, taking long, slow drags as he sank to his knees. He knew when he had opened the door that he had let the atmosphere of this world in and this is what had killed the creature. Which was probably a good thing, because facing off against a healthy individual of that species would have surely been dangerous.

"If you look in there now," he told himself in a quiet voice, "it'll be gone. Nothing but a stain on the floor and in time even that will fade."

As he finished his cigarette in the chilly October air, he knew this was only the beginning. This was a warning. Toddy and Bones' version of leaving a dead fish on your doorstep. Next time, it would be something worse and it would keep getting worse until they got what they wanted.

Or he did something to stop them.

26

He took a drive that afternoon and it was no real surprise to him that he found himself driving past Daryl Smites' old house. It still looked the same except that one of the big oaks in the yard was now a stump and the porch was gone, replaced by a garish shit-ugly terraced redwood deck.

He kept driving.

Sometimes if he squinted his eyes, it could almost be 1981 again and he would be young and healthy with his entire life in front of him, instead of a fifty-two-year-old man that was most assuredly haunted by the sins of his past and most assuredly scared shitless. He sighed as he watched the houses passing by. How had it happened? How had he become old? That was for other generations; his generation was supposed to be young forever. They were supposed to be eighteen and fit, young and sassy until the end of time. But age had caught up with them just like it caught up with the generation before them and the one before that and a thousand before that. He was now (he knew) in the final stage of his life where middle age segued into elderly and infirmity and ultimately death.

That was fucked up.

That was so fucked up.

If he had another thirty youthful years, he could change the world. He laughed at that as he supposed everyone did at some point in their old age. If he were given another thirty years of youth, he would waste it away like everyone else. It would just be another thirty years of poor choices and foolishness.

He drove on until he found the little windy park across the street from Henry Elementary. This is where he'd gone that day so long ago when Bones and Toddy had been after him and the Skylark died and he ended up at Daryl's. That was also the day you finally stood up to those monsters. True. And that incident had been like a rock dropped in a pool, the ripples still battering the sinking ship of his life.

He parked the car and trudged through the leaves until he found the bench he sat on that day. It was still there. It was painted blue now instead of green, but it was there by God. As he sat in the wind, smoking, shaking inside, his soul as cold and barren as the playground across the street, he listened to the trees creaking and the flagpole rope dinging behind him.

He thought: Chad. Fucking Chad Reese. If he was here right now, I'd goddamn well strangle him. He caused all this. He's the one that got me into this mess and, lookit me, thirty-odd years later I'm still paying for it. And if I don't think of something and think of it quick, the only thing I truly love in this world will be taken from me. Either I offer it freely like Chad or I'll be joining Marjorie Halloween night for a little trick-or-treating.

He laughed out loud.

So loud that a woman passing by looked at him as if he was some kind of lunatic. She moved away quickly and he didn't blame her. If she only had any idea what was going on inside his head or the evil that crawled beneath the surface of the town, she would have run.

Chad, fucking Chad.

Flynn found it interesting how he made Chad shoulder 99% of the blame. Now wasn't that amusing? Chad had offered and he had accepted. That's all there was to it. All he had to do was say no. Yes, reject them. Nullify their power. Daryl's words. But he hadn't done that because he was hungry for revenge and lusting after status. That's what had created this entire clusterfuck. Watching the leaves blowing around him, he thought about Daryl. Good old dependable, loyal, intelligent, and, yes, wise Daryl. He wondered were he was now. Definitely not in this pissant town. Probably involved in research or engineering or teaching.

Flynn knew that Daryl would be doing well wherever he was.

Good for you, Daryl. Good for you.

The wonderful thing about that is Daryl would have done it all on his own. He wouldn't have needed another agency to intercede on his behalf to tip the scales in his favor.

Not like me.

He wondered how long this could have conceivably been going

on. How long Toddy and Bones had been manipulating lives, twisting fate and destiny, creating luck where none existed...and damning souls in the process. Decades? Centuries? There was no way to really know. Maybe it was a phenomena of recent vintage, but Flynn didn't think so. If their original appearance was any indication, they must have started back in the 1950s, which gave them many, many puppets to toy with through the years. All it takes is one person, he thought then as the leaves blew over his shoes and tangled in his hair. Just one unhappy/miserable/bullied/tormented/teased/much-put-upon person who wants, no needs, to make their life better. And that person could be a kid or an adult because they both were fed equal rations of shit in our merry society. But a kid would work best because status and popularity are tied so inexorably to their self-esteem, ego, and sense of worth. They were the perfect victims. No adult experiences or wisdom or rationale to impede their ambitions or greed or petty self-indulgence. And nobody should know that better than you, Flynn, because you were one of them.

Yes, yes, he was.

As much as the idea sickened him and made him want to crawl inside his own shell, he figured that there had to be something there, some strength, some advantage he could draw from his own miserable fucked-up experiences. It had to give him an of edge. But what?

He remembered Daryl saying, Once they've entered your life, you can always see them and they can always see you. You can't hide from them and they can't hide from you. Did that mean that if he looked for them that they'd be where he expected them to be? He wondered. If he hopped in his SUV and drove down Main until he reached the building that had housed Clyde's Barbershop once upon a time and cut back toward the old National Fruit Building (if it was still there) and took the alley alongside it, would he find them by the loading dock? Would they be in the same place after all these years? Would the '59 El Dorado be rumbling in wait, AC/DC's Back in Black or Def Leppard's High 'n' Dry cranking from the speakers?

He had no doubt.

They'd be there.

They'd be waiting for him.

Sitting on the bench, he sighed and closed his eyes. This was a fucking nightmare. How could any of it even be true? He forced himself to relax a bit, at least as much as was possible. He had to keep his head. That was the important thing. Fear, uncertainty, and anxiety would strengthen his enemies and weaken him.

As he sat there with his eyes closed, he could hear the leaves and the wind and it was so much like that day he had run from Daryl's that he expected Daryl to come walking up. In a strange way, when he opened his eyes, he was surprised he wasn't there with that goofy smile on his face.

But Daryl was long gone, living a life far away, no doubt and Flynn was completely on his own here...save for Chad, that was. Chad. He was the guy who brought him into all this and his only real connection to Toddy and Bones. Yes, he was blaming Chad again, but fuck it. Chad was dangerous. For all he knew, Chad had targeted him (with the help of Toddy and Bones) back in 1980. Maybe none of it had been coincidence or shit luck, maybe it had happened because it was meant to happen. It had been orchestrated, manufactured, engineered, scripted...call it what you want. This wasn't the first time Flynn had thought these things. It had occurred to him again and again over the years and when he was a teenager he was almost certain that he had been groomed as a fall guy, a sucker, an offering. If that was the case, then he most certainly was a victim and Chad most certainly was the real criminal here. Toddy and Bones were monsters. They were what they were. But Chad was a human being. And if he had targeted people back then for them, then that made him something beneath contempt. You don't blame a shark for eating someone in the open ocean; but you do blame the guy who throws someone overboard to it.

But was it true?

That was the question.

Was a shitbag like Chad low enough to do something like that?

You do the math, hotshot, a voice in his head said to him. He gave them his brother, his wife, his girlfriend, and, inadvertently, his unborn child. You can't honestly think for a moment that there's anything a guy like this is above. He has no standards, no morals, no ethics. He's a walking piece of shit. He's like one of those Jewish kapos in a concentration camp that tormented and sold out his own people to gain favor from the Nazis. Don't put anything past him. He's a predator and he's protected his lifestyle by handing over others for many, many years. Even those he supposedly loves.

There. It was said.

Flynn had thought it for many years and now it had been aired. He told himself such things as coincidence, timing, and plain bad luck also had a hand in things, but he was beyond believing they were solely responsible. Toddy and Bones had a way of manipulating things, bending them to their will to serve their purpose. And the more he thought this the more he was certain that he had been purposely targeted.

"And what if you were?" he said under his breath. "Does it really change the outcome?"

No, but it changes the rationale.

That was for sure. And in some small way it also changed his culpability because not only had he been young and stupid and fully capable of making the worst possible choices, but he had been carefully manipulated by Chad and his puppet masters to achieve a desired result—desperation. He had been beaten down to a point where he would have accepted just about any way out.

Okay.

But just suspecting these things was not enough; he wanted proof. In fact, he wanted Chad to admit to him that, yes, it had all been manufactured, that he had been selected and then put through the shit (with a little help from Toddy and Bones) because he was what they needed: another victim to extort.

He walked back over to his SUV.

What he was going to do now required careful planning because he had no interest in ending up in jail. First, he had to find Chad. He had to find him alone and not with a lot of witnesses about. Then he was going to ask him quite nicely if what he suspected was true. If Chad refused to cooperate, then he was going to beat the truth out of him. He knew what he was planning was wrong, but Chad was far from being right. He was a predator, a monster, a fucking worm. Chad had every intention of seeing that Marjorie was delivered to Toddy and Bones with or without Flynn's help.

You either offer her or I'll do it myself. Either way she's going…

Flynn drove off, knowing full well that it wasn't Marjorie who was going away but the only person that Chad really loved: himself.

27

When he got home, Marjorie was not there. No note, no nothing. Her car was gone, which probably meant she was out shopping or having dinner with one of her friends. Or, perhaps, she had been summoned to some desolate location and was now en route to Planet fucking X.

Just stop. Clear your mind. Do what has to be done.

And there was no question of what that was. As far as Flynn was concerned, there was one person who had started this unhappy excursion to hell and that person was going to answer for it. What that might entail he was not sure. Not just yet. There were ideas forming in his mind of a very dark variety but he refused to think about them. Not until there really was no other choice.

Finding Chad's house wasn't too difficult.

He lived in a turn-of-the-century Victorian monstrosity just outside town replete with towers and gingerbread and wraparound porches and widow's walks. It was an ostentatious, pretentious show horse that screamed position, money, and blatant greed. Then again, Flynn had always found Victorian architecture to be uglier than an ape's hairy ass.

He parked down the road from the gates and, after a few moments in which he asked himself just what in the hell he thought he was doing, he walked over. The gates were open. He walked in and up onto the porch. The front door was open and, again, he let himself in.

Inside, the house was about what he expected—high ceilings, narrow corridors, lots of imported stained glass, and dark oak. That and the pervasive musty smell you just couldn't get out of those old dinosaurs.

After a bit of exploration (he still couldn't believe he was doing it), he found himself facing a set of sliding French doors through which guttering firelight could be seen. Ah, of course—The study. A man of means had to have one of those.

He gripped the door and slid it open maybe ten inches. Then he waited there, his heart pounding, his breath catching in his throat. He was committing a crime. This was breaking-and-entering, yet it didn't seem to bother him. And maybe that was because if things got bad, there would be far worse crimes committed this night.

"Go ahead, Flynn," Chad's voice said. "Come in. I know it's you."

Flynn just stood there, his hand on one of the sliding doors. He tried to swallow but his throat was too dry. It felt as if it had been sandpapered. He thought that if he coughed, sawdust would come out in a powdery down. Well, you've got your invitation. Take it. Sure. Only this was not what he had planned. He wanted the element of surprise to be with him, not the other way around.

"Come on, Flynn. The chairs are comfortable, the booze is the best money can buy, and the cigars are good."

Sighing, Flynn stepped in and found Chad lounging in a high-backed velvet chair like lord of the manor.

"Somehow," Flynn said, "I never expected to find you in a place like this."

Chad laughed, sipping off his drink. "It was my wife's dream house. You know how women are about these old barns. They play with doll houses when they're little girls and when they grow up, they want to fucking live in one. I'm putting it on the market next week. Drafty as hell in the winter."

Flynn was not sure what to do or what to say. This wasn't how he had envisioned things. He supposed, in a way, he had imagined something out of an old film noir. The guy who had been used, abused, and terribly exploited broke out of prison to even the score and now here he was, frustrated, angry, disenfranchised, slipping out of the shadows. But before he had his cold dish of revenge, he wanted answers. He wanted hows and whys. He wanted to know why him. Of all the suckers out there, why was he tagged to suffer. The scenario of this playing out in his head nearly made Flynn smile because in many ways it was too close to the truth.

"I knew you'd be coming," Chad said. "I just knew it. That's why I left the front door open."

So smug, so sure of himself. Flynn decided that if he'd brought a gun, he would have killed him. No hesitation. No remorse. He would have been better for the experience.

As if reading his mind, Chad said, "Did you bring a gun? A knife?" The smile on his lips was practically a smirk. "Or were you planning on using your bare hands?"

"Neither."

Chad looked disappointed. "That's too bad. Like I told you in my office that day, I admire you. You were my hero. You beat them. Then they called you back."

"They didn't call me, I—"

"Yes, they did. They summoned you and you came." Chad finished his drink. "No matter. I still admire you. You have guts. You stood up against them once and I think you're going to do it again. It's completely suicidal...but, God, how I admire you." He shook his head. "But, hey, sit down and smoke my cigars and drink my booze."

He's schmoozing you, Flynn thought. You've seen it in a dozen boardrooms: the guy with everything to lose kissing ass on the only man who can save him. They always look the same...shifty rodent's eyes, sweaty desperate faces, and reaching oily hands.

It was true.

Chad might have actually admired him a bit—the same way you admired the guy in a war movie that suicidally charges a machine gun nest with nothing but a couple hand grenades—but mostly he was playing his hand, trying to level the playing field and get on the same page with his uninvited guest. That way he could make Flynn see that, hey, he wasn't such a bad guy after all and they had a lot in common. Mutual suffrage perhaps. Once that was established, Chad would bring him around, make him realize that sometimes sacrificing the thing that you loved best was the right thing to do... even if it made you bleed inside.

Bullshit.

"In the top drawer of that cabinet behind you," Chad began, breathing hard now, "there's a gun. Get it. It's a little .32 Smith. It's loaded and ready to go. Put the barrel up to the back of my head and squeeze the trigger. It's the right thing to do and we both know it."

"I didn't come to kill anyone."

Yes, you did. It was in the back of your mind the entire way over here.

Chad's eyes were full of tears, wet stones in his tanned, handsome face. "Please, Flynn. Don't make me beg to die. It's not in me. You hate me almost as much as I hate myself. Just do it."

Now he's working the sympathy angle. He'll do whatever it takes to steer you in his direction. He's a lawyer for chrissake—and a damned good one by all accounts. He knows how to play people. He's got a dark bag of tricks at his disposal and he knows how to use them. He's the kind of guy that can make a jury think a pedophile or a serial rapist is nothing but an unfortunate, misguided soul.

"Do it already!" he demanded and for a moment there—just one brief moment—the slick reptilian lawyer's skin slid away and revealed the frightened human being beneath. But only for a moment.

"I have no intention."

Now Chad laughed—dryly, cynically. "No, you wouldn't, would you? Not Flynn Connors. He's too moral, too ethical, too above it all. Why, if he did something like that, he'd be no better than me."

Baiting you now. Trying to piss you off. Trying to make you mad enough to grab that fucking gun and shove it in his face. Because if you do that, you've already conceded loss, haven't you? You've committed the first irrational act.

Flynn lit a cigarette and stared down at what was in the chair. No, Chad wasn't really smug or sure of himself, he was scared. In fact, he was scared shitless. He was ready to squirt lemonade down his leg. But he was running every play in his greasy well-thumbed book so his guest might think otherwise.

Now he relaxed.

He effused calm, understanding, maybe even something approaching wisdom. "No, I knew you wouldn't kill me. That's not the person you are or could ever be. You like your life and you don't want to throw it away, old friend. Which is exactly why we need to talk, to understand each other. Because we both stand to lose a lot. There's a way to handle our problem. All it will take is some careful bartering. I can make them listen to reason."

"Can you?" Flynn asked.

"Yes."

"And all it will take is my wife."

Chad, not breaking character, shook his head. "No! Not that. I was thinking of something else. Someone else. A surrogate, let's say."

Flynn, already not liking it, suppressed his ire. "A surrogate?"

Chad smiled, flashing a winning million-dollar grin of blinding white teeth that were perfectly straight like books on a library shelf. That smile must have made juries swoon. "Sure, my friend. You keep Marjorie and they get what they want. Everyone's happy. You pay your debt and your luck comes back in spades, right? It'll be easy," he said, gesturing expansively with his wonderfully tanned hands and their pristinely manicured nails. "Listen. Now, you're a great-looking guy. Hell, you look like you're in your thirties. So take a ride out into the boonies to some shithole bar and work your magic on some hot young thing. Lay on the charm. Flash some money. Let her know you're loaded and she's just what you've been looking for. Three, four drinks into it, you'll have her out in your car. Tell her you're taking her back to your place. Then take her to where you first met our friends. They'll be there day or night. They're expecting you. Hell, I've brought them little treats like this before and more than once."

I'll just bet you have.

"And they'd go for it?"

"Of course they will! Just a little something to whet their appetite. That's all they want. In fact—" and here Chad dropped him a little wink to signify that this was nothing more than a mischievous prank like peeking into the girl's shower room at summer camp "—I took the liberty of mentioning it to them and they like the idea…as long as it's delivered by your hand."

Flynn said nothing.

It had all been leading to this. Chad had it all planned out. Make the situation seem dark, grim, and hopeless, then drop the surrogate idea which, under the circumstances, would seem almost reasonable. Just some bar slut in exchange for Marjorie. Why not? The question was why? Why the change? Part of it, he figured, was because he was in a desperate place and Toddy and Bones knew that when he was desperate, he was unpredictable as all men were under pressure (save Chad). He might not knuckle under properly. He might make a fight of it. They didn't really want that because regardless of what cosmic pond they'd spawned in, they were still essentially bullies. They liked to hit people where they were vulnerable, not get hit. That was part of it. Maybe they still remembered him going after their car.

Yes, he was certain that was part of it.

But only part.

The rest was that if they got him to commit the immoral, depraved act of kidnapping an innocent girl and offering her up to them, then it would damn him, push him down that much closer to Chad's level and when that happened, whatever they demanded of him next time would be that much more palatable. Because there would be a next time. It would build rotten brick by rotten brick into a crooked house until he crawled into its cellar like a certain reptile named Chad. And once that happened, when they asked for Marjorie down the road, he'd give her to them.

"And that's all I'd have to do?"

"That's it, man."

Now Flynn did sit down. He wouldn't smoke the man's stogies or drink his liquor, but he would use one of his chairs.

"That's all you need to do," Chad emphasized.

No more than that.

Marjorie would be saved from an unimaginably hellish fate and all it would take was the life of a young woman who got into a car with the wrong man. Sorry, hon, but my skin and that of my lady love is vastly more important than the one covering your marvelous young curves. In the end, you see, your hide will be peeled from your bones about the same time your mind flies apart inside your skull during an eye-opening fact-finding tour of Planet X.

"I'll keep it in mind," he promised Chad's oh-so-hopeful face. "But first, you're going to answer a few questions."

"Anything."

Don't be so eager, asshole.

"Why me?"

"What do you mean?"

"You know damn well what I mean. Back in 1980, why did you pick me?"

Chad shook his head. He was caught off-guard and he was

scrambling to get his composure back. "It wasn't like that. You needed help back then. That's all there was to it."

"Bullshit."

"Flynn…"

"Tell me why."

Chad's face went hard. "Nobody forced you."

"I didn't say they did. But you picked me for a reason and I want to know what that reason is. Now tell me or I'll fucking take you to them. I'm not screwing around."

Chad sighed. "Because they wanted someone and I owed them. I picked you because you were new. You didn't have any friends. You didn't have anyone to help you or fall back on. You were the perfect choice."

Flynn nodded. It was pretty much as he had always expected. He had been selected and once that happened, Toddy and Bones worked their magic and turned everyone against him.

"Sorry, Flynn. That's just how it was."

"I'm sorry, too, because we're both going to go down because I'm not going to bring them a fucking thing."

Chad was sitting up now. "Then they'll take it."

"And they'll take you, too. And that's all I really want."

"You crazy fucking asshole. You'll throw away everything and for what? The life of some whore in a bar whose greatest contribution to this world will be the children she pumps out of her loins to burden the welfare system? You better fucking think again because I won't allow it."

No composure now. Chad's face was bright red, sweaty, drool on his mouth. His hands were balled into fists and it looked like he wanted to use them, which was something Flynn was hoping for.

"It's not your choice to make, now is it?"

"Flynn…" Chad slowly recovered himself. "I know what they put in your garage. Next time it'll be in your bedroom, and it'll tear Marjorie in half. You better think of what you're doing."

"I have thought about it and that's why the answer is no," Flynn said, standing up. "They killed my parents, Chad, when they couldn't get what they wanted. Do you think I can forgive something like that? And do you really think I want to become trash like you?"

Chad said nothing. He only trembled and it wasn't with rage.

He was a man on the edge with no options. He breathed in and out. Finally, licking his pale lips, he said, "Take that gun, Flynn. Take it and kill me now. If you don't, I'll come for you. I'll come for your wife. I'll sell you, I'll sell her to them. Whatever it takes."

"Why don't you stand up and fight them?" Flynn put to him. "Why don't you be a man for the first time in your fucking life?"

The insult was lost on Chad.

He seethed.

He raged.

He shook with terror.

Flynn took it down a notch. "We can fight them, Chad. I know we can. I did it once and I can do it again. I've been thinking this over for thirty years. You see, I always thought they were parasites that feed on fear like in the movies, but that's not true. They're just shitheads. They get off on toying with other life forms, with debasing them and breaking them wide open. They're addicted to it. They're just monsters. That's all they are. Fucking bullies. Intellect with no discipline. They might have the technology, but they're just rotten little brats that kick puppies and step on frogs and throw firecrackers at cats. They torment the weak," he ranted, flying by the seat of his pants but liking it, feeling it was somehow true. "They can be fought. That car or craft or whatever the fuck it is, it's their only way back to where they came from. Maybe if we destroy it, we destroy them."

Chad kept shaking his head. "You're completely out of your fucking mind."

"No, I'm not. Didn't you notice—even when we were teenagers—how they disappeared for weeks on end? That was because they had to go back to where they came from to recharge their batteries. If we destroy that car, we destroy them. We unplug them. They can't survive here for long."

"But what they'll do in the meantime is what you should be thinking about," Chad told him. "Because they will fuck you up in ways you can't begin to imagine."

But he was wrong.

Very wrong.

Because Flynn had been imagining those very things since he was sixteen and he was shit tired of it.

28

That night, he slept at Marjorie's side. She did not leave and sleep on the couch as usual, but neither did she get within two feet of him. He wanted so badly to tell her the way things were, but every time he moved closer to her, she slid away. He knew if he kept pushing it, she would run out of bed and angrily head to the couch. And he did not want her down there where he could not watch over her.

He opened his mouth to admit it all to her no fewer than three times before he fell into a heavy, drugged sleep. But at the last moment he lost his nerve. He wasn't sure what scared him more—the idea that her knowing might endanger her or the fact that she might despise him the way, down deep, he despised himself.

He didn't really think he'd sleep, but when he finally did, it was complete devastation. He went under, sinking into the black mud of unconsciousness and down further into the deeper darkness of his subconscious mind where the wild things dwell.

29

The dream came, not gradually or even subtly, but with great force, hitting him like a wave, bowling him over and sending him tumbling into a field of grayness like a kid rolling down a grassy summer hill. And then he saw he was in his room. The same room he slept in. The room he shared with Marjorie. Everything looked so positively normal, that he was not sure if he was dreaming or awake. A voice in his head assured him it was a dream, but another told him it was anything but.

He lay there, feeling paralyzed.

Next to him, Marjorie slept.

He heard a gurgling, phlegmy breathing like a man on his death bed. It was coming from the closet. It was silly. He was a grown man…wasn't he?…and he was certainly not afraid of anything in the closet; that was something you left behind in third grade. Yet as he listened to that perfectly awful liquid sound of tubercular lungs rasping and drowning in foul secretions, he was terrified. He could barely breathe himself. In fact, it felt like he was suffocating. The calm and logical voice—the one that assured him this was only a dream—started giggling. Oh really, Flynn. You're afraid of the boogeyman at your age? You're afraid of things in closets and midnight creepy-crawlers under the bed? The laughter of the voice increased until it became not exactly hysterical with mirth but rather high-pitched and neurotic. Just what do you think is in there? Some tall, narrow rotting creature dressed in black? Its face coming apart, viscous fluid bubbling from its lips each time it exhales a rattling breath? Is that what you think? Is that what you REALLY think is in there? Some malefic haunter, some saw-toothed monster that has come to tear your throat out? Well, you sir, are…RIGHT!

He was aware in the dream, or perhaps out of it, that his body was drenched with cool sweat. This scared him because he remembered Bernie Pauls back in Chicago saying that, right before he suffered his first coronary, his body was suddenly awash in chilly sweat. But even as this scared Flynn, he knew that a heart attack was the least of his problems.

Because there were worse things.

And one of them was about to make itself known.

The door swung open—not slowly with great drama as he would suppose—but quickly and forcefully. A tall man in a shiny, greasy-looking black motorcycle jacket stood there. He wore scuffed engineer's boots, a black T-shirt, and pegged jeans. It was Toddy, of course. His hair was longer and scraggly, not the flattop he'd sported when Flynn first met him, but it was Toddy all right.

He was here.

He had come in the dead of night.

"Hello, Flynn," he said in a perfectly awful voice that was shrill and cutting like a rusty gate creaking in the wind. He put his hands on the edges of the doorframe, his fingers oozing a chalky white paste as if he was dissolving.

"You can't be here," Flynn's dream-voice said. "Not here. Not in my house. You can't just come in here."

Toddy laughed and it sounded like a man vomiting out his own stomach. "Sure I can. I can come here anytime I want, and I can take anything I want."

In his sleep paralysis, Flynn could do little more than thrash his head back and forth on his pillow. He was powerless. Completely powerless. Terrible things were about to happen and there wasn't a damned thing he could do about it.

Toddy pulled himself out of the closet a few more inches, steadying himself there, and Flynn gasped when he saw his face. His first thought was that it was wrapped in dirty gray bandages that were coming loose and leaking puss and all manner of foul septic drainage...but there were no bandages; it was just his face. Something awful was happening to it and he had no doubt that it was something from inside rather than the result of some horrible accident. It was not only rotting, but sloughing off the skull beneath in ragged strips of tissue that dangled like the wrappings of a mummy. The left side was swollen purple-blue in a suppurating mass that leaked tears of black juice. His left eye looked like a steamed gray oyster that was ready to slide from its shell. When he grinned, the stress split open his right cheek and another sheet of flesh sloughed free like a snake skin.

"And there's your wifey sleeping next to you," he said, a clot of jelly dripping from his lips. "How nice. How fucking convenient."

Toddy's grin widened and Flynn noticed that he was missing teeth.

"What's happening to you?" Flynn asked him.

"Let's just say I overstayed my welcome."

This came as no surprise to Flynn because it was exactly what he'd told Chad that day—Toddy and Bones needed to return home now and again to recharge their batteries. Though, in his dream, he knew that comparison wasn't very apt; it was more a matter of regeneration because the skins they wore and the forms they took definitely had an expiration date on them. And when they didn't go back when they were supposed to, this was the result: they decayed in their own bodies. They became walking sacks of putrescence.

Toddy feigned checking his watch even though there was no timepiece there, only a yellowed knob of bone.

"Pressed for time," he said, a pink bubble expanding from his nostrils. "Gotta get my job done, then I gotta go, gotta jam, gotta be history. You know how it is."

Flynn didn't really, but he figured he was about to find out.

Toddy walked around the bed and as he did so, Flynn writhed like a worm on a hook. His dream-self kept alternating between the sense that it was a dream and that it was anything but. Toddy hovered over Marjorie. He reached out a hand and caressed her breast through her nightgown. Despite the dimness of the room, Flynn clearly saw that the hand looked like a frayed leather glove with popped stitching. There were white squirming things on it.

Marjorie shifted uneasily in her sleep. Her gown had hiked up, revealing her left thigh in all its glory.

"Is this some sweet shit or what, son?" Toddy said, grinding his teeth together with a sound like a knife on a sharpening stone. "Is this what you been keeping from us? Well, no wonder! This was my hole, I wouldn't let anybody paw it up either."

Marjorie chose that moment to wake up, even though Flynn cried out in his head, Please, oh please, not now, baby, don't open your eyes. Too late. She was awake and she clearly saw the hunched-over, grotesque thing standing over her that looked like a badly-used scarecrow that was splitting its seams.

Then Flynn was awake.

Really awake.

He was lying there in the dark, Marjorie sleeping peacefully beside him. It took several minutes before spiking panic subsided and when it did he wondered if it had been a dream at all or if Toddy had psychically attacked him. He had a mad desire to check the closet, but the idea of doing so terrified him.

Some time later, knowing that sleep was done for the night, he went downstairs and sat there in his recliner, smoking and drinking and wondering vaguely what kind of toll this sort of stress was taking on his middle-aged body. By the time the sun started to rise, he knew there were really only two choices available: either he tried to get Marjorie out of town (which would be next to impossible without coming clean and even then, unlikely) or he took a ride and visited his friends. If he did the latter—and it would take guts, real fucking guts—he would need to accept the idea that he would not be coming back, that he would be leaving his wife a widow. That was not easy to take. And if he died…well, there was no guarantee they wouldn't come after Marjorie anyway.

By seven A.M. he still didn't know what the hell to do.

Caught between fear and anger, the idea of making the wrong choice scared him. So much hung in the balance—not only his life but his wife's.

But he had to think fast because Halloween arrived at midnight.

30

By two that afternoon, Marjorie simply couldn't take it anymore. Flynn's drinking and chain-smoking, brooding and secret despair, were too much. All her married life she had one by-law and that was that she did not give in when she knew she was right. She put up with shit as any wife did, but that was a standard she held. But now...well, it had gone too far and the man she loved was sinking into a bottomless abyss of fear, self-pity, and depression. She couldn't stand for that. So, finally, she ate some crow. She took Flynn by the hand and led him to the couch and forced him to sit down.

"Let's hear it," she said. "I've had enough. Either tell me what the hell's going on or I walk out that goddamn door and I don't come back."

This was mostly bluff, but as she said it she believed it.

"I want you to leave," he said.

"What?"

"I mean I want you to get out of this town. It'll be safer that way if you do. I can't leave. It's not possible...but I think you can get out because you're not hooked up in this."

She sighed. "Explain."

Flynn sat there next to her, hearing the pain in her voice; how it had become the dull, listless timbre of a proud woman who had been beaten by her own emotions. How could he hope to explain it without sounding like a crazy man?

It was his turn to sigh. He stood up and walked over to the window, staring out at Candlelight Lane and remembering, once again, when it had been simple old Norton Avenue on the edge of town before the yuppies took over; before the old businesses were bulldozed along with the distinctive hills, and McMansions sprouted like toadstools. He studied what he saw out there, all the houses, the flat lots and evenly squared streets. The rolling grassy hills of Norton existed only in his mind now.

Sighing yet again, he lit a cigarette, turning back to his wife and wondering how he was he was going to frame this in a sensible way for her, yet knowing such a thing simply wasn't possible. So he didn't bother.

He started talking, spinning horror stories, teenage tales, and science-fiction yarns. The more he talked, the more it came spilling out of him, and the more it spilled out of him, the easier it became. He told her everything: moving to Compton, how as much as he tried, he didn't fit in; how he was targeted and tormented and bullied, and about how Chad came into his life. That's when it got a little tougher. But he pushed on, telling her about Toddy and Bones and the '59 Caddy. And that, of course, led to awful things like Bobby Swinn and Daniel Harms, Norm Kinder and Mr. Martin, Danice McKerran and Mr. Upright Concerned Citizen…hell, all of it. He also touched on Chad's brother and what Chad had been doing since to keep the Gruesome Twosome happy, and his own good luck rolling straight and smooth.

"But…but Flynn," Marjorie said after a few minutes of guarded silence, "these memories…they're the memories of a confused, hurting teenage boy. They're probably not even accurate."

"Oh, they're accurate, dear. The disappearances of those people is public record. Trust me, it happened. I know it's easier to believe I was a teenage crackpot that has morphed into an adult neurotic with anxiety issues, but it's not true. I don't expect you to believe me. I'd never believe it myself if somebody told it to me. No matter." He kissed her on the mouth and hugged her. "This is why you have to leave, baby. You have to get out of here. Tonight will be Halloween."

She held his hand tightly. "Flynn, please, I'm not about to abandon you over…over something like this. All that was thirty years ago."

He shook his head. "No, it's happening now, too. They've been calling me since I got back and Chad and I have had more than one chat about what it is they want from me."

"Which is?"

Oh, Jesus, why did he even start any of this? "You," he said without emotion. "They want you. You're the payment. They want to take you to that awful place, they want to take you trick-or-treating."

"Flynn…"

"They took my parents, Marjorie. Now they'll take you."

It was obvious that she didn't understand any of it. She was trying, bless her, but all of it was so far beyond ordinary human comprehension that she simply couldn't wrap her brain around it.

He tried another approach. "Do you remember when we sat on this very couch not so long ago and talked about how our luck was going to shit since we got here?" He saw that she did. "I think what you said is that up until our arrival in Compton we had frighteningly good luck. I tried to talk you away from it because it was too close to the truth. But you were right. Your intuition was spot on."

She folded her arms across her breasts and he knew that was her way of retreating. He'd seen it many times before. He pitied her. He really did. Because in her mind she was seeing the complete mental collapse of someone she loved. The pain of it was etched on her face.

"Maybe we could go to the police."

Yeah, bring the authorities in. That'll do it.

"And tell them what? That there are monsters from Planet X living in fair Compton and they want me to offer you as sacrifice to them?"

"This is just so…far out."

"Then believe I'm a raving lunatic who's going to murder you in your sleep. Whatever. Just go. Grab a few things and drive out of town. If I get through this, I'll call you tomorrow."

"I'm not leaving. I'm not leaving because I love you and because this is insane and you have to be made to see that," she said, getting up and fixing herself a drink, which was rare for her that early. "I'll be with you and we'll expose this for what it is."

"No, honey. No way."

"Maybe we should call your friend Chad."

"It won't do any good. He's a consummate liar. He won't admit to any of it. But if I don't offer you, he will."

Standing there, she raised her glass of Seven-and-Seven to her lips and it promptly slipped from her hand and thudded to the rug, spilling. "Shit. I'm so clumsy."

"It's a lot more than that, Marjorie."

She looked at him.

"Our luck has nearly all run out," he said.

31

1981

With Daryl at his side, they walked back over to Norton Avenue and the '77 Skylark waiting at the curb. To Flynn's surprise, it started right away. "I'll be damned," he said. "Thought she was going to need a jump."

"Don't be too surprised," Daryl said. "When your friends pulled into my driveway, the TV died and the digital clock blanked out. They emit something that disrupts the grid like a power failure."

Flynn smiled at that because he knew that this was like some role-playing fantasy to Daryl. This was the stuff of the novels he read and the TV shows he watched. This was a plot straight out of Dr. Who or the Outer Limits or maybe even Kolchak: The Night Stalker. He was living his secret dream. Problem was, those shows generally had the hero coming out of it alive…but that might not be the case here.

Daryl had changed from the guy who wanted to know nothing about Toddy and Bones and said sensible things—Say no. Reject them. Nullify their power—to someone literally obsessed at the idea that they were alien monsters with the keys to the stars. And therein lay his naiveté. He was courting serious danger but his personal infatuation with all things otherworldly and science fictional was clouding his mind. He was no longer the wise, seasoned sage, but a fan that had to see those things that he had read so much about.

Flynn kept trying to talk him out of it.

In fact, he brought him home before they went anywhere else but Daryl absolutely refused to get out of the car. In many ways, Flynn was glad he wasn't alone in all this, but in others he was terrified that something perfectly awful would happen to Daryl for sticking his nose in where it didn't belong. Toddy and Bones usually targeted the enemies (or perceived enemies) of their "friends" but that didn't mean they wouldn't sort out anyone they saw as a threat.

"You might be setting yourself up for something bad," he said.

Daryl shrugged. "I'm not worried."

But he was and Flynn knew it. He was wearing his skin firmly and fervently, but underneath he was scared and they both knew it; they just didn't speak about it.

The McKerran house was outside town and the closer they got to it, the more something began to stir inside Flynn that he acquainted with menace. He refused to give it any credence because if he did that, if he let common sense win out, he would turn the car around and go back home and hide under his bed. He'd done something today that had changed everything. He'd shown Toddy and Bones that he was not Chad in any way, shape, or form, and he had to build on that in the slim hope that they would move on to easier pickings.

But as he drove, his anxiety increased.

Daryl didn't help, of course, because the entire way he prattled on endlessly in a jittery, nervous voice about life on other worlds and the level of intelligence it would take to create something like the parsec-hopping '59 El Dorado. Flynn ignored him for the most part because whatever Toddy and Bones were, he didn't see them as being particularly intelligent. His gut feeling was that they didn't understand the technology of their vehicle any more than a rich brat understood the technology of the Jaguar he tooled around in. Hell, maybe they had stolen the damn thing. To him, they were like a couple of lowlife, inbred rednecks who had discovered a laser gun and went around disintegrating everything that moved simply because they could.

Maybe they're smart, he thought. Maybe. But their intellect has no morals or ethics and no discipline. They're cowboys shooting up a cow town on a Saturday night. Human beings are nothing but game to them. Toys to be played with.

About ten minutes later, they arrived at the McKerran house. It was set off the road, flanked by tall pines and maples; the yard blown with brown leaves, yellow fields spreading out to either side. As he pulled into the driveway, Flynn was struck not only by the apparent desertion of the place, but by the fact that the house, a plain and ordinary midwestern two-story, seemed to embody every haunted house he'd seen in every B-movie at two in the morning. It managed to get under his skin quite easily.

"Now what?" he said.

Daryl sighed. "Now we go knock on the door."

"And say what? 'Has Danice been acting odd lately?'"

"I don't think anyone will answer so don't worry about it."

Flynn stepped out into the chill October air. The wind was hissing through the pines above. There was a Ford Bronco parked near the garage. It was plastered with autumn leaves and it looked like it hadn't been brushed off in weeks. They moved up the drive and stood before the porch. There were a dozen rolled-up newspapers near the door.

"It looks like the McKerrans are on vacation," Daryl said, as if he was looking for a good reason to get out of there.

Flynn swallowed. I hear Planet X is lovely this time of year, a smart-assed voice said in his head. "Nobody home, I'm guessing."

But inside, he wasn't so sure. He studied the withered climbing ivy on the walls, the leaves on the porch steps, the dark windows that seemed to leer at them. He was certain at that moment that while the house was certainly empty it did not mean that it was not occupied. That made no sense, yet it made all the sense in the world.

"Are we gonna stand here or what?" Daryl asked.

Flynn shrugged and moved up the steps, kicking a newspaper aside. He went to the door and rapped on it five or six times very hard. His knocking echoed through the house. Something about the reverberating sound of it unnerved him—it was like there was nothing inside but a great hollow.

They waited for two or three minutes.

There was no sound from behind the door, no footsteps approaching. Only that even, unbroken silence that seemed terribly wrong in every way.

Flynn tried the doorknob. It was unlocked.

"We can't just barge in there," Daryl warned him.

"Why not?"

To that, Daryl had no good argument. There were reasons why

you didn't barge into people's houses, but at that moment neither of them could think of what they were.

Flynn turned the knob, then pushed the door in…and there was a sudden hissing like the seal on a vacuum jar had been broken, followed by a hollow boom that made them both jump. Leaves were sucked through the doorway and Flynn nearly was, too. That kind of suction was not normal. Houses weren't sealed that tight. Maybe bathyspheres or decompression chambers, but not houses.

"This is messed up," Daryl said by way of scientific observation.

"No shit."

"What I'm saying is that the only thing that could cause a suction like that is if there were no air in the house to begin with," he explained. "If it was a vacuum."

"And that boom?"

"Do you know what causes a sonic boom?"

"No."

"When a jet breaks the sound barrier, it's going so fast that it leaves a channel. When the air collapses back in to fill the void, you hear the boom of the shock wave it produces."

"And that's what that noise was?"

"Yes, I think so. When we opened the door, air rushed in to fill the void."

Flynn wasn't going to argue with him. It made sense in a way, but no ordinary house could be sealed tight enough to keep air out. It just wasn't feasible. But maybe that was the answer—no ordinary house. He decided he better move before he lost his nerve.

He stepped through the door and Daryl followed behind him. There was a dank, musty smell inside the way Flynn imagined a buried pipe might smell. It was very strong at first, but within seconds it had dissipated as if the air sucked in from outside had displaced it.

On first inspection, there was nothing unusual about the house. They saw a set of stairs leading to the second floor, a corridor to the left that must have led to the bedrooms, and an archway to the right that showed them a living room. Again, nothing unusual.

Flynn stood there hoping Daryl would suggest what it was they were supposed to do next because he was absolutely clueless. He felt…strange for some reason. Jittery, nervous. A low-grade headache was beginning to throb at his temples and his eyes were so wide they felt painted on. He had to consciously hold his jaws open so his teeth did not chatter. It felt like something inside his skull wanted to fly out through his ears. He saw it in Daryl, too. He was clenching and unclenching his hands. He continually licked his lips and his eyes seemed to tremble in their sockets.

"You feeling it?" he finally asked.

Daryl nodded. "Weird. I feel very wired, really wired. Agitated or something."

Flynn was going to say he felt like he had just washed down a handful of speeders with a six-pack of Mountain Dew. Everything inside him was drawn tight—ringing, tweaking. There was no other way to describe it. This is what a lightbulb must feel like when you screw it in, he thought and giggled at the idea.

"What's so funny?" Daryl asked, smiling drunkenly.

"I don't know. I feel like I want to bounce off the fucking walls."

"The air. There's something funny with the air."

That gave Flynn pause. "You think it's bad?"

"Not exactly."

"Maybe there's not enough to breathe?"

Daryl shook his head. "No, if there wasn't enough or if it was bad, it would make us dizzy, put us to our knees. This isn't that. It's almost like there's too much air, too much oxygen in it."

Flynn looked into the living room. Nothing there. He needed to relax, unwind, or he was going to run right out the front door. The house was just a house. It was empty and that always made houses seem more threatening. But there was no threat here, not really.

"C'mon," Daryl said.

Flynn followed him into the living room…and was it his imagination or did his stride feel oddly lumbering? Even the sound of his shoes making contact with the floor made an odd, vibrating sound that reminded him more of a struck tuning fork than actual footsteps. He stood there with Daryl, his mouth dry, his heart racing. The air felt heavy around him. Not humid exactly, but thick. He saw a sofa with a few fringed pillows on it, a recliner, and a couple of wing-backed chairs by the fireplace. Some landscape prints hung on the walls, next to a shelf of Reader's Digest Condensed Books. The picture window looked out into the yard, and a huge console

TV took up a good section of the wall. Nothing strange.

"Danice?" Daryl called out.

Flynn tensed at the sound. He could hear her name echoing through the house. It seemed that it took some time to die away—longer than it should have. Daryl stepped toward the archway that led into the austere dining room. He stopped and stared blankly at the big TV. He seemed fixated on it as if he was seeing something Flynn could not.

"What are you looking at?"

Daryl shrugged. "I'm...I'm not sure."

Flynn was all for leaving because even if he couldn't put a finger on what it was, there was still something out of sorts about the McKerran house. He had the worst suspicion that like Chad and Danice, the house had gone trick-or-treating. He looked back the way they had come and he gasped. The sofa had moved. He had walked past it a minute before, but now it was set lengthwise, blocking his path. He would have had to climb over it to get where he now was. The recliner, too. It was sideways. And that picture had been on the other wall and the bookshelf was now to his left and—

No, nothing's moved. Look. Look! You're just viewing it from a different perspective. You're not standing where you were. You're now standing clear across the room.

He blinked his eyes and it was true.

His position relative to the room had shifted dramatically, but Daryl was still over there staring at the TV. Or was he? For one frightening moment, his image seemed to flutter as if it was going to dissolve completely. Flynn had to blink his eyes a few times to make sure he wasn't hallucinating. He wasn't.

"Flynn?" Daryl said. "What are you doing over there?"

"I haven't moved. The room did."

Daryl looked concerned, but certainly not panicked like Flynn. He looked around, taking it in and trying to process it.

"I think we better get out of here," Flynn told him.

But Daryl didn't seem interested in that at all. "I think...I don't know what happened here...but I think this house is somehow caught between our world and another. It's sort of out of phase, you know?"

Flynn did not know, but he could guess. As Daryl rambled

on excitedly about spatial shifts and interdimensional voids, he kept watching the room. Like Daryl's image, it seemed to flutter, losing solidity, fading like a picture on a TV screen. Whatever was happening, it started in the corner of the room, then spread out. Everything would fade and look misty, indistinct, then it would flicker and return with sharp clarity. Only when it did, the perspective of the room had changed. His greatest fear was that one of these times it—and they—wouldn't come back at all.

"Let's go," he said, as Daryl continued his monologue about hyperdimensional passage, the fourth dimension, and interspatial teleportation, which somehow segued into a Star Trek episode called "The Tholian Web" in which Captain Kirk found himself trapped between two dimensions. Flynn seized him by the arm and whirled him around so they were facing the archway that had brought them in…only it wasn't there. At least, not the way it had been. It was oddly crooked now, tilting down a 40° angle, so distorted that it looked like a reflection from a funhouse mirror.

Holding onto each other, they moved forward and there was the door . It seemed unable to hold its shape. One second it was perfectly ordinary and the next it had elongated into a slit and the ceiling appeared to be thirty feet above them. When it gained solidity again and was compressed down to something like a hatch, it looked the right size but was warped in its frame like the archway. It kept moving.

When it phased back in, Flynn reached for the knob with a visibly shaking hand, but Daryl slapped his hand away.

"If you get caught in it when it changes, you'll warp out of shape, too, and I don't think you'll survive it."

Flynn felt the warping of reality in his brain, too. With no consistent geometric frame of reference, his thoughts were muddled and a deep-set paranoia began to settle in. It felt like something in his brain wanted to scream.

Daryl led him away, but the corridor before them was in constant motion as if it was breathing. It went from being perfectly rectangularly symmetrical to something like a parallelogram and then a trapezium and finally a scalene triangle. It was insanity. Flynn could feel his mind beginning to flake away. His face was wet with sweat and his guts were tied in sheepshanks.

I'm gonna lose it, he kept saying inside his mind. I'm really going to lose it.

Daryl turned them away from the corridor and they moved back into the living room, which suddenly had become a corridor itself. It was long and narrow. The archway leading into the dining room looked as if it was fifty or sixty feet away. They moved towards it and despite the apparent distance, they seemed to glide with great speed towards it. It was as if each step launched them forward with amazing velocity. They stumbled through the dining room and stopped at the window looking out into the backyard.

Except the backyard wasn't there.

What they saw through the window was a grotesque, blurring world of tall stone towers and jagged black crevices and things like trees that were upside down, their struggling roots reaching into a purple-hued sky like wriggling vines. Flying specks darted through the air and immense fungal toads with red crystalline eyes seemed to hop into the sky and never come down. It was like looking through a telescope to some vastly distant place. When they shifted their position at the glass, the images whirled by rapidly as if they were looking out of a train window. They had to stop and focus on the same pinpoint for several seconds before the outside world stopped flying past. When it did, they saw yellow, almost liquid ground that was turgid and bubbling like a primordial swamp. Bubbles broke free from time to time and rose up only to split into more bubbles. There were things inside them, moving things, but neither Flynn nor Daryl could see exactly what they were. What they did see was something like a massive, viscid and gelatinous worm rising from the yellow soup. It was composed of interconnected cuboids that were liquid then gas then plasma, reshaping and reforming themselves at will. And then it, too, vaulted into the sky and was no more.

"Please, Daryl, get me out of here," Flynn said, and his voice was broken, begging. "Get me the fuck out of here."

"Getting in was one thing, but getting out might be a bit more complicated," Daryl said.

Flynn was ready to grab him and shake the stuffing right out of him...then he saw something else out there. Whatever they were, they were big, very big. They stood on stout black tripods, above which was a socket that held an immense glistening, silvery eyeball with a golden pupil. Above this was a branching collection of feelers that looked like the dendrites of a nerve cell.

"They know we're here," Daryl said in a hollow voice. "They're looking right at us."

Flynn knew he was right. The terror he felt was like being doused in ice water. He went cold inside and out. The things were moving closer to the house. As they did so, their massive eyes shifted, the golden pupils glowing, ripples playing out over the corneal surfaces.

Daryl reached out and pressed his hand to the glass, jerking it away. "It's hot. Really hot."

Flynn took his word for it.

Maybe they would have stayed there, transfixed by the tripod things but something landed on the glass, making them jump back. It was a bug. A bug that could have only evolved in a place much different from the one they knew. It was about three feet long, like some gigantic crazy dragonfly whose entire body was made of the same transparent, veined material as its wings. It was ribbed and chitinous-looking like a living exoskeleton made of diamonds. Flynn was staring at its three spherical pink eyes and watching its feathery jointed legs flexing as it moved about. From its mouth it extended a serrated tongue that rasped against the glass. It made the entire window vibrate as if it was going to break at any moment.

Daryl pulled Flynn away and for the first time he looked genuinely frightened, genuinely confused, and genuinely disturbed. A bead of blood ran from his left nostril and it looked redder than any blood Flynn had ever seen before. It was followed by another drop, then another and the sheer brilliance of it was mesmerizing. Suddenly, he knew why: Daryl's face was pale. Hell, more than pale. It was the washed-out color of wax paper and the blood was the only thing that made it look alive. With a sinking feeling of horror, he realized it wasn't just Daryl's face but everything.

The color's fading. It's fading from everything.

And it was. He looked frantically around the kitchen that, like the rest of the house, was clicking in and out of phase, blurring then becoming more distinct. But each time it did, there was less color to be seen. The change had been so gradual that he barely noticed. On the fridge there were several large apple magnets that had been bright red when they first arrived—he remembered them distinctly, thinking how kitschy they were, how they were the kind of thing his mom would like—but had now faded to a dull pink. Above the kitchen table there was a still life featuring a bowl of bright yellow pears, except they were not bright yellow anymore, but fleshy and pallid like organs removed from a corpse. And above the stove there was a chalkware hanging of a bunch of grapes. The vivid purple had faded and the grapes looked like a cluster of blanched eyeballs.

Panicking, Flynn glanced at his hand and it looked like a white rubber glove.

"Your nose is bleeding," Daryl said.

Flynn wiped it with the back of his hand and the red smear on his knuckles was vivid, startling. "So is yours. This place is fading out and we're fading with it."

Now it was Flynn's turn to take charge because Daryl was starting to lose it. Not only had he gone pale outside but he had become listless inside. The spark that invigorated him, the life force, was diminishing now.

Flynn felt it in himself, too.

He wanted to sit down and close his eyes. He couldn't remember feeling so sleepy or sluggish before. It was as if he'd just pushed away from a Thanksgiving feast. He felt heavy and glutted with excess. Except it wasn't that but the fact that he was being drained dry, just like the house.

Fuck this!

As they dragged themselves toward the dining room, Daryl suddenly stiffened, eyes wide, and mouth gasping.

Flynn turned and saw the back door leading out to the patio. But that wasn't all he saw. Looking in through the window was a hideous, mutant face that was white and wispy as if it were made of cobwebs. There were dark depressions for eyes and a puckering indent for a mouth. Though it had no eyes, it was watching them. And what was worse was that it didn't seem to be connected to a body.

They went through the dining room, ducking as the ceiling canted down at them and the walls bowed and stretched like taffy.

In the living room, Flynn pulled Daryl to him. By that point, Daryl was stumbling about like he was drunk. He couldn't stand up straight and each time he spoke, his words became distinctly slurred. It wasn't just him, though. With a sense of alarm, Flynn realized that while his thinking seemed relatively unimpaired, he was having trouble turning those thoughts into words. His tongue felt slow in his mouth.

Yet, he managed to utter, "Look."

Daryl saw and he flushed a bit with fear. There were two bodies in the room that, of course, had not been there before. The insane thing—or maybe not insane at all, considering where they were—was that they were fused inside the walls so that it was hard to say where one began and the other ended. Their heads, upper bodies, and reaching hands seemed to grow from the wallpaper without disturbing the pattern. Both were dead, thank God, and both seemed to be made of something like gray ash. Even so, it was easy to see that one had been a man and the other a woman.

Danice's parents.

There could be no doubt of it.

But there were worse things happening in that room and what they were, Flynn was not really sure. Not at first. The wallpaper was moving. In fact, it was infested. There were numerous small oval bodies moving across it, skittering. He had to look, really look to see them. Spiders. He thought they were spiders. At least, spider-like. They were translucent things with round flattened bodies about the size of teacup saucers ringed with spindly creeping legs. When they moved, it looked as if the wallpaper moved because their pellucid bodies were like running drops of water that magnified what was beneath. Yet even though they seemed to be composed of some limpid material, they held their shape.

There were clusters of them on the ceiling.

The only time they truly disappeared is when they crawled over the picture window and even then they distorted the glass.

Daryl let out a little cry when one of them lowered itself on a thread between Flynn and him. It dangled there, swinging back and forth like a hypnotist's watch on a chain. It camouflaged itself even in the air, creating a blurring form but nothing else.

"MOVE!" Flynn shouted, grabbing Daryl's arm and towing him toward the foyer as more of the transparent spiders began to lower around them. Others abandoned the walls and crawled over the floor in their direction.

They ran into the foyer. One of the spiders' legs grazed the back of Daryl's neck and left a pink welt as if he had been scalded.

The foyer was acting much as it had before, flexing in and out of phase, losing solidity and then sharpening with clarity. But it was happening faster now and the walls and the carpet were completely colorless as if they'd been bled white. The door leading outside was still there, elongating, widening, becoming normal for a few seconds before completely losing its shape again.

Flynn saw Daryl staring behind him and turned to look.

The staircase leading up was wavering and guttering like a candle flame. It looked like some crazy heat mirage in the desert. Then, as he watched, it began to glow with a lambent illumination. And the reason for that was the luminous form that was standing at the top of the stairs. Like the rest of the house, it could barely hold its shape. What he saw—he thought—was a woman, because he could see long hair blowing around that was lit like electrical wires. A pulsating diaphanous shroud enclosed her in a membrane, and through it, he could see her skeleton, the bones of which were phosphorescent like glowing fuel rods pulled from a reactor. Her skull was cocked almost playfully to one shoulder, the death mask of her face grinning and sparkling, crackling with hellfire. Like the staircase, she was flickering and moving like a greasy plume of smoke. She seemed to be fragmenting…shining bits of her filling the air, swirling and circling, moving down the stairs at them.

Flynn looked away; her aura was as bright as the sun at midday.

He took hold of Daryl's arm.

He didn't need to tell him that they had to be out of there before the wraith came down the stairs and that their only chance of that was the way they had come in. Flynn pulled him to the door. Behind him, he could feel a building heat. The walls around him were shining as the wraith crept closer and closer. When the door blurred, then gained solidity, becoming normal once again, he jumped forward, turned the knob and they were sucked out into a whirpooling darkness.

They hit the ground.

Solid ground.

It was night and the house, amazingly, was forty feet behind them. But above, the stars were right. There was the Big Dipper and the North Star. All was right. Though, it had been daytime when they went in, now it was night.

They were both sore and tired and it took them some time to catch their breath.

"You know who that was, don't you?" Daryl said, lying next to Flynn.

"Yes. It was Danice."

"Part of her is here and part of her is…wherever."

No more needed to be said. Daryl checked his digital watch and found that it was nearly eleven. Which meant they had been inside the house over five hours. They knew it wasn't true, but temporally, their dimension and the other were not strictly aligned.

They lay there for a while and then piled into the Skylark. Daryl was concerned about what he was going to tell his mom, and Flynn told him just to be glad that they'd made it back so he could tell her.

As they pulled out of the driveway, the house began to move on its foundation. They both saw it and Flynn stopped. It was shivering and then it began to crack open like an eggshell, spokes of blinding blue-white light shooting up into the sky, searchlights announcing a premier. Gradually, within seconds, the lights died out and the house fell into itself. Flames licked up slowly and engulfed it.

By then, the Skylark was racing down the road toward Compton.

32

"Okay, Mr. Pouty Pants, out with it."

It was two days since the events at Danice's house and Halloween was coming fast. Flynn dreaded this as he lay on the couch, which pretty much seemed to be his station these days when he wasn't at school or at work. What he didn't need was his mom standing there like this, glaring down at him.

She knows. She knows something.

He was panicking, of course, because there was no way his mom could have known about any of it. Still, it disturbed him. He rarely saw his dad—he was always busy and three, four days a week he was out on the road for his job—but Mom was always there. She was the cement of their lives, the bedrock, and she was aware of the fact. That's why she took any and all problems as an affront to her rule. She was continually jabbing and parrying, trying to catch Flynn off-guard, forever searching for a problem that needed her immediate attention. And he knew this, yet the idea that she somehow, someway knew what was going on made him curl up inside. She was the last person in the world he would ever want to put in harm's way.

"Who's pouting?" he said, trying to sound unconcerned. "I'm just relaxing."

"It seems to me that you do a lot of relaxing."

"I go to school. I work. I recycle cans for a living, lady. I get tired."

He thought it sounded pretty good—calm, breezy, a bit of playful banter. Still…there was that nagging, illogical worry that she knew exactly what was going on or suspected it. And that filled his mind with a fog of dread. For what if those fucking animals started toying with her, too? Because if they really wanted to hurt him, that would be the way to do it.

She sat on the sofa by him, lifting his feet up and placing them on her lap.

"What's wrong, Flynn?"

"Nothing."

"Oh, there's something. You can't lie to the maternal unit."

He sighed. "I'm tired."

"Why is it," she asked, "that just a month ago you had more girls and more friends than you knew what to do with and now you're back to where you were a year ago?"

"I'm busy. I don't have a lot of time for that stuff."

"Flynn, the phone was ringing off the hook all summer for you. Now you never get a call. Did something happen?"

Yeah, my luck has gone sour in ways you can't imagine. "Of course not. It's just the way things are."

"Are you still not fitting in?"

He shrugged. Lie! Lie! Lie! But he couldn't. There just wasn't anything left to lie with. "Not really. I still feel kind of out of place here."

She laughed. "We had this identical conversation last year. I remember you laying here, denying everything, watching Godzilla movies."

"Shows what you know." He pointed at the Curtis Mathes console set across the room. "That's Gamera the flying turtle, not Godzilla."

"Ha, ha, so funny. One guy in a rubber suit is the same as another guy in a rubber suit."

"That just shows your ignorance of Japanese monster movies. Godzilla is not Gamera and Gamera is not Rodan and none of them are King Ghidorah."

"Oh, good lord."

He was trying to lead her away from the subject, keep her off balance with a steady stream of pop culture bullshit because inside he was still panicky. Panicky? No, it was more than that. There was self-loathing for who and what he'd allowed himself to become—a popularity addict who had to have his fix at any price—and the people he'd gotten involved with; guilt for the awful crimes they'd committed that he kept secret; and terror for what might be coming next and what form it might take. His apathy over the whole situation had cost people their lives and he couldn't stop hating himself for it any more than he could pretend that there wasn't a fatalistic turn to his mind now. He saw death everywhere. Jesus, some days he could smell it.

"Sometimes I feel guilty for ever bringing you here," she said.

Are you happy, butt-munch? Is this what you wanted? To make her feel bad? "No, Mom, c'mon, it's nothing. Don't worry about it. I've got friends. Sometimes I'm just too busy."

"I get the feeling you're patronizing me."

"Hardly. Besides, I don't know what that means."

"Is English your second language?"

"Sometimes I think so."

He was trying to sell her hard but she wasn't buying and he knew it. Mothers had a sixth sense about things like this. They knew instinctively when something was wrong and there was no way you were going to talk them out of it. And Flynn's mom was particularly intuitive. What he didn't know was that she stood outside his bedroom door many nights over the past year while he cried out in his sleep. That she wanted desperately to hold him as she had when he was a boy and had a bad dream, but she knew she couldn't. She knew he wouldn't appreciate it at his age. So she stood out there, wringing her hands helplessly, her eyes moist with tears, knowing—feeling—that something terrible was overtaking her son but not knowing what to do about it or how to fight it.

She grabbed his foot and began to tickle it. "Ve have vays of making you talk," she said.

"No…Mom…stop it…no, you can't…don't….gaaah! No, no, no!"

She knew his weaknesses, but even under prolonged tickling, he would not speak what was on his mind so, frustrated, she went back to her clown paintings. Which, he had noticed in an offhand way, were beginning to look more than a little sinister.

"If you ever need to talk," she said, "I'm here. I might be old, but I went through it all, too, and I know exactly how it is. Trust me, Flynn, the teenage world is no different now than it was in my day. Keep that in mind."

The sad look in her eyes as she departed the room nearly broke him. He was inches from spilling his guts to her. But he couldn't.

He just couldn't. It would put her in danger and, maybe worse, she might wonder what sort of a monster her son indeed was.

And he couldn't have that.

Her disapproval was acid to him.

He would do anything to avoid it.

33

The next day, he heard the telltale rumbling of the El Dorado and his skin instantly began to crawl. This was it. They had come for him. They had come to take him for a ride and he either did as Daryl suggested and got a round-trip ticket to Planet X or he went with it. He accepted what they offered and gave them the sacrifice they demanded.

These were the things going through his head as the car pulled to a stop and Toddy stepped out. He looked older. He was no longer the rejuvenated teenage hood. He looked much like he had when Flynn first met him: his face seamed by a hard life, the skin sallow and blotchy, the lines deep-cut. There were streaks of gray in his hair. His lips had pulled back from his teeth like those of a corpse shriveled by death. That pervasive stink of rot that Flynn had been smelling for days emanated off Toddy in hot, rank waves.

"We need to have a chitchat," he said, his voice gravelly. His eyes were dark and oily like the sucking mud at the bottom of a cold black pond. "Get in the car."

Here it was.

Here was his opportunity to do the right thing, to deny Toddy and what he was, to nullify him. This was his chance to stand up. Toddy had already yanked the carpet of good, hell, great near-supernatural luck from under his feet and taken away the Midas touch and the golden key, now was the time to complete his descent from the popular to the shunned.

"Flynn. Get in the car."

But Flynn just stood there, eyeballing him, knowing he was risking a lot and something inside him demanding that he risk a lot more before he became vermin like Chad, a writhing heap of refuse bought and paid for like a spineless dirty politician or a corporate yes-man.

Walk away. Walk away right now. If you even acknowledge this monster, you are inviting him into your life.

Toddy looked like he was going to start snorting steam at any moment. His eyes were not just dark, they were black holes leading into dead-end space. The lines in his face were knife cuts. He was trembling. Manic desperation reverberated through him and Flynn sensed it. He knew right at that moment that Toddy needed him a lot more than he needed Toddy.

"Get in the fucking car."

"So you can take me trick-or-treating like you did to Chad?"

Toddy fired up a cigarette, smoke blowing from his nostrils. "It's not like that. This is just a chat. Five minutes. Then you can be on your way."

"Really? Did you let Danice McKerran go on her way?" Flynn asked, knowing he was not just tempting fate but getting downright suicidal. "You know what? I went over to her house. I saw what was going on over there."

"Your pal Chaddywhacker gave her to us. We performed a service and we expect payment."

"I'm not paying you."

"Yes, you will."

"No, I won't!"

He expected Toddy to go absolutely ballistic or possibly psychotic, but he didn't. He only stood there, blinking his eyes, looking oddly fatigued as if it was getting to be too much for him.

"Please, Flynn, just get in the fucking car. Nothing'll happen to you."

It was crazy, but Flynn was going to.

He actually was going to.

Even after all he'd seen and experienced and after that horrifying adventure in Danice McKerran's house, he was still going to get inside that fucking car and take a cosmic ride to an armpit of the universe like Rigel-12 or Altair-4. He was really going to do it. At first, he wondered if Toddy was exerting some subtle mind control over him, but he didn't believe that. It was curiosity. Nothing but stark, mindless curiosity. Even the memory of what Chad had been through in the Caddy did not stay him. I was defiant, man, and they were going to make me pay. They were going to punish me. So they took me trick-or-treating. He wanted to take the ride. Some self-destructive thing inside him practically demanded it. Whether that was a death wish or some macho bullshit posturing to prove to Toddy that he had no fear of him (building upon the incident with the baseball bat, of course), he just didn't know.

You do this, you're asking for it.

You're just fucking asking for it.

Though his paranoia told him it was a trick, a trap, and he was waltzing right into it, his common sense told him that would come later. So he walked over to the car, but he could barely make his hand grab the door handle. It did not want to touch it. Something in him recoiled as if the Caddy was a loathsome, putrid dead thing creeping with carrion-swollen worms. The fear that owned him at that moment told him in no uncertain terms that there was corruption beyond physical death, that there were far worse things than being beaten or stabbed or strangled, that there was something inside him, something vastly important and unique, and Toddy needed it. He needed to stuff himself with it. He was willing to barter to get it.

He needs your participation and you know it. Just taking it is no thrill—it must be offered. You know that. You've always known that.

Flynn gripped the door handle and he could feel the terrible energy of the vehicle right up to his shoulder. He opened the door. As he did so, he took stock of what he was carrying, which was nothing. The only weapon he had was a pocketknife. If it came down to it, he would use it. It would be his final act of defiance. As the door swung open in his hand, a hot stink came wafting out at him, the stink of blood, oceans of it, as if there was a carcass in the backseat slowly bleeding out. It was the same awful, pervasive stench of death that had been haunting him for weeks and this was its source.

He didn't see Bones in there.

He sat down and touched the seats; they felt like warm meat beneath him. Under his fingertips, they were oily like the hides of snakes. They gave off an unpleasant, musky odor. Then the door was closed and he couldn't even remember shutting it. Toddy pulled away from the curb and Flynn noticed that there was blood at his ear and in his hair.

"You're bleeding," he said.

"In more ways than you know, little brother. What I need is a breath of fresh air."

As he drove, Toddy did not even watch the road; he stared at his passenger. Despite this, his course was straight and narrow, picking up speed as he made for Norton Avenue at the edge of town. Beyond that…Flynn didn't want to think about what was beyond that.

Toddy looked like shit.

There was no disguising it. It wasn't only the blood in his hair drying in uneven spikes nor the gauntness of his frame. His face looked like a living skull, the nose beginning to cave in, the skin sucking to the bone beneath like wrinkly yellowed parchment. It was even worse than it had been mere minutes before.

"Flynn, shit has been good for you. You're our friend and we like our friends to be happy," he said. "That's why we tweak their luck, we make their lives easy, we make the money fall into their hands and the grades come without trying; we make them a natural magnet for the hottest pussy and the most powerful allies. We make our friends succeed and that's something you can never take too lightly in a cold, hard world like this. You see what I'm saying?"

"You want something back. You want payment."

Toddy glared at him and Flynn felt something inside him shrink. "Not payment, fuckhead. A favor. Friends don't pay friends; they do 'em favors. We do you favors, you do us favors."

"What do you want?"

Toddy was opening up the Caddy on Norton Avenue as if his anger required speed. "See? I don't like that. I don't like when you fucking talk to me like that. It's like you're not my friend and when you're not my friend that means you're my enemy and that means I have to bury you and everything you ever fucking cared about."

Flynn swallowed. "And you said nothing would happen to me."

"But you got in the car anyway, didn't you?"

The truth of that was inescapable. Why had he gotten into the car? He told himself it was curiosity, but in his heart, it was more complicated than that. Maybe if he was going to fight them, he needed to know what they were, how they were, and why they were.

"I'm not giving you anything," Flynn said, feeling afraid, yes, but also defiant and pissed-off. "You better understand that right now."

"Oh really?"

"Yeah, fucking really."

Something hit him and he saw stars and he realized Toddy had cuffed him and so fast he hadn't seen it coming. There was blood on his mouth. He could taste it on his teeth. As his right hand began inching toward the knife in the pocket of his jean jacket, he wiped his mouth with the left. "Is this the point where I begin cowering and begging?" he snapped. "Well, fucking guess again. You want something, take me."

Toddy hit him again, but this time he saw it coming.

He's getting slower.

Somehow, the pain and the blood only served to strengthen him and harden his resolve. "You'll have to do better than that. I've been bullied and harassed by the very best."

Toddy brought his hand up again, but he dropped it at his side with a slow weariness. He was used up. He was drained. Flynn had a feeling that the longer he fenced with him and mouthed off, the weaker he would become.

"We're gonna take a ride, Flynn. Just you and me in this here street-hungry shark, which calls itself the El Dorado," Toddy said, his mouth grinning like a jagged knife cut in his pallid face. "Yes, sir, just a nice little drive in the country to distant places and while we drive, you're going to do some thinking. You're going to decide who lives and who dies. Just like the Grim Reaper, you're going to make a choice because life is all about choices, now ain't it?"

"Kiss my ass."

Toddy giggled about that as he opened up the El Dorado right there on Norton, going faster and faster until everything was a blur. The speedometer was pegged at 120 halfway across the dial, just as Chad had said. This was it. They were going fucking trick-or-treating. He saw the red luminous numbers that made up the other half of the dial—P12, P25, P75, P125, P250. And now Toddy was edging beyond 120 and Flynn felt something peculiar happening: the air had the consistency of gelatin and he was not sure he could have moved even if he wanted to. The moon was beginning to rise.

A full, fat harvest moon and now they were driving right at it and it became larger and larger, filling the windshield until it looked like an immense diseased eye and then…he wasn't sure, not exactly…there was a sensation of speed, of incredible velocities like being a bullet fired from a gun.

Then he blacked out.

For seconds, minutes. He could not be sure.

His eyes sought and found the speedometer and the needle was passing P125 and there was a sudden, grinding, deafening sound like a saw biting into sheet metal and the noise of it erupted and his ears felt like they would blow out. The pain was intense and he tried to scream, but it was so loud that he didn't know if he honestly had. This was followed by the popping sound Chad mentioned. He likened it to a cork blowing off a bottle of champagne and there was some truth in that, but to Flynn it was more of a booming sound like he'd heard when they opened the door to Danice McKerran's house…only much louder. It seemed that he heard it in the distance, as if it occurred many miles away, then the echoing noise of it rushed right at them and the car shook as its sound waves struck them like the aftershock of an earthquake.

Flynn went out cold.

When he came to, it felt like his guts were in a blender. It was like the worst puking flu he'd ever had, except that it passed in seconds, leaving him there lying back in the seat, gasping for breath as ice-cold sweat ran down his face.

"Sometimes it's a little rough," Toddy said, and it sounded like he was shouting from a faraway rooftop.

Flynn sprawled there, panting, sweating, feeling burning hot one moment and freezing the next. He saw his breath coming out in rolling white clouds. The air felt thick like slow-bubbling jelly around him. It was all as Chad had said right down to the numbness of his limbs and the pins-and-needles in his extremities to the crushing atmospheric pressure that paralyzed him. It felt like he was being squeezed between concrete plates. He wouldn't survive. He was going to die.

Toddy turned his head slowly, mechanically, and started speaking, only Flynn could not hear what he was saying. The air had gone liquid, it seemed. It had become a slightly phosphorescent greenish medium and as Toddy spoke, there was no sound, only a series of ripples shivering through it. Flynn felt them bounce off him—some ran down the length of his body, and others simply broke apart.

Then the atmospheric pressure was equalized and outside the windows there was darkness, unbroken darkness. Though he couldn't see anything out there, now and again something bumped against the Caddy or slid over its roof. He was aware of movement out there, of immense forms passing by, but he could not see them. Some of them made a low moaning sound and others passed with the creaking, rasping noise of dozens and dozens of tree branches rubbing together. Then he heard a swishing, gushing sound similar to that of a washing machine agitator spinning a heavy load...and a point of light like a blue ball sped at them. It passed over the car with incredible speed, but Flynn caught a glimpse of it—it looked like a pulsating blue eyeball that was nearly bigger than the El Dorado itself.

By that point, he wasn't smarting off anymore.

He kept his mouth shut because he knew he was completely at Toddy's mercy. The cockiness and anger and all the rest of it was gone. All that was left was...terror. He was a hollow vessel slowly filling with it. Everything he knew, everything he thought he knew, all those many things he had taken for granted on the insignificant ball of dust called Earth, had been turned upside down and inside out. The physics of what he deemed reality were inverted. He was experiencing everything that Chad had—right down to the weird ghostly trails his limbs left when he moved them.

"I guess we're here," Toddy said and although Flynn could hear his voice, it still seemed to come from a great, echoing distance. In fact, when he looked over at Toddy, he looked like he was about fifteen feet away; as if whatever this place was, it had stretched the volume of the car, tripling its dimensions.

Flynn wanted to ask him where they were, but something in him just didn't have the heart; he honestly did not want to know and would he have understood anyway? Toddy was looking worse than ever. Like an old man afflicted with black lung, each time he drew in a breath he had to get his entire body into the act, his chin lifting up, his shoulders arching back, his belly thrusting forward.

The rotten, black decayed stink coming off him had changed to a sharp, pungent chemical reek that reminded Flynn of the jars of formaldehyde in bio class where the frogs were stored. It seemed to steam out of him in plumes of nauseous vapor.

But the most startling thing—and the thing that made Flynn press himself up against the door—was that there was something moving at his throat…in fact, not one thing but many things. They were like black worms the thickness of thread. They stitched in and out of his neck like sutures, always on the move, making it look like Toddy's head had been sewn back on.

"Well, home sweet home," he said, attempting a low chortle that became a ragged cough. "Smell that air! Ain't nothing like it!"

The flesh of his face was wrinkled and corrugated, several of his teeth blackened and pitted with holes. He looked like a mummy from one of those black-and-white horror magazines, Creepy or Eerie. His left eye had turned turtle in its socket, the pupil staring up at the ceiling, drowning in an oozing pocket of brine. There were pink sores at his lips and a jagged crevice had split his forehead in half.

"You don't seem to be…saying much now," he said.

Flynn's throat was so dry he couldn't get up enough spit to let any words fly. His tongue felt so swollen it seemed to fill his mouth. He could not talk around it. His hands were balled into fists and he honestly did not know what to do, so he did nothing. He waited there, riven white with fear, his entire body tense like a flexing muscle. So when he finally did speak, no one was more amazed than he was.

"What…what the hell are you?"

Toddy laughed and then coughed some more. There was a rattling, fluid sound from inside his chest. "I'm a man with a plan, buddy boy, and you are definitely part of that plan."

"Where are you from?"

"I'm from here."

"Where's here?"

He coughed again and sputum sprayed from his lips and struck the windshield. It wriggled like maggots.

"Long way from Compton."

"Tell me," Flynn said. "Where is this place and what are you?"

"Why do you want to know so badly?"

"It's not like aliens visit Earth every day."

"Don't they?" Toddy scratched at the thread worms infesting his throat. "Besides, we're not exactly on Earth anymore, are we?"

Flynn trembled.

The stars had come out now, not just above but to both sides as if they were high above the world—whatever world they were on. As Chad had said, they were almost globular-looking, arranged in intricate geometric patterns and each larger than the sun back home. But for all that, they cast no visible light. They did nothing to illuminate the landscape. He remembered from physics that in order for something to be detected by the naked eye it either had to absorb or reflect ultraviolet radiation. This place did neither.

Toddy licked his lips and the sound was hideous. It was as if he were sucking a snake into his mouth. "Scared, eh? You're stronger than Chaddy was, I'll give you that much."

He reached over and gripped Flynn's wrist and even through the sleeve of his denim jacket, Flynn could feel the iciness of his grip. His hand was beaded like the skin of a collared lizard. The bones were beginning to stick out and they were almost like an interwoven lattice of fine sticks.

"Looks like we're attracting some of the local wildlife."

Flynn was now seeing things: a broken, battered landscape of jagged escarpments and mounds and towers that rose high up into a boiling sky that was sometimes green and sometimes purple, but scudded with strange brown clouds that crawled across the ceiling of the world, extending gaseous pseudopods and dragging themselves ever forward. Sometimes they were visible, sometimes they were obscured by immense tangled growths of vines that grew up into the sky, which seemed oddly convex. Just like looking through the window at Danice's, if he moved his head even slightly, everything blurred and his point of perspective was changed. He saw skittering things about the size of squirrels running up the vines. They looked like ants made out of red crystal.

But none of this was what Toddy was talking about.

He was referring to something much larger, something unbelievably vast that was moving in their direction. To call it an insect would have been like calling a saber-toothed tiger a kitty cat.

It was really hard to say if it was an insect as Flynn understood insects. It was more of a hybrid between a gargantuan bug and a deep-sea jellyfish. First off, the thing was blue—bright blue and skeletal as if it was made out of glowing neon tubing. At its posterior, there was an immense bell that seemed to expand and contract like the siphon of a squid, sucking in air—or what passed for air out there—and releasing it in a jet.

From the back end of the bell there trailed fifteen or twenty long ribbon-like tendrils that looked either like party streamers or the stinging tentacles of a Portuguese man-of-war. He couldn't possibly guess what their possible function was. The creature was easily the size of a tractor-trailer and the tendrils were three or four times that in length.

Amazing.

Utterly amazing.

Forward of the bell, there was a thorax shaped like a Victorian hourglass corset made of hundreds of constantly wiggling electric-blue cilia. From either side grew clusters of wiry legs that went from an indigo to a brilliant scarlet as the thing moved. Forward of that, at the anterior end, there was a head. It was immense, flattened out, and shovel shaped. Four wavering appendages like antennas or eyestalks protruded with diamond-shaped orbs at the ends. Were they eyes or another sort of sensory apparatus? It seemed likely, but who could really say?

Like the clouds above, it was crawling over the ether like a beetle on a laboratory slide, clinging to something, but what that was Flynn could not say. Despite its mass, it was silent, completely silent. It was basically transparent save for a bright blue exoskeleton—if that's what it was—and the blue outline of the bell itself. Inside the thorax and head, there were things he could not make out that were made of deeper blue, edging toward purple.

Now and again, it turned sideways so that he could get a good idea of its form, then it turned straight toward them again. The closer it got, the faster it moved like a train in the distance that seems to stand still until it's almost on you and then rockets forward with incredible, dizzying speed.

"Get us out of here!" Flynn told Toddy.

Toddy giggled. "Make me an offer first."

"An offer?"

"Yes. Tell me what you're going to give me when we get back. That's what I want to hear."

"You...fucking ASSHOLE!" Flynn screamed and then the thing was hovering right over them. He tensed, waiting for the car to be crushed like a pop can but that didn't happen. Up close, the creature was blindingly bright. He had to shade his eyes as it passed over them and as it did so, he heard its legs skittering over the roof and a series of electrical shocks made him jump and twist in his seat.

Then it was gone.

"We stay here long enough," Toddy said with dire amusement, "other things'll come. Worse fucking things."

Flynn's skin was crawling and his breath would barely come. It felt like there was immense pressure bearing down on his temples and a worse, equalizing pressure coming from inside his skull. It was building and building and as it did, it seemed as if his eyes would blow from their sockets. His thoughts were convoluted and irrational, one stumbling over another until nothing made sense and he wasn't sure if he was dreaming, awake or maybe in both states at the same time. He didn't know where he was or even who he was. And for one hysterical, stark moment, he was not even sure what he was.

"You gotta give us something, man," Toddy's voice said, bouncing around the inside of the car, ghostly and unearthly sounding. Flynn was nearly certain that if he reached out, he could have held one of those words right in the palm of his hand.

"Payment is due. Delivery to be made by your own hand."

Bright white lights were spiking inside Flynn's head like burning staffs, and he thought he heard himself scream with the agony of it all and a voice, maybe his own, was crying out in his mind for him to hang on, just hang on...a...little...bit...longer.

"Choose," Toddy said, and his voice was like a razor that slit Flynn's throat and a blazing sword that slid into his belly and then... and then—

34

A nd then he must have gone out cold. Because when he again opened his eyes, he saw Main Street, Compton. Home. There were the businesses lined up side by side like boxes: Schulman's Shoes and the A&P; the Rialto theater and Rexall Drugs; the A&W root beer stand and B.F. Goodrich, Jiffy Dry Cleaners and the Zephyr station at the end. Everything was closed up for the night, which meant it was late. He glanced at his watch and it was just after midnight. Time loss again.

In his head, memories of where he had been competed against one another. If there was an insane asylum in the universe—or out of it—he had just been there. It was hard to know what was fever-dream and what was reality; what was fantasy and what was cold hard fact. He could not be objective about any of it. His mind was a whirlpooling cyclone of hallucinations, some psychological and some horribly physical. What was and what had been were conflicting and confused. He felt much the way he had after visiting Danice's house.

"Where are you taking me now?" he finally asked, surprised, shocked even, at how old and brittle his voice sounded.

"Where you need to go," Toddy rasped.

He hung a right past Clyde's Barbershop and its ever-rotating barber pole. It was obvious where they were going. No, no, not here. Not to this fucking place. He reached out for the door handle so he could toss himself out, but the handle would not move. He wasn't getting out until the driver said so. Here was the industrial backwater of Compton: mills, machine shops, boarded-up warehouses, a couple of seedy-looking bars, a lumber yard…and the red brick National Fruit building. If Compton had an asshole, this was it. Everything here was old, run-down, buildings crumbling, storefronts boarded, the old railroad hotel leaning precariously to one side and looking as if it might fall. Toddy pulled the El Dorado into the alley next to the Fruit building and pulled to a stop in the grassy, leaf-blown courtyard. A bonfire was burning and a single shape stood before it, nodding its head.

Flynn heard a barely audible whimpering in his throat.

Toddy turned to him, grinning like a corpse three weeks in the ground. "Now you got to choose, my friend. There's nothing left but the choice itself."

In the moonlight flooding in through the windshield, Flynn could see that Toddy was in rough shape. The trip must have been very trying on him. He was a spongy, flyblown cadaver, black and green and gray. Yellow nets of grave fungus had grown up the side of his face and filled the triangular hollow where his nose had been. His left eye had slid out of its socket and congealed at his cheekbone like an especially slimy, rotting egg. His dark hair jutted up in spikes and clock springs, most of it missing, his skull showing through rents in his scalp. Huge flying insects like palmetto bugs crawled out of his mouth and nested in his hair. Corpse vapors hissed from him like open gas jets.

"Let's warm ourselves by the fire," he said, his voice nearly unintelligible with his tongue lying in his mouth like a well-fattened dead leech and his larynx collapsing in on itself.

Flynn nearly fell out of the car in his need to escape. He made it maybe four feet before his legs went weak and his head spun— then down he went. Down into the yellow, dew-sparkling grass that smelled so fresh, so clean. The dry heaves that had been wracking him in the car subsided and his mouth was no longer filled with sweet, pooling saliva. He breathed in and out.

You got into that car of your own free will, a voice in his mind whispered. Nobody forced you. Like most things in your life, shit-fer-brains, you brought that all on yourself. I told you—you were asking for it.

Using the car, he finally pulled himself to his feet. He hated the feel of it…like smooth, polished bone. After a few seconds, his head cleared. He was thinking again. He was on his turf now. Not fucking Planet X. In this place, physics worked with him rather than against him.

"Come over here," Toddy said. It was not a request.

"You heard him," Bones chipped in. "We need to talk fucking business. We do you favors, you do us favors. You know how it works. Now you make good on your end. That's what has to happen now."

Flynn stood there, feeling it all boiling inside him—fear and disgust, rage and apprehension, pure terror and purer anger. "Yeah…and what is it you want?"

"What you love best," Toddy said. "Nothing more, nothing less."

"Tomorrow night's Halloween. You bring your mommy to us or we'll come and get her and you won't like that."

There it was. Just as he'd suspected. They really thought he would lead his mom down here and hand her over to them, to two fucking drooling monsters from Planet X. The arrogance of that. They knew he wouldn't do it so they were throwing everything they could at him—bad luck, loss of social status, girls who loved him a month ago but wouldn't give him the time of day now, friends who turned out to be no friends at all. And if that wasn't enough, there was a little trip into the Twilight Zone at Danice's house and a worse trip into the Outer fucking Limits in the '59 Caddy. It should have broken him. Part of him (the weak and sniveling part that cared only for its own skin) wanted him to relent and give them what they wanted, but he was not about to. Denying them was the only real power he had. And giving Mom to them…ridiculous. Sometimes she could be bossy and downright belligerent when she didn't get her way, but that was just crust, a barrier against the cold, harsh, unforgiving world. Under that crust, she was soft as butter and sweet as whipped cream. Maybe she gave his dad a fair amount of trouble (as all wives do one way or another) but to him, her boy, her little man (as she'd called him when he was a little kid) she was a mama bear, she was all honey. They were more than mother and son; they were friends; they were allies; they were pals and compadres. Mom had nursed him through everything from chicken pox to the flu to a burst appendix when he was in seventh grade. When he broke his leg at fourteen and missed nearly an entire summer lying in bed, she was the one who made it fun, listening to music with him, watching movies, ordering pizza and making him French toast and grilling out hamburgers in the backyard and arranging parties so all the kids could come over even though he was laid up. She was the one who made him those absolutely rocking Fluffernutter sandwiches and would spend all day making her great aunt Luianna's orgasmically delicious spaghetti sauce. Though she was a folkie at heart, she always came home with new albums by Judas Priest and AC/DC, which she would crank loud enough on the stereo to scare the birds out of the trees. She would stay up all night long for monster-movie marathons and she would lie on the floor with him on cold January afternoons and read comic books. Maybe her heart belonged to her kitschy clown paintings and Peter, Paul, and Mary records, but her soul was all about Asteroids and Space Invaders and she could kick just about anybody's ass at them. She was golden. She was untouchable. And if Toddy and Bones thought they would lay a fucking hand on his ma...they were about to step into a world of shit.

"You won't get her now and you won't get her later," he said through clenched teeth, feeling like he could have single-handedly kicked the shit out of the Chicago Bears defensive line at that moment.

Toddy chuckled...but he was in such bad shape it sounded like he was gargling with oatmeal. He made a motion to Bones with one skeletal hand. The skin hung off it in loops like Spanish moss. Bones stepped away from the fire and started toward Flynn, who stood there waiting for it without really knowing why. He was about to be beaten to a pulp, taken apart and put back together in the worst possible way.

Here it comes, here it comes.

Bones looked like he had the first day Flynn had seen him. He was tall and mean-looking, his blond flattop crew cut bristling like porcupine quills. He wore greasy pegged jeans, studded engineer's boots, and a white T-shirt. He tossed the cigarette he'd been pulling on and came in for the kill. His eyes were blazing funeral pyres and the tattoos on his forearms, scorpion on the right and skull-and-crossbones on the left, suddenly looked luminous. They were evil ghosts that would own his soul.

"You're going to get in that car, you fucking pussy," he growled. "And we're going to take a ride to your house and when we get there, you're going to bring that cunt out to me or I'll bury both of you."

"Fuck you," Flynn said.

And as the words left his lips, he heard a thumping, then a

bumping in the car behind him. He whirled around and saw…he was not certain at first what it was. A writhing form, a spasmodic shape moving and jerking with agonal convulsions. Then he knew. It was Danice McKerran. He was certain of it when a cool pale blue luminosity lit up the backseat of the car and he saw her jerking and jumping back there, head whipsawing on her neck, back and forth, back and forth, her entire body twitching and quaking as if she were being electrocuted. And maybe she was because she looked like some kind of gruesome x-ray: her skeleton was glowing inside her, shining right through the skin, pulsating with a weird sparkling radiance. She was smoldering. Steam was pouring out of her as if she were boiling inside and when she slapped one hand against the window—the metacarpals and phalanges within lit like hot neon—it began to melt.

Flynn let out a wild, ragged cry and then he ran.

He ran like he had never run before in his life, legs pumping like pistons and heart pounding away in his chest. He vaulted past the '59 Caddy and across the courtyard and into the alley. He knew in his deepest, darkest fear that Bones would overtake him and bring him to ground, but that didn't happen because the hound of hell was called back at the last moment.

"Let him go," Toddy's voice called out. "We'll take it out in trade."

And this mere seconds before Bones' yellow and scabrous buzzard's claws would have dug into his back and opened him up. Flynn kept running, emerging from the alley that ran alongside the National Fruit building, looking back once and seeing the form of Bones standing beneath the lone streetlight at the corner. It was an image he would carry with him in the back of his mind for the rest of his life. But on that lonely, windy night before Halloween, he kept running until he was out of breath and his face was damp with sweat. He stood before the darkened A&W, panting, hunched over, hands on his knees. Exhilarated that he had escaped but knowing he only did so because that's what Toddy had wanted.

Let him go. We'll take it out in trade.

Standing there before the darkened root beer stand, he knew he hadn't escaped at all.

35

That night, the worst of his life up until that point, he did not sleep. In fact, he found it nearly impossible to attempt it because his eyes would not stay shut for any length of time. He lay there, listening to the chill October night, waiting for the wraith of Danice McKerran to come for him or for the sound of strangers entering the house, for his mother to start screaming down the hallway as things from beyond space and time took her off into the night. None of it happened, of course. The night was silent save for the sound of his dad snoring and a dog barking off and on a few streets over. The only other noise was the wind blowing along the eaves.

Even so, Flynn could not sleep.

He had to stay on guard.

He had to keep watching.

If he slept, that's when they would come and by the time he came out of it, it would be too late to do a thing. So he lay there, waiting, tensed, ready, terrified in the depths of his soul, an awful feeling of dread and impending doom tying him in knots.

When the sun started coming up, he closed his eyes. It was Saturday and he had no school and no work, so he slept until almost noon. When he awoke, it was a cool but bright sunny day. Outside his window, the yards were filled with leaves and carved pumpkins stood sentinel on porches.

It was Halloween.

36

"Your father and I are going on a dinner date. It'll be the first time in over a year," his mom said that evening in between handing out candy to the local ghouls and ghosties. "We shouldn't be home too late, though. What kind of movies are lined up tonight?"

Flynn was sitting on the couch, his eyes heavy as they had been all day. He grabbed the TV Guide, noticing with some amusement that his dad had torn off the address tag with his usual gusto and severed the cast of Hill Street Blues nearly in half. "Let's see… we've got War of the Worlds and…this one sounds good: Children Shouldn't Play with Dead Things. After that, a couple of those teenage movies: I Was a Teenage Werewolf and I Was a Teenage Frankenstein."

"Ha!" Mom said. "I saw both of those in high school at the drive-in when they were new."

"Makes you feel kind of old, eh?"

She glared at him. "It makes me feel no such thing, smarty-pants." She sat down by him. "So what's on your busy social schedule tonight? Let me guess. You'll sit around and watch TV until around eight, then you'll brood for a few hours, watch TV again, then go to bed. That sound about right?"

"Well, don't blame me. It wasn't my idea to come here."

"Don't be like that. You know we had to."

"Yeah, I know."

He sighed. It wasn't anyone's fault. He'd been over this ground a hundred times in his head and in the final analysis he knew that his mom and dad did what they had to do to put food on the table. The only true perpetrator of anything was himself and his innate weakness that led him to make all the wrong choices. And now it was all about to come home.

Mom went to the door and answered the cries of "TRICK OR TREAT!" and then sat back down again. "I worry about you."

"You don't have to."

"Yes, I do. You have no idea. But I have to."

"I'm doing okay," he told her, trying to calm her fears. "This is my senior year. In six months or so I'll graduate and that'll be that. I'll go away to college and my high school years will seem silly."

"They're not silly. They're important."

He wasn't buying that. "Really? Do you or Dad chum around with any of the old gang from high school?"

"No."

"See? It's all infantile stuff. When you're at the bottom of the pecking order like me, there's nowhere to go but up. The popular kids? When they graduate, there's nowhere to go but down."

"Well, listen to you. The sage of the ages. Mr. Wisdom himself."

"It's true and you know it."

She handed out more candy and came back. "Maybe it is true, but you have to enjoy the fantasy while it's there. You only get one shot at being a teenager."

He grunted. "And we can be thankful for that."

She didn't like what he was saying but he wasn't going to back down on it because he knew that, essentially, he was right. High school was bullshit. It didn't prepare you for the world. It didn't prepare you for anything. The only thing you came away with was the sure conviction that people were generally selfish, narcissistic assholes under the skin who worshiped only what they saw in the mirror. Watch me strut about, I'm popular and socially desirable. Witness me preen the lovely feathers of my letter jacket and strut about in my short cheerleading skirt. I am pretense. I am a spectacle. It's all stagecraft, of course, because inside I'm just as unsure and fractured as you are, that's why I belittle you and treat you like shit because the more I step on you, the higher it lifts me up. But please don't tell anyone I'm a compete douche bag. He grinned at his pessimistic view of high school mentality. But he didn't grin too long because it was all too close to the truth.

"Boy, are we going through the candy tonight," Mom said.

He could tell by the look on her face that the time for clever banter was over with. She had something very serious she wanted to broach and he waited for it.

"Flynn," she said, "are you on drugs?"

He didn't mean to, but he burst out laughing. "What?"

"I said, are you on drugs? Are you a junkie?"

"A what?"

"You heard me."

"No, Mom, I'm not a junkie. Why would you ask me something like that?"

If he found it amusing, she certainly did not. "It's not funny, Flynn. You're tired all the time. Stressed out. Moody. You cry out in your sleep. You don't seem to have any ambition to do anything. You don't socialize with anyone."

"Stranger in a strange land," he told her, thinking of the title of a science-fiction novel he'd read in tenth grade. "I'm not a junkie. I don't even smoke pot." Not exactly true, but it was what she needed to hear. "I don't do drugs, so relax."

She sighed. "The reason I ask is because I've seen it before. When your uncle Ritchie came back from Vietnam, he was using heroin. I watched it nearly destroy him. He ended up in a clinic. In fact, he ended up in a clinic twice. The second time was in prison."

Flynn had only met him a couple of times. He seemed like a pretty okay guy. The black sheep of his mother's somewhat strict Italian family, but a pretty funny guy.

"Well, he straightened out. He's doing good."

"Sure. After six years on the needle and five years in prison for running a chop shop in Milwaukee and selling stolen cars. Now look at him. He's down in Miami, spending money like it's water, probably involved in something illegal, and living with a twenty-year-old stripper. And him at forty-five."

"Sounds good to me."

"Flynn!"

"I'm just kidding."

She went off to hand out more candy and he took her absence as an opportunity to slip upstairs to his room. He wasn't up to the third degree. Maybe tomorrow, but definitely not today. Not on Halloween. He lounged around for a few hours and listened to music. Then there was a knock at the door. It was Mom and she was all dolled up in her black sequined dress and gold chains.

"Well, look at you," he said.

"We're leaving in a few minutes. There's frozen pizzas in the freezer if you're hungry." Shoulders slumping, she walked over and gave him a big hug and planted a kiss on his cheek. "My little fella's all grown up." There was a tear in her eye and she wiped it carefully away before her makeup ran. Her arms around him felt really good. He felt stronger—like he could do anything. She smelled like lilacs and coconut shampoo. "I hope I didn't get too heavy on you before," she said, "but, hey, I worry. It's my job. It's what I do."

"Nothing to worry about, Mom. Tomorrow night I'll probably be hanging out with Daryl, so my social life will be fine."

She hugged and kissed him again.

"Stop it, lady," he said. "What will your husband think?"

They both laughed.

She stepped to the door, opened it, paused. "I should be back in time for the teenage monster movies. I can regale you with amusing stories of a 1950s teenager hanging out at the drive-in. So keep a candle burning, chum." She dropped him a wink. "See ya then."

When the door closed, he felt chills run up his spine and over his arms. Something inside him seized up and his mouth went dry. As he watched his parents pull out of the driveway and take off down the street in the Olds Ninety-Eight, there were tears in his eyes. Mom, he thought. Oh, Mom. He sat on the bed, filled with conflicting emotions. He kept thinking about how she looked when she was standing in the doorway. The smile on her face. The love in her eyes. The wink she dropped him.

It was the last time he ever saw her.

37

NOW

By 11:30 that night, he couldn't take it. Marjorie—bless her kind heart—was still in denial and still refusing to leave. Nothing he said made any sense to her and she was treating him in a very polite, very understanding, very condescending way, like he was possessed of dangerous delusions. What could he do? What could he say? In thirty minutes it would be fucking Halloween and then they would come. He was willing to stand and fight...but not with her there. The idea that something might happen to her took the fight out of him. It weakened him and deteriorated his resolve.

He was trying to go easy on the booze so his head could be as clear as possible, but the ashtray was filling fast, which always annoyed the shit out of Marjorie. But tonight, like everything else, she was willing to overlook it because her husband—poor thing— was on the verge of mental collapse.

"We'll stand together," she kept telling him. "Then midnight will come and pass and you'll see there's nothing to worry about."

This was her standard stout-hearted, level-headed stalwart speech, but each time it passed her lips as the clock ticked closer to All Hallows' Eve, he was certain that there was less conviction in it. Something was beginning to take hold of her. Maybe it was her well-tuned woman's intuition and maybe it was simple doubt— sure, it's just teenage trauma channeling itself as the boogeyman and he's going to need therapy...but what if it isn't? What if what he says is true? What then?

He sat in his recliner watching her, waiting for her to crack because he knew it was coming and when it did she'd be that much easier to deal with. Her stubborn streak would melt and her rationality would become impotent in the face of the darkness that—she knew—was making ready to reveal itself.

About 11:45, when it felt like his stomach was filled with tacks, his Nokia rang and he winced. A sour nausea bubbled in his stomach and crept up the back of his throat. He looked over at the phone as if it were a black widow spider that he was contemplating picking up.

"Are you going to answer it?"

He looked over at her with red-rimmed eyes. "Do you really want me to?"

"Yes."

She didn't even hesitate. That meant she still did not believe. Not all the way. Not yet.

"All right." He pushed the button. "Yeah?"

"Do what's right, Flynn. Your time is almost up. Do you hear me?" Chad said. "Do you fucking hear what I'm saying to you?"

"I hear you. I'm not letting them have her."

"Then they'll take all of us, you sonofabitch! We'll all go into the trunk and we'll—"

He shut the phone off and put it in his pocket. He looked over at Marjorie. "That was Chad. I think you know what he wanted."

She was chewing her lower lip now. Classic Marjorie indecision. "Flynn...this is crazy. You know it is." That was what she said and he could hear it beneath her words—a mounting dread. She didn't believe and yet she did. Something in her was ready to panic and she was fighting it down with everything she had.

She can feel it. She can sense it growing around her.

He felt it himself, something cold and inexplicable threading into the very marrow of his bones and filling them with crystals of ice.

"Flynn, dammit!" she cried suddenly. "If this is bullshit, just say so! If this is all a joke or a delusion, just admit it already before I lose my fucking mind!"

Leaves blew against the picture window and she jumped. He didn't, but his heart bumped in his chest.

"It's real, baby. That's why I want you to leave. There's still time."

She sat there, eyes flicking about in their sockets, teeth worrying her lower lip. She brushed her hands against her legs, folded her arms, scratched at her scalp, interlocked her fingers, then let her hands fall limp into her lap like dying blossoms.

"I'm scared," she said. "I'm really scared."

"That's why you need to go. They can't stop you from leaving... at least, I don't think they can...but I have to stay. They'll be coming and I'd rather you weren't here. This is my problem. I created it. I let it happen. And only I can stop it."

He was no hero; the idea of meeting them and fighting it out—if such a thing were truly possible—terrified him. Yet, he knew it had to be done. He'd been running from this his entire life and now it was time to face it.

"You have to get out of here," he emphasized.

She shook her head. "This is fucking insane and you know it. Even if this is true, what good will it do? Why wouldn't they just grab me down the road? Or in Rockford or Beloit? If they're as powerful as you say they are, they can probably do anything they want."

"No," he said, grasping her by the shoulders. "It doesn't work that way. They could do anything they want, but there's no thrill in it for them. They need me to offer you. They need me to hand over what I love most. They need me to destroy myself. They need me to humiliate myself, debase myself, degrade myself...that's the thrill of it. That's how they exploit us—by giving us what we want and making us pay the most horrible price imaginable. A price that damns us, fills us with self-loathing and disgust. Then we're easy to manipulate because our ethics and morals have crashed and we're barely human. We're like horses they ride to death for sheer amusement."

"I can't...abandon you." There were tears in her eyes.

"It's not like that. If they can't get at you, I'll be stronger and I need to be strong. Stronger than I've ever been before." He kissed her. "Now I want you to get in your car and drive out of town. Call me when you're well away. If I don't answer within a couple rings, call 911 and get them over here. Tell 'em...tell 'em you were on the phone with me and somebody was breaking in. That'll get 'em moving."

She was caught between the real need to flee and the need to stand at his side. "This isn't right, me taking off."

"But it is. This is something I have to do alone. I can't fight them with you here. I have to face my past alone. It's the only way." He held her in his arms, squeezing her tight, his love for her at that moment nearly overwhelming him. "Hurry. We have to get you out of here."

It was 11:53.

38

Marjorie spent about thirty long seconds throwing some things into a bag. She still didn't want to leave, but Flynn did not give her time to think about it. That was the important thing. Give her the old bum's rush before the dust settled and she had time to reason things out. When she had her bag, he pulled her out the back door and dragged her out to the driveway. Her eyes filled with tears but he got her into her little Nissan.

"Flynn…" she started.

"Go!" he said.

He shut the door and she turned the key. Click, click, click. The battery was dead. He went through the usual bullshit. She popped the hood and he made sure the cables were connected to the terminals and there was no corrosion. Everything was fine and he was wasting time. They tried his SUV next. It was just as dead.

It was 11:57.

They were out of options.

Of course you're out of options. You spent all day trying to talk sense into Marjorie but she wouldn't listen. Nothing you said convinced her of anything but the fact that you needed a good, long rest away from Compton. And by the time she accepted…well, it was too fucking late, wasn't it?

Together, they ran back through the yard, leaves blowing around them in whirlwinds. It was a wild night. Chill, gusty, the moon like a grinning white mouth, and the wind moaning like the voices of the dead crawling up out of their graves. Even when they got up on the back porch, they had to hold on to each other so it didn't blow them back out into the yard. Tree limbs were creaking and leaves skittered over rooftops. Finally, after some fumbling, they got inside, pulling the door shut behind them.

He locked it, threw the dead bolt.

"Now what do we do?" Marjorie asked, the terror making her voice so fragile he thought it might shatter.

"Go upstairs and make sure all the windows are locked," he said as he raced away, double checking to see that the front door was locked and bolted. He went through the downstairs making sure every window was secure. It was. Weapons. That's what he'd been thinking about all day. He had a golf club, a baseball bat, and an axe. That was it except for a few hammers out in the garage and the cutlery in the kitchen. He wished he had a gun but Marjorie would never allow one in the house.

Not that, in the final analysis, it would do him much good.

"Everything's locked," Marjorie said when she got back downstairs. "What now?"

A voice in Flynn's head wanted to say something dramatic like, Now we pray. Was that from a movie? He couldn't remember. His thoughts were buzzing around in his head like wasps.

"They're going to come soon," he told her. "I don't think they'll try to sneak in. I think they'll come right to the front door and demand what's theirs. That's how they'll do it."

"I'm calling the police," she said, grabbing her cell.

"Go ahead. And five minutes after they leave, we'll have visitors."

He ran out to the garage, grabbing the baseball bat and the axe.

Then the phone rang.

This time it was the landline. Marjorie looked at Flynn and he could see there was no longer any doubt: she believed. The terror was real and it was etched onto her face. She gave him a desperate look, seeming to plead with him not to answer the phone.

He picked it up off its cradle. He didn't bother saying hello and there was no point. What came over the line was something like a needle scratching over a dusty record, a sound of wind and thunder and screams, the buzzing of hornets, and something like a car crash—all of it punctuated by growling and slurping sounds like the big bad wolf licking its chops in an old cartoon. All of it played at deafening levels. And was he completely losing his mind or did he hear something like a military induction ceremony—in his own voice—buried in the mix? I, Flynn Connors, do solemnly swear that as I have been given, I shall give, as has been offered and accepted,

I, too, shall offer with hopes of acceptance. I shall lay my bloody offering at the feet of those—

He threw the phone against the wall and when it hit the floor, it kept ringing. It couldn't possibly, but it did. His cell started ringing. So did Marjorie's. Whereas her ringtone had been the perfectly harmless "Walking on Sunshine" by Katrina and the Waves, now it was the macabre piano of Chopin's funeral march. She tossed it away with a scream.

The lights began to flicker.

There was a groaning sound from beneath their feet as if the house was about to split in half. About the time it stopped, the knocking at the front door began. It was slow, booming, and insistent.

Marjorie had clasped her hands to her ears now and she was shaking her head back and forth. "No, no…no," she kept saying, trying to deny the reality of what was happening.

Flynn grabbed her by the arm and she violently pulled away from him. She looked like she was capable of just about anything at that moment. In fact, he thought she would scratch his eyes out given half a chance.

"Marjorie! Marjorie," he shouted at her. "Snap out of it! Do you hear me? Snap out of it!"

She let out a cry and then nodded her head.

The pounding was still coming from the front door, only now it was delivered with more force and the door panel began to split. A fist wouldn't have been capable of making that sound. Maybe a sledgehammer or a battering ram. But it wasn't the only thing they were hearing.

Now there was something else.

Something even worse.

A gnawing.

It was coming from outside, like mice chewing at woodwork or rats clawing inside narrow walls. It seemed to be coming from everywhere at once, as if something was trying to gnaw its way into the house. The only question was: Would they eat their way into the house before the front door came down? Or would it be the other way around?

Flynn grabbed the phone from the floor, but it was still playing the same noise and gibberish. They were on their own. Absolutely on their own.

"Flynn!" Marjorie cried out. "Look!"

As impossible as it was, the gnawing was getting louder until it seemed he could hear nothing else. In the living room, plaster dust was falling from the wall. Now there was an opening and he saw a shiny, black, hook-like tendril push through and waver about like the antenna of a slug. It withdrew and there was another bout of fresh gnawing. A huge crevice appeared and a humped, worming shape pushed itself through. It was hard to say what it was at first, only that it filled him with a crawling repulsion. It was about three feet long and made of the same black material as the tendril, like wet neoprene rubber. The creature had a thick, muscular vermiform body, sharply ribbed, and was as big around as a football midline, tapering to a sharp worm-like tail at the rear. It moved with an inching motion. At the anterior end, its body swept upward into the tendril he had first seen coming through the wall. And as he watched, the tendril opened, splitting into three stalk-like prongs, each of them lined with stubby, serrated teeth.

"FLYNN!" Marjorie cried out. "FLYNN! PLEASE!"

She was tugging at him by the elbow, trying to pull him back… but like the thing he'd found in his garage, it was as fascinating as it was repellent.

Now it was moving toward him, inching over the hardwood floor with a moist suckering sound. It had closed its prongs into a single elongated tendril again and as it did so, eyes popped open like bubbles. They were serous orbs, deathly yellow, and seemed to lack anything like a pupil. There were six of them. Three to each side of the tendril's base arranged in vertical lines. Against its dark oily skin, they looked bright like the running lights of a freighter seen by night.

Marjorie cried out again because three more of the creatures had gnawed their way into the living room and others were definitely on their way. The front door was split wide open and he could see a hunched-over form standing out there that he did not believe was either Toddy or Bones.

But something else.

Something called down from another place to seed fear and

anxiety here on this night of nights.

The creature before them closed its eyes and the tendril opened much like a thumb, forefinger, and middle fingers spreading apart. Its teeth were glistening.

Marjorie grabbed a pillow and threw it at the thing. The triple prongs came together like scissors and cut the pillow neatly in half. Two more creatures were coming from the kitchen, their egg-like eyes glaring with a toxic, flat hatred.

The front door was hanging by a single hinge. He saw a malformed hand like a crimson, flaccid starfish reaching in.

The creatures were coming through the walls everywhere and Marjorie was going out of her mind, starting first in one direction, then turning and starting in another. But there was nowhere to run. Nowhere but upstairs. He grabbed her by the hand and towed her in that direction but one of the things waited at the foot of the steps. Flynn didn't even think. He swung the axe at it with everything he had. One of the creature's prongs was sheared off, then the axe was buried in its body. Despite its muscular appearance, it was unbearably soft and spongy. It moved away from them, making a whistling sound, leaving a trail of fluid as dark as ink. It made it maybe four feet…then it erupted. There was no other word for it. Its skin went flaccid, then sheared open with a gushing expulsion of slime and globby liquid anatomy.

Breathless, stunned, Flynn and Marjorie raced side by side up the steps. When they got to the top, he looked down and saw what appeared to be dozens of them marching toward the stairs.

It was pointless, he knew, to try and hide in one of the bedrooms. The creatures would get up the stairs and they would gnaw through the doors. Holding Marjorie's hand, he got her into the master bedroom and then out onto the balcony. This was the only way out. Not ten feet below there was a flat roof overhang above the kitchen. He went first, landing solidly, the impact hurting his ankles. Marjorie followed and he broke her fall. Then they lowered themselves to the ground, which wasn't too bad. He expected the yard to be filled with the creatures, but it wasn't.

They ran into the wind, leaves blowing around them, and for some reason, he tried his SUV again. Miraculously, it started.

It shouldn't have. This is a fucking trap. I know it's a fucking trap.

He suffered a moment of indecision as to whether they should risk driving it. He originally had no intention of even trying...then the idea jumped into his head and he was compelled to try.

Was it his idea or a thought placed in his head?

"Flynn!"

Marjorie was already climbing in. The thing that had been standing outside the door was coming through the yard...he could not see it clearly but it was humpbacked and swollen, vaguely man-like in form but with a jerky, hobbling gait. He could not have sworn that it had only two legs.

Then they were both in the SUV with the doors locked and he was backing into the alley. The manlike shape was following and as the headlights swept over it, Flynn caught a glimpse of a creature with shivering folds of black corrugated skin that sparkled as if they were embedded with sequins. It didn't like the light and pulled membranous webs of itself over a greasy, nodding hood that might have been a head.

More of the slug-like creatures fell from the sky, thudding against the roof. Several others tumbled off the hood and one investigative creature tried unsuccessfully to climb the windshield. The wipers knocked it free.

Flynn drove away down the alley and squealed into the street, flooring it.

"Get us out of here," Marjorie said. "Just get us the fuck out of here."

39

They were driving and neither of them were talking. At this juncture, there was nothing to say and no way to apply any real world logic to what they had just been through. Flynn realized after a few minutes that he was feeling dopey. Was he that tired out from their escape or was it something else entirely? He had an urge for a strong cup of black coffee. Since he lacked that, he lit a cigarette, hoping that the nicotine would wake him up inside. Every second made him feel drowsier, almost drugged.

"Are you all right?" Marjorie asked as he swerved in the road.

"Sure, fine."

But he wasn't fine. Something was going on. Something was happening here. He felt positively narcoleptic as if he might nod off at any moment. He had to get them out of there, though. He had to get them out of this town before...he couldn't seem to remember. Before something.

Aren't you getting sick of this shit? a voice said inside of his head, and he couldn't be sure if it was his voice, Chad's or maybe even Toddy or Bones or maybe a combination of them. How long do you think you can keep going on like this? Driving around, running away from your own past? Sooner or later, you have to face it. And here's something to think about: maybe facing it wouldn't be as bad as you think.

He tried to shake it from his head. He lit another cigarette, determined to quit for good when this was all over. The SUV was filling with smoke and Marjorie was waving it away, saying something to him about why he was slowing down and he heard his voice tell her that he wasn't about to pile them up now.

The urge to nod off was getting stronger and he had to force his eyes open. Jesus, what the hell was wrong with him? It made no sense. He should have been tense, terrified, agitated...but he was none of these things. He felt peaceful and easy with things. If he hadn't known better, he would have thought he didn't have a care in the world.

See how easy it can be? Why go on fighting when it's so simple to throw in the towel and give in. Don't listen to that woman. Just take her where she needs to go to see the people that are waiting for her. What can be easier?

"No," he said under his breath. "I know what you're doing. I know what your game is. You can't make me do something I don't want to do."

The wind was blowing hard, making the SUV rock, and Marjorie kept asking questions. She wanted to know why he was talking to himself. Funny, but he heard fear in her voice. He was so relaxed that such a thing seemed inconceivable.

"They're...they're trying to mess with me. They're trying to take over my mind," he explained to her. "But they can't pull one over on me. I won't allow it."

She kept grabbing him, shouting at him, saying so many things that made no sense whatsoever. She was becoming hysterical so he told her in a calm and soothing voice how it was. How he had been called home like a sailor returning from a long voyage because he was needed. Now that he had seen the world, it was time to come back and pay tribute to those who made it possible. At this point, as she cringed away from him, he began to laugh with a high, demented sound, telling her how he had been summoned back by his old friends who demanded payment and that's why they had returned and that's why he let her fall in love with the town and the house and settle in like a hen brooding over an egg because she was needed, oh God yes, needed by those who had given and would now take. For she—at this point her name escaped him—had been brought back for one reason and that was to be given in expiation as a blood offering—

Look how she squeals and sobs and cries out that you have lost your mind! Her eyes are opened for the first time since birth and she sees the world for what it is. Its anatomy has been laid raw and bare to her as she herself shall soon be laid most raw and most bare.

Flynn was having trouble driving now because the woman was

pitching a fit, clawing at his reaching hands and slapping at his face. It was no good. He would have to pull over so he could fix the bitch good and proper. When he brought her to the place of sacrifice, he wanted some fight left in her, yes—a bit of sport after all—but he also wanted her submissive, served on a platter, well-tied, well-greased, an apple in her lovely mouth.

How's that for eats, boys?

As he slowed down, hugging the curb, the woman did the most curious and painful thing. She picked up the cigarette he had dropped and she jammed the glowing end right into his cheek. He cried out and let go of the wheel, popping the curb and sideswiping a tree.

"Marjorie?" he said.

And she promptly slapped him across the face.

40

Before he could say anything, her door was open and she was half jumping/half falling out, crawling away through the grass of someone's lawn as fast as she could go, scrambling off like a spider frightened from its sleepy midday ruminations.

She didn't understand.

She just didn't know.

The faster and farther you tried to run, the more you tangled yourself in their web and fell into their arms. He called out to her, but she kept going, finding her feet and sprinting flat out down the sidewalk.

He told her to stop, to slow down, to let him explain because he was the only one that really could. But she kept going. He went after her. When he caught up to her, he would tackle her and hold her down. He had to make her understand that things were happening. They were happening right now. Didn't she see how the shadows were different and how the stars were rearranging themselves in the sky? Moving and shifting and rumbling as the world went out of phase and then reassembled itself?

"MARJORIE!" he shouted. "YOU HAVE TO STOP! YOU'RE ONLY MAKING THINGS WORSE!"

He kept after her, the thoughts in his head colliding like atoms as he tried to make sense of what was and what was not. If only he could catch her before something terrible happened, if only he could make her realize that what she thought she knew was not true. That things were being played now by an entirely new set of rules.

Main Street.

It was all lit up, lots of neon, stores open and ready for business… except as Flynn walked past them, there wasn't a single person in any of them. Ahead, Marjorie had stopped. She was realizing now that there was something desperately wrong with the Compton she was seeing just as she was realizing that the stars overhead did not look right. They were huge and pulsating, arranged in geometric patterns that were so complex they taxed the brain. Sometimes, it almost seemed as if they pulsed to the beat of your heart. Poor Marjorie. Stranger in a strange land, a germ on a Petri dish being watched, always watched by…by intellects vast and cool and unsympathetic. Flynn giggled at that. What was that? Had he read it somewhere? Seen it in a movie? No matter because there was truth in it. She was realizing it now. Just as she was realizing the wisdom of the shopworn cliché that she was definitely not in Kansas anymore (or anywhere else men had ever mapped for that matter). This was Compton, yes, from foundation to rooftop…but not the Compton she knew, but one as imagined on Planet X, pulled from Flynn's own memories. The makers of this anti-Compton had done their best…but somehow, things were off kilter, grotesque, and out of sorts. Yes, his memories but as transcribed by them, the out-worlders, the alien monsters known as Toddy and Bones. She was discovering (as Chad had) that things were not so ordered in this Compton, not so…tidy in many ways.

Flynn could see it himself—everything was too crowded, too narrow, too tall, too leaning, too everything.

They pulled this from your mind or Chad's and they did a pretty good job of it for the most part…except they don't see things as you do. Three dimensions are great, but they see beyond that.

He had the distinct feeling that he was only seeing part of the town, the part his limited vision and limited mental acuity would allow him to see. But there was more, much, much more, but his senses were limited to five.

Marjorie was clutching a light post now, shaking and sobbing.

She had never seen this Compton before. This was not the Compton of now, but the Compton of 1981. Amused, scared, disoriented, feeling as if his atoms would soon fly apart, Flynn stared up at a giant wooden boot hanging above him. Yes, Pearson's Cobbler Shop. And down the way, Chip's Diner and the A&P. Across the street, Montgomery Ward, the old Kresge building, and Rip's

Sinclair Station with the giant green dinosaur on the roof. As he kept walking, he saw the old Woolworths. He peered in the door and at the back he could see the fish tanks where you could buy goldfish and tetras for your tank. He could hear the bubblers. There was the counter and the red vinyl stools waiting empty. He could smell the ghosts of burgers and fries.

He stepped outside again and passed Freedberg's Mobil. The red Pegasus still spread its wings over the door as it had when he was a teenager. Next door to it was the associated Red Horse Diner. Down the way he even saw A&W. He knew in reality (in the real-world Compton, that was), that there was a car wash now where A&W once stood and Freedberg's and the Red Horse had been demolished to put in a new sparkly Farm Bureau Insurance. Montgomery Ward had been broken up into shops and where the Sinclair Station had stood in 1981, there was now a parking lot.

Still…to see it all again, the way he remembered it…amazing. It nearly took his breath away.

Marjorie saw him coming and shook her head back and forth, whimpering.

"Don't run away," he said. "Don't wander off. You can get in all kinds of trouble here."

She started moving, slowly backing away down the sidewalk and he wished she'd stay put so he could explain where they were and how this place could be, and particularly how time and space could be manipulated by entities like Toddy and Bones as easily as a man manipulated dry kindling and matches to make his fire.

"Marjorie…wait…just wait," he called out to her, keeping the panic from his voice so he did not alarm her and make her bolt. "Just listen to me, please. I won't hurt you. I only want to help."

She looked at him and screamed.

Only she wasn't looking at him, he realized, but at something behind him. In fact, something behind and above him. He saw it, too. Some of the wildlife of Planet X were intrigued by this facsimile of Compton. He saw a swarm of phosphorescent creatures passing high above the streets in a crackling field of pink static electricity. They looked like moths, but with the wings of bats. And above the rooftops something about the size of a two-story building towered. A chimerical creature, part jellyfish and part squid. Its head or mantle was oblong and made of a quivering transparent gelid material, storms of blue, red, and purple lights exploding within. Each time they did, he could see an intricate network of segmented veins. Beneath the mantle itself, there were countless flowing diaphanous indigo sheets of tissue that resembled butterfly wings stacked up like books. They fluttered and flowed. And beneath those, coiling delicate tentacles limned violet. All these appendages moved with slow, fluid grace as if they were underwater.

It was a lovely creature really, a living kaleidoscope of chromatic vibrancy.

Beyond it, approaching stealthily was something that appeared to be covered in metallic green scales. It had huge pink-yellow eyes like glowing sodium lights seen through fog.

Marjorie turned and ran and a shape stepped out of a seam of darkness to claim her. It was Bones. He grabbed her by the arm and forced her down to her knees. She gasped and whimpered but it did her no good. The offering had been received and he'd never let her go now.

"Atta boy, Flynn," he said in an evil, thick voice. "You wanted and you got. We wanted and you delivered. See how easy it was? See how fucking easy it all was?"

Easy?

Had it really been easy?

Flynn's head wasn't right and he knew it…still, none of it was easy. He looked over at Bones—scuffed engineer's boots, motorcycle jacket, pegged jeans, hair thicker now and swept back in a greasy duckbill, sneering reptilian grin on his face—and he thought about what he had lost even as some gluttonous, greedy, sociopathic voice told him in an oily voice about how much he was about to gain.

"A month from now you'll be a rich man in Pebble Beach or Pago Pago," Bones told him, "sipping rum punch as a couple swimsuit models fight over who gets to sip from your dick. Healthy, happy, well-fed and well-fucked, leggy college girls climbing all over you because you're a fucking billionaire with a yacht, a beach house and a private jet. A fucking rock star who never loses."

And yes, Flynn knew exactly that's how it would be. And it would start with winning the largest lottery in history, which would grow through shrewd investments into a pile that would make shitheads like Mark Zuckerberg look like chump change.

It's gonna happen. It's beginning right now. Ten years from now you'll be in your sixties but you'll look like you're thirty.

A cloudy grayness filled his head and he swooned, going down to his knees on the sidewalk. Everything was spinning and he was about to go out cold. It was only Marjorie's agonized shriek that brought him out of it and made the world swim back into view.

She wasn't screaming because of what Bones was doing to her.

It was because Bones was changing.

His form rippled like water, first narrowing, then filling out and flowing like dark jelly. His blonde hair turned white and fell out. One of his ears curled up and blackened like a dead orchid. His face collapsed into a sunken death mask, then pushed back out again, becoming something totally alien. His entire body quivered and quaked, oozing and liquid like a bubbling cauldron of flesh stew and gurgling fat. It sucked into itself and then it opened like a flower, budding, germinating, sporing in a storm of yellow fuzz.

It's showing itself, Flynn thought. It's finally showing its true self. This is Bones. This is the real Bones. This is what has been hiding under the skin the entire time.

Standing over Marjorie, there was a hunched-over figure like a bloated, pulpous toadstool wearing a monk's black habit, only ragged and webby and viscidly alive like a living greasy pelt. Its head was a pulsing oval mass with a crest of fine white spines like whale bone toothpicks, the face blubbery and shifting, the lips swollen obscenely into a pale fleshy ring like the sucker of an octopus but big around as a mason jar. It sucked in and out, fine hairs webbing it together, gray saliva gushing out with each breath…if it was indeed breathing at all.

It had no nose, only a vertical ridge, a bony excrescence. Eyes that were milky and yellow glistened from narrow slits that looked like gashes in the pulsating pallid face.

Marjorie screamed again because Bones was holding her with a three-fingered hand like a catcher's mitt. It was covered in sores and carbuncles the size of nickels. Whenever she moved, white threads like living cobwebs came out of the hand and knotted her up so that she could not move.

The creature held up its other hand, palm extended, to stay

Flynn from any foolish heroics. It was nothing like the other one—it was fine and slender, the fingers ending in suction cups like the toes of a tree frog.

Slowly, very slowly, making a sound like a rooting hog, it dragged Marjorie off into the shadows.

Flynn called out her name, but his voice was weak and wheezing. They had done something to him. He felt drugged, deadened, numb from head to toe. His limbs were like rubber. He tried to give chase but he was awkward, stumbling and useless. He felt the way a spider must feel when a hornet stings it. Filled with toxic venom, the world tilted this way and that.

The Bones-thing had dragged Marjorie into the shadows near Rexall Drugs, and as he tried to follow, he found a long black corridor that stretched for hundreds of feet. At the end there was light and he saw Bones pulling Marjorie into it.

Fumbling, drunken, he gave chase even as the strength ran out of him and he felt himself plummeting into unknown Stygian depths.

41

He was sinking. He was drowning in mud, sucked into quick-sand, pulled down into a bottomless bog where a blackness waited that was beyond anything his feeble mind could comprehend. This was it. This was Endsville. The big exit. Fade to black. He knew it. He understood it. He screamed but he had no voice. He could feel everything that made him who and what he was begin to fly apart. It was happening, he knew with a blinding eruption of pure lunacy, at the subatomic level. Toddy and Bones had distorted time and space, they had warped it and bent it, bringing the Compton of Planet X to the real Compton, letting them join together in an impossible transgalatic interface for a few moments...but now it was all springing back like a tree limb pulled to the breaking point. The intersection of what was and what could not possibly be was ending and he was caught in the dark spaces between, falling into some nameless void—

Then he was caught.

He felt hands that burned like nuclear fission take hold of him and tow him away with an incredible velocity, taking him back... and back...and back.

And he heard a voice he knew, say, It's okay now. This is the return trip. Your work is not yet done and I am the instrument of destruction. Call me.

"I don't know...I don't understand," he heard his voice say. "HELP ME! I DON'T UNDERSTAND!"

You will. When the time is right, you will.

That voice. That voice. He knew it, he remembered it. It was the voice of someone you didn't mess with and someone you did not cross. If only he could remember. It was a calm and soothing voice on the surface, but beneath it was pure vengeance, it was snake venom, it was a bomb waiting to go off, a blade waiting to stab and a bullet waiting to shatter a skull.

But who?

Who?

Who could it be?

His mind went blank and he rested, for the time of retribution was close at hand.

Call me.

42

When Flynn woke up, he was facedown in the grass. What brought him out of it was his own groaning, miserable voice. He was in the grassy courtyard by the National Fruit building. This was the place. This is where it all happened. He had not dared come here since he got back to Compton, but now here he was. He licked his dry, cracking lips. Last night...had it been last night?... he remembered escaping with Marjorie and then, and then awful things happened. His mind was subverted by them, it was changed until his thoughts were their thoughts. It was all foggy. He could recall the town of 1981; Marjorie, then Bones taking her.

You gave them what they wanted. You offered your wife with your own hand.

"No, no, no," he said under his breath. "It wasn't that way. It wasn't that way at all."

Breathing in and out, he looked at the place where he had first seen the El Dorado, Toddy and Bones. The car was not there. This was not 1981, it was...was now. Yes, the old decrepit railroad hotel was gone, torn down years ago. National Fruit was still there, a big imposing red brick building, but it was long closed.

He began to sob, to whimper. He wanted to open his wrists and let all the filth run out of him at long last.

Marjorie.

Marjorie.

Gone now, taken away to some awful place to suffer, to be squeezed dry of pain and sanity. There was no helping her. There was no helping himself. Yet, even as horrible and despairing as it all was, he could hear Daryl Smite's voice from so long ago. He could remember the words. Once they've entered your life, you can always see them and they can always see you. You can't hide from them and they can't hide from you. But he couldn't see them. They weren't here. They were somewhere else.

But before him, he could see that the grass had been pushed down and rutted by tire treads. Someone had driven through here not just once, but many times. He swallowed. He tried to think. He tried to reason. Rows of pigeons sat atop the Fruit building, cooing ceaselessly.

Follow the ruts, follow them.

Feeling numb and confused, he did just that. They led to a row of boarded-up warehouses that were gray and slouching and, according to signs posted, condemned. The ruts stopped dead at a brick wall. Think, think. He walked farther down until he found a door that was askew. It was roped off with yellow tape. He kicked it in. It didn't take much work. It smelled musty inside, dirty and mildewing, with a strong after-odor of old piss and rodent droppings. Sections of roof were missing and rays of dusty sunlight speared down. Very high above in the rafters, more pigeons gathered as if in audience to what would now take place.

You know. You know what must happen now.

But he didn't.

There was something.

There was a voice.

But he just couldn't remember.

The further he went, the stronger the smell became, like some fusty, closed warren of mud and straw. Although he did not see Toddy or Bones, he sensed they were here and that this was their smell.

The warehouse was about sixty feet long and forty wide. There was nothing in there besides a few rotting crates and rusting metal drums pushed up against the walls. There was nowhere to hide. If Marjorie was here, he would have seen her. He kept walking and looking, though he knew with an icepick of pain in his heart that he was wasting his time.

"Gone," he finally said, his eyes moist. "She's gone."

Standing there, defeated, on the fractured weed-sprouting, grime-coated concrete floor, he knew he was beaten. They had summoned him back to Compton to give them what they desired. He had been nothing but a puppet.

He heard what he thought was a dragging footstep behind him. He turned and there was nothing. At least, nothing he could see. Yet…he felt a presence. Something very near.

You can't hide from them and they can't hide from you.

That voice. Was he really hearing it? Daryl's words, but definitely not his voice. He was long gone, living well and doing good things.

Not like me, he thought. I'm still here wallowing in my own shit, tethered to this fucking town. It's conjoined to me like an evil twin.

No, the voice was female. It was comforting and calm yet authoritative. He knew it…but from where? He couldn't think. He was broken inside, his heart bleeding, his soul raw as an open wound. There was nothing left without Marjorie. Nothing at all.

You can't hide from them and they can't hide from you.

Dammit, that voice! He stood there, trembling, feeling something gaining power around and within him. They can't hide from you. They're here and you can smell them. Yes, now that he relaxed, something shifted and the doors of perception were thrown wide.

There.

Look!

Right there!

He could see the '59 Caddy. At first, the image wavered like a heat mirage, but now it was solid and three-dimensional. It was no hallucination. The car waited there for him, an exotic and deadly alien machine, long, black, and shining, its tail fins sharp enough to slit a throat. Its headlights leered at him, its grill grinned with a terrible mocking hatred.

Flynn walked over to it, his insides gone to sauce. He expected that at any moment it would leap out at him like a tiger and bite him in half. Sweating now, he moved in closer, the smell of his enemies stronger, almost violent now. As if to prove that the car indeed existed, he reached out one trembling hand and touched it. Gah. It didn't feel like metal at all. In fact, it felt oily and scaled and unbearably repellent like snakeskin. The energy in its shell crackled along his fingertips like a static charge. There was power in it, immense unbelievable power. Unleashed, it could cut wormholes through space-time and split worlds in half.

His heart in his throat, he looked inside and gasped.

He wasn't sure what he expected to see, but certainly not this.

Not some brown, wrinkled sack that was veined like a leaf. A chrysalis that breathed from the hideous life gestating within. This was Toddy...or the entity that called itself such. There was another in the backseat that had to be Bones. They had not gone back to Planet X, but had merely hibernated, gone dormant to rest and repair themselves. They looked like huge seed pods.

The car. It has a heart. Find it.

Yes, but where did he look? It wasn't in the front or back seat. He opened the door and Toddy's chrysalis quivered. Nearly gagging on the stink in there, he pulled the latch and popped the hood. He went around to the front and opened it. The engine was unlike any engine he had ever seen before. Where was the filter? The battery? The hoses? The belts? All he saw was a pale sphere sitting in a formfitting cavity like an egg in a nest. No wires, no connections, no vacuum lines. Nothing but the sphere. Was that the heart? He swallowed...it looked alive. Was that possible? Logic told him it wasn't, yet it did not look like a machine. Steeling himself, he reached out and prodded it with his forefinger and recoiled in disgust. Partly because it was soft like a gelid mass and partly because it quivered as if it didn't like being touched.

It was madness.

He didn't know what it was, but his instinct told him it was not the heart. Maybe it was the brain. He rejected that instantly because the very idea stripped his gears and made him want to cackle hysterically.

Breathing hard, he shut the hood as carefully as possible. He went back and popped the trunk. Toddy's chrysalis was beginning to writhe now. Something terrible was about to happen.

Open it!

Now! Do not hesitate!

He pulled the trunk open and there was a fleshy, tearing sound, and he soon saw why. The trunk was filled with a huge jiggling mass of jelly that looked much like an egg, a gigantic birth sac. It was veined, slimy, and pink...and inside it, he could see things, shapes, forms, a liquid shifting. They seemed to be moving with a slow rolling motion. Gelatinous threads were adhered to the inside of the trunk, rooted right into the metal. The stink was hot, fungal, and revolting.

The heart? Is this the heart?

Good God…was the car a living thing? Maybe not living as he understood it, but a biomechanical hybrid of machine and organism? Again, he wanted to reject the idea. Still, hadn't he thought that very thing more than once? Hadn't he thought the seats felt like warm meat? Yes. Just as when he touched the hood a few moments before, it had felt like reptilian flesh. And he wasn't forgetting the sphere… that was no fucking machine.

But I've sat inside it.

Which meant, of course, that he had been inside a living thing, a mechanical composite, a cyborg. It was completely insane.

Now there was movement in the car.

Don't waste time! the voice commanded him, but he wheeled around, needing to see what was going on. Toddy's chrysalis had slid out of the open door. It was splitting open and a white four-fingered hand emerged, the appendages like wiggling worms. Now his face pushed free, glistening white and bulbous like a mushroom. The puckering, blubber-lipped mouth opened and closed in what looked like agony.

DO IT! DO IT NOW!

He went back to the trunk, facing that immense pink ovum. Without thinking, he thrust his hands at it. It was slippery like wet rubber, sweating a vile ooze. He punched it, trying to drill his fingers into it but it was remarkably elastic.

Toddy was emerging completely from the sac now, unzipped like a garment from a laundry bag. He was struggling to throw off the remnants, the gluey threads that tethered him to it.

Flynn! Think, Flynn! Think of what we've done for you and what we can still do! It's not too late to stop! Don't ruin everything now that the cycle is nearly complete! PLEASE, FLYNN! DON'T DO THIS!

It was Toddy's voice in his head. Not tough and threatening and arrogant. No, now it was shrieking and pained. It was begging.

And that more than anything made Flynn attack that egg-mass with everything he had, jabbing his fingers into it, clawing, ripping, tearing, shredding the glossy, gooey membrane, opening it wide as he shouted and screeched out his anger, his hatred, his burning rage. There was an eruption of cold slime and warm bubbling goo, then clotted gushing waste. It blew him back off his feet. He hit the concrete floor hard. Everything inside the egg-mass came out in a gurgling, boiling grisly wave of tissue and drainage. He saw... he saw bodies tumbling over one another in an embryonic flood of limbs and faces and placental pulp—Bobby Swinn and Daniel Harms, Chad's kid brother and his unborn baby and his wife...and yes, there was Flynn's mom and dad and Danice McKerran and finally Chad himself, too many others Flynn did not recognize. The others dissolved as they struck the floor. Chad tried to creep away. And a single hand emerged from the trunk, trying to pull itself free.

It was Marjorie.

Flynn ran over and gripped her gooey fingers, then her hand, and finally her whole arm. Something in there had her and it was pulling her back in but the depth of feeling and love for his wife gave him a strength beyond anything it could know. With one final gargantuan pull, he yanked her free and they fell to the concrete floor.

She looked drunkenly at him, eyes flickering open in her be-slimed face. "Ga...ga...ga...ah...ahhhhh..."

He dragged her away across the floor, ignoring Chad because it just wasn't in him by that point to save the man.

Toddy and Bones—or the horrible things they were—were clinging to the El Dorado, looking broken and bent, ruptured and shrunken like dying insects caught in a radiator. They were foul yellow things drowning in their own waste.

Flynn heard Toddy scream in agony and then his face bulged like a blood blister, popped in an expulsion of maggoty serum and hissing black ichor.

But it wasn't quite over.

As Toddy and Bones squirmed among the wreckage they had created, a wind rose up, howling and blowing, gathering up anything that wasn't tied down and turning the warehouse into a tunnel of cacophonous violence. Clouds of dust spun in whirlwinds. Moldering crates blew apart. Iron drums rolled across the floor. Beams creaked and cracked overhead, splinters of wood raining down. The howling storm was pure wrath and pure devastation. It had form and intent. It grew louder and louder until Flynn had to cover his ears even as he covered Marjorie with his own body.

It was deafening.

Freight trains and burst steam pipes and echoing explosions and then, in the flying gray storm of debris, he saw the thing that had been coming down the stairs at Danice McKerran's house all those years ago and the owner of the voice that had led him to the car, the entity that had plucked him from the void and delivered him here, the one you did not mess with and you never crossed: Danice herself. Trapped between this world and the next, neither here nor there, a creature of the void, she had seethed with stark, immense hatred for a long, long time and now that rage, that mindless fury had come to even the score.

She was a voltaic wraith, an electrical storm in the exaggerated skeletal form of a woman that billowed and swelled like a sheet on a line. She flickered like a dying lightbulb, on and off, and each time she reappeared she was closer to the car and her enemies. She agitated the windstorm. Planks of wood spun like boomerangs and drums flew through the air, dust and dirt and grit blowing like sea fog. Pigeons caught in her maelstrom were divorced of their feathers and spun ground-ward like plucked chickens ready for the pot. A shattered crate was sucked into her mass and ejected out the other side as flaming debris. She sparked and crackled and threw out forks of blue lightning that started the walls burning. Her eyes were huge white-hot suns and her reaching fingers arcing rods of fissile material.

But before she reached the car, she had another matter to settle.

Chad, who was still trying to crawl away, broken like a stepped-upon toad, saw her and screamed. He was her target. She had waited a long time to even the score. Just like at her house that day with Daryl, Flynn saw that she was fragmenting…except, that wasn't it at all. A swarm of flickering, radiant insects lifted off her, buzzing and swooping. They were all two or three inches long, living, leggy exoskeletons blazing with luminosity that hurt the eyes to look upon. They were part of Danice. Maybe in the realm she came from, that awful black void, they were the equivalent of carrion flies whose purpose was to dispose of carcasses. They kept swarming around her, sparking and flashing.

Then they went right for Chad.

They hit him like a volley of bullets, dozens and dozens of them, drilling through him, covering him, infesting him. He became a strobing flesh bag, bursting with steaming spouts of blood as they took him apart.

Flynn, covering his eyes against the glare, peered through his fingers and saw Chad writhing and twisting, the insects like tracer rounds whirling about him. His eyes were gone and his face was a bleeding flap. The majority of them had burrowed—or burned— into him, devouring him from the inside out. Flynn could see them through his flesh, blinking lights under his skin. They were incinerating him and within seconds he was a cremated, animate skeleton trembling with outstretched digits...then he hit the floor and broke into carbonized bits and pieces.

After that, Flynn couldn't be sure.

The air was an envelope of smoke and heat and searing wind.

Danice moved closer to the car, the flashing electrical stasis of her form growing brighter and brighter, her yawning mouth opening as wide as a sewer cover. She reached for the car and made contact and—

There was an explosion and a blinding flash of light, then she was no more. She went out like a fused circuit and the car went with her. Both were just...gone.

And the warehouse was burning.

43

It was nearly an hour later when Flynn finally got Marjorie home. She slowly came out of her fugue and he put her in a hot shower and scrubbed her clean. Then they both dressed and packed. They didn't fuck around. They took only what they couldn't live without. The movers could pack up the rest.

They kept driving until they reached Chicago where they took a suite at the Renaissance hotel in the Loop. For days they did little but sleep and rest, eat and swim. At night, they lay in bed in each other's arms and tried to make sense of the senseless.

Had the car been somehow energized by the life force of those in the egg-mass? Were they a battery of sorts from which it drained energy?

There were no good answers.

Knowing it was over was enough.

As the days passed, they kept waiting for their luck to totally go to shit, but it didn't happen. Their luck was good sometimes and bad sometimes—like everyone else. That was the best thing. Unplugged from the enchantment (for lack of a better word) of Toddy and Bones, they were perfectly ordinary and there was something satisfying about that.

Two weeks later, they were down at their place in Key West and it was hard to believe any of it had happened. At least during the long, sunny days. At night, however, the nightmares still came with frequency and they accepted that.

Time would take care of that.

"The furniture will be coming down from Compton this week," Flynn said to her one day.

"I'm envisioning a bonfire."

"Me, too."

He wondered what would happen to Compton now. In some way, Toddy and Bones had been part of that place, empowering it, making it shine and gleam. He figured a long, slow process of decay would set in. That the town would eventually fail and dry up. The idea didn't make him sad. There were good places in the world and bad places.

And here with Marjorie, he was in a very good place.

ABOUT THE AUTHOR

Tim Curran is the author of the novels Skin Medicine, Hive, Dead Sea, Resurrection, Hag Night, Skull Moon, The Devil Next Door, Doll Face, Afterburn, House of Skin, and Biohazard. His short stories have been collected in Bone Marrow Stew and Zombie Pulp. His novellas include The Underdwelling, The Corpse King, Puppet Graveyard, Worm, and Blackout. His short stories have appeared in such magazines as City Slab, Flesh&Blood, Book of Dark Wisdom, and Inhuman, as well as anthologies such as Shadows Over Main Street, Eulogies III, and October Dreams II. His fiction has been translated into German, Japanese, Spanish, and Italian. Find him on Facebook at: https://www.facebook.com/tim.curran.77

Curious about other Crossroad Press books?
Stop by our site:
http://store.crossroadpress.com
We offer quality writing
in digital, audio, and print formats.

Enter the code FIRSTBOOK
to get 20% off your first order from our store!
Stop by today!

Printed in Great Britain
by Amazon

39064180R00133